While the Billy Boils by Henry Lawson

Henry Archibald Hertzberg Lawson was born on the 17th June 1867 in a town on the Grenfell goldfields of New South Wales, Australia.

As a youth an ear infection had left him partially deaf and by fourteen he had lost his hearing completely.

He immersed himself in books to make up for the difficulties of a classroom education but later failed to gain entry to a University.

His first published poem was 'A Song of the Republic' in The Bulletin on 1st October 1887. This was quickly followed by other poems with one recognising him as "a youth whose poetic genius here speaks eloquently for itself."

In 1892, The Bulletin engaged him for an inland trip where he could write articles about the harsh realities of life in drought-stricken New South Wales. This resulted in his contributions to the Bulletin Debate and became the experience for a number of his stories in subsequent years. For Lawson this was an eye-opening period. His grim view of the outback was far removed from the romantic idyll of contemporary poetry and literature.

In 1896, Lawson married Bertha Bredt, Jr. but the marriage ended in June 1903. They had two children.

Despite this Lawson was finding his way in the literary world and achieving recognition. His most successful prose collection 'While the Billy Boils', was published in 1896. In it he virtually reinvented Australian realism.

His writing style of short, sharp sentences with honed and sparse descriptions created a personal writing style that defined Australians: dryly laconic, passionately egalitarian and deeply humane.

Sadly, for Lawson despite his growing recognition and fame he became withdrawn and unable to take part in the usual routines of life. His struggles with alcohol and mental health issues continued to drain him. His once prolific literary output began to decline. At times he was destitute mainly due, despite good sales and an enthusiastic audience, to ruinous publishing deals he had entered into.

Henry Archibald Hertzberg Lawson died, of cerebral hemorrhage, in Abbotsford, Sydney on 2nd September 1922.

Index of Contents

FIRST SERIES

AN OLD MATE OF YOUR FATHER'S

You remember when we hurried home from the old bush school how we were sometimes startled by a bearded apparition, who smiled kindly down on us, and whom our mother introduced, as we raked off our hats, as "An old mate of your father's on the diggings, Johnny." And he would pat our heads and say we were fine boys, or girls—as the case may have been—and that we had our father's nose but our mother's eyes, or the other way about; and say that the baby was the dead spit of its mother, and then added, for father's benefit: "But yet he's like you, Tom." It did seem strange to the children to hear him address the old man by his Christian name—considering that the mother always referred to him as "Father." She called the old mate Mr So-and-so, and father called him Bill, or something to that effect.

Occasionally the old mate would come dressed in the latest city fashion, and at other times in a new suit of reach-me-downs, and yet again he would turn up in clean white moleskins, washed tweed coat, Crimean shirt, blucher boots, soft felt hat, with a fresh-looking speckled handkerchief round his neck. But his face was mostly round and brown and jolly, his hands were always horny, and his beard grey. Sometimes he might have seemed strange and uncouth to us at first, but the old man never appeared the least surprised at anything he said or did—they understood each other so well—and we would soon take to this relic of our father's past, who would have fruit or lollies for us—strange that he always remembered them—and would surreptitiously slip "shilluns" into our dirty little hands, and tell us stories about the old days, "when me an' yer father was on the diggin's, an' you wasn't thought of, my boy."

Sometimes the old mate would stay over Sunday, and in the forenoon or after dinner he and father would take a walk amongst the deserted shafts of Sapling Gully or along Quartz Ridge, and criticize old ground, and talk of past diggers' mistakes, and second bottoms, and feelers, and dips, and leads—also outcrops—and absently pick up pieces of quartz and slate, rub them on their sleeves, look at them in an abstracted manner, and drop them again; and they would talk of some old lead they had worked on: "Hogan's party was here on one side of us, Macintosh was here on the other, Mac was getting good gold and so was Hogan, and now, why the blanky blank weren't we on gold?" And the mate would always agree that there was "gold in them ridges and gullies yet, if a man only had the money behind him to git at it." And then perhaps the guv'nor would show him a spot where he intended to put down a shaft some day—the old man was always thinking of putting down a shaft. And these two old fifty-niners would mooch round and sit on their heels on the sunny mullock heaps and break clay lumps between their hands, and lay plans for the putting down of shafts, and smoke, till an urchin was sent to "look for his father and Mr So-and-so, and tell 'em to come to their dinner."

And again—mostly in the fresh of the morning—they would hang about the fences on the selection and review the live stock: five dusty skeletons of cows, a hollow-sided calf or two, and one shocking piece of equine scenery—which, by the way, the old mate always praised. But the selector's heart was not in farming nor on selections—it was far away with the last new rush in Western Australia or Queensland, or perhaps buried in the worked-out ground of Tambaroora, Married Man's Creek, or Araluen; and by-

and-by the memory of some half-forgotten reef or lead or Last Chance, Nil Desperandum, or Brown Snake claim would take their thoughts far back and away from the dusty patch of sods and struggling sprouts called the crop, or the few discouraged, half-dead slips which comprised the orchard. Then their conversation would be pointed with many Golden Points, Bakery Hill, Deep Creeks, Maitland Bars, Specimen Flats, and Chinamen's Gullies. And so they'd yarn till the youngster came to tell them that "Mother sez the breakfus is gettin' cold," and then the old mate would rouse himself and stretch and say, "Well, we mustn't keep the missus waitin', Tom!"

And, after tea, they would sit on a log of the wood-heap, or the edge of the veranda—that is, in warm weather—and yarn about Ballarat and Bendigo—of the days when we spoke of being on a place oftener than at it: on Ballarat, on Gulgong, on Lambing Flat, on Creswick—and they would use the definite article before the names, as: "on The Turon; The Lachlan; The Home Rule; The Canadian Lead." Then again they'd yarn of old mates, such as Tom Brook, Jack Henright, and poor Martin Ratcliffe—who was killed in his golden hole—and of other men whom they didn't seem to have known much about, and who went by the names of "Adelaide Adolphus," "Corney George," and other names which might have been more or less applicable.

And sometimes they'd get talking, low and mysterious like, about "Th' Eureka Stockade;" and if we didn't understand and asked questions, "what was the Eureka Stockade?" or "what did they do it for?" father'd say: "Now, run away, sonny, and don't bother; me and Mr So-and-so want to talk." Father had the mark of a hole on his leg, which he said he got through a gun accident when a boy, and a scar on his side, that we saw when he was in swimming with us; he said he got that in an accident in a quartz-crushing machine. Mr So-and-so had a big scar on the side of his forehead that was caused by a pick accidentally slipping out of a loop in the rope, and falling down a shaft where he was working. But how was it they talked low, and their eyes brightened up, and they didn't look at each other, but away over sunset, and had to get up and walk about, and take a stroll in the cool of the evening when they talked about Eureka?

And, again they'd talk lower and more mysterious like, and perhaps mother would be passing the wood-heap and catch a word, and asked:

"Who was she, Tom?"

And Tom—father—would say:

"Oh, you didn't know her, Mary; she belonged to a family Bill knew at home."

And Bill would look solemn till mother had gone, and then they would smile a quiet smile, and stretch and say, "Ah, well!" and start something else.

They had yarns for the fireside, too, some of those old mates of our father's, and one of them would often tell how a girl—a queen of the diggings—was married, and had her wedding-ring made out of the gold of that field; and how the diggers weighed their gold with the new wedding-ring—for luck—by hanging the ring on the hook of the scales and attaching their chamois-leather gold bags to it (whereupon she boasted that four hundred ounces of the precious metal passed through her wedding-ring); and how they lowered the young bride, blindfolded, down a golden hole in a big bucket, and got her to point out the drive from which the gold came that her ring was made out of. The point of this story seems to have been lost—or else we forget it—but it was characteristic. Had the girl been lowered down a duffer, and asked to point out the way to the gold, and had she done so successfully, there would have been some sense in it.

And they would talk of King, and Maggie Oliver, and G. V. Brooke, and others, and remember how the diggers went five miles out to meet the coach that brought the girl actress, and took the horses out and brought her in in triumph, and worshipped her, and sent her off in glory, and threw nuggets into her lap. And how she stood upon the box-seat and tore her sailor hat to pieces, and threw the fragments amongst the crowd; and how the diggers fought for the bits and thrust them inside their shirt bosoms; and how she broke down and cried, and could in her turn have worshipped those men—loved them, every one. They were boys all, and gentlemen all. There were college men, artists, poets, musicians, journalists—Bohemians all. Men from all the lands and one. They understood art—and poverty was dead.

And perhaps the old mate would say slyly, but with a sad, quiet smile:

"Have you got that bit of straw yet, Tom?"

Those old mates had each three pasts behind them. The two they told each other when they became mates, and the one they had shared.

And when the visitor had gone by the coach we noticed that the old man would smoke a lot, and think as much, and take great interest in the fire, and be a trifle irritable perhaps.

Those old mates of our father's are getting few and far between, and only happen along once in a way to keep the old man's memory fresh, as it were. We met one to-day, and had a yarn with him, and afterwards we got thinking, and somehow began to wonder whether those ancient friends of ours were, or were not, better and kinder to their mates than we of the rising generation are to our fathers; and the doubt is painfully on the wrong side.

SETTLING ON THE LAND

The worst bore in Australia just now is the man who raves about getting the people on the land, and button-holes you in the street with a little scheme of his own. He generally does not know what he is talking about.

There is in Sydney a man named Tom Hopkins who settled on the land once, and sometimes you can get him to talk about it. He did very well at his trade in the city, years ago, until he began to think that he could do better up-country. Then he arranged with his sweetheart to be true to him and wait whilst he went west and made a home. She drops out of the story at this point.

He selected on a run at Dry Hole Creek, and for months awaited the arrival of the government surveyors to fix his boundaries; but they didn't come, and, as he had no reason to believe they would turn up within the next ten years, he grubbed and fenced at a venture, and started farming operations.

Does the reader know what grubbing means? Tom does. He found the biggest, ugliest, and most useless trees on his particular piece of ground; also the greatest number of adamantine stumps. He started without experience, or with very little, but with plenty of advice from men who knew less about farming than he did. He found a soft place between two roots on one side of the first tree, made a narrow, irregular hole, and burrowed down till he reached a level where the tap-root was somewhat less than four feet in diameter, and not quite as hard as flint: then he found that he hadn't room to swing the axe, so he heaved out another ton or two of earth—and rested. Next day he sank a shaft on the other side of the gum; and after tea, over a pipe, it struck him that it would be a good idea to burn the tree out, and so use up the logs and lighter rubbish lying round. So he widened the excavation, rolled in some logs, and set fire to them—with no better result than to scorch the roots.

Tom persevered. He put the trace harness on his horse, drew in all the logs within half a mile, and piled them on the windward side of that gum; and during the night the fire found a soft place, and the tree burnt off about six feet above the surface, falling on a squatter's boundary fence, and leaving the ugliest kind of stump to occupy the selector's attention; which it did, for a week. He waited till the hole cooled, and then he went to work with pick, shovel, and axe: and even now he gets interested in drawings of machinery, such as are published in the agricultural weeklies, for getting out stumps without graft. He thought he would be able to get some posts and rails out of that tree, but found reason to think that a cast-iron column would split sooner—and straighter. He traced some of the surface roots to the other side of the selection, and broke most of his trace-chains trying to get them out by horse-power—for they had other roots going down from underneath. He cleared a patch in the course of time and for several seasons he broke more ploughshares than he could pay for.

Meanwhile the squatter was not idle. Tom's tent was robbed several times, and his hut burnt down twice. Then he was charged with killing some sheep and a steer on the run, and converting them to his own use, but got off mainly because there was a difference of opinion between the squatter and the other local J.P. concerning politics and religion.

Tom ploughed and sowed wheat, but nothing came up to speak of—the ground was too poor; so he carted stable manure six miles from the nearest town, manured the land, sowed another crop, and prayed for rain. It came. It raised a flood which washed the crop clean off the selection, together with several acres of manure, and a considerable portion of the original surface soil; and the water brought down enough sand to make a beach, and spread it over the field to a depth of six inches. The flood also took half a mile of fencing from along the creek-bank, and landed it in a bend, three miles down, on a dummy selection, where it was confiscated.

Tom didn't give up—he was energetic. He cleared another piece of ground on the siding, and sowed more wheat; it had the rust in it, or the smut—and averaged three shillings per bushel. Then he sowed lucerne and oats, and bought a few cows: he had an idea of starting a dairy. First, the cows' eyes got bad, and he sought the advice of a German cocky, and acted upon it; he blew powdered alum through paper tubes into the bad eyes, and got some of it snorted and butted back into his own. He cured the cows' eyes and got the sandy blight in his own, and for a week or so be couldn't tell one end of a cow from the other, but sat in a dark corner of the hut and groaned, and soaked his glued eyelashes in warm water. Germany stuck to him and nursed him, and saw him through.

Then the milkers got bad udders, and Tom took his life in his hands whenever he milked them. He got them all right presently—and butter fell to fourpence a pound. He and the aforesaid cocky made arrangements to send their butter to a better market; and then the cows contracted a disease which was known in those parts as "plooro permoanyer," but generally referred to as "th' ploorer."

Again Tom sought advice, acting upon which he slit the cows' ears, cut their tails half off to bleed them, and poured pints of "pain killer" into them through their nostrils; but they wouldn't make an effort, except, perhaps, to rise and poke the selector when he tried to tempt their appetites with slices of immature pumpkin. They died peacefully and persistently, until all were gone save a certain dangerous, barren, slab-sided luny bovine with white eyes and much agility in jumping fences, who was known locally as Queen Elizabeth.

Tom shot Queen Elizabeth, and turned his attention to agriculture again. Then his plough horses took bad with some thing the Teuton called "der shtranguls." He submitted them to a course of treatment in accordance with Jacob's advice—and they died.

Even then Tom didn't give in—there was grit in that man. He borrowed a broken-down dray-horse in return for its keep, coupled it with his own old riding hack, and started to finish ploughing. The team wasn't a success. Whenever the draught horse's knees gave way and he stumbled forward, he jerked the lighter horse back into the plough, and something would break. Then Tom would blaspheme till he was refreshed, mend up things with wire and bits of clothes-line, fill his pockets with stones to throw at the team, and start again. Finally he hired a dummy's child to drive the horses. The brat did his best he tugged at the head of the team, prodded it behind, heaved rocks at it, cut a sapling, got up his enthusiasm, and wildly whacked the light horse whenever the other showed signs of moving—but he never succeeded in starting both horses at one and the same time. Moreover the youth was cheeky, and the selector's temper had been soured: he cursed the boy along with the horses, the plough, the selection, the squatter, and Australia. Yes, he cursed Australia. The boy cursed back, was chastised, and immediately went home and brought his father.

Then the dummy's dog tackled the selector's dog and this precipitated things. The dummy would have gone under had his wife not arrived on the scene with the eldest son and the rest of the family. They all fell foul of Tom. The woman was the worst. The selector's dog chawed the other and came to his master's rescue just in time—or Tom Hopkins would never have lived to become the inmate of a lunatic asylum.

Next year there happened to be good grass on Tom's selection and nowhere else, and he thought it wouldn't be a bad idea—to get a few poor sheep, and fatten them up for market: sheep were selling for about seven-and-sixpence a dozen at that time. Tom got a hundred or two, but the squatter had a man stationed at one side of the selection with dogs to set on the sheep directly they put their noses through the fence (Tom's was not a sheep fence). The dogs chased the sheep across the selection and into the run again on the other side, where another man waited ready to pound them.

Tom's dog did his best; but he fell sick while chawing up the fourth capitalistic canine, and subsequently died. The dummies had robbed that cur with poison before starting it across—that was the only way they could get at Tom's dog.

Tom thought that two might play at the game, and he tried; but his nephew, who happened to be up from the city on a visit, was arrested at the instigation of the squatter for alleged sheep-stealing, and sentenced to two years' hard; during which time the selector himself got six months for assaulting the squatter with intent to do him grievous bodily harm-which, indeed, he more than attempted, if a broken nose, a fractured jaw, and the loss of most of the squatters' teeth amounted to anything. The squatter by this time had made peace with the other local Justice, and had become his father-in-law.

When Tom came out there was little left for him to live for; but he took a job of fencing, got a few pounds together, and prepared to settle on the land some more. He got a "missus" and a few cows during the next year; the missus robbed him and ran away with the dummy, and the cows died in the drought, or were impounded by the squatter while on their way to water. Then Tom rented an orchard up the creek, and a hailstorm destroyed all the fruit. Germany happened to be represented at the time, Jacob having sought shelter at Tom's but on his way home from town. Tom stood leaning against the door post with the hail beating on him through it all. His eyes were very bright and very dry, and every breath was a choking sob. Jacob let him stand there, and sat inside with a dreamy expression on his hard face, thinking of childhood and fatherland, perhaps. When it was over he led Tom to a stool and said, "You waits there, Tom. I must go home for somedings. You sits there still and waits twenty minutes;" then he got on his horse and rode off muttering to himself; "Dot man moost gry, dot man moost gry." He was back inside of twenty minutes with a bottle of wine and a cornet under his overcoat. He poured the wine into two pint-pots, made Tom drink, drank himself, and then took his cornet, stood up at the door, and played a German march into the rain after the retreating storm. The hail had passed over his vineyard and he was a ruined man too. Tom did "gry" and was all right. He was a bit disheartened, but he did another job of fencing, and was just beginning to think about "puttin' in a few vines an' fruit-trees" when the government surveyors—whom he'd forgotten all about—had a resurrection and came and surveyed, and found that the real selection was located amongst some barren ridges across the creek. Tom reckoned it was lucky he didn't plant the orchard, and he set about shifting his home and fences to the new site. But the squatter interfered at this point, entered into possession of the farm and all on it, and took action against the selector for trespass—laying the damages at L2500.

Tom was admitted to the lunatic asylum at Parramatta next year, and the squatter was sent there the following summer, having been ruined by the drought, the rabbits, the banks, and a wool-ring. The two became very friendly, and had many a sociable argument about the feasibility—or otherwise—of blowing open the flood-gates of Heaven in a dry season with dynamite.

Tom was discharged a few years since. He knocks about certain suburbs a good deal. He is seen in daylight seldom, and at night mostly in connection with a dray and a lantern. He says his one great regret is that he wasn't found to be of unsound mind before he went up-country.

ENTER MITCHELL

The Western train had just arrived at Redfern railway station with a lot of ordinary passengers and one swagman.

He was short, and stout, and bow-legged, and freckled, and sandy. He had red hair and small, twinkling, grey eyes, and—what often goes with such things—the expression of a born comedian. He was dressed in a ragged, well-washed print shirt, an old black waistcoat with a calico back, a pair of cloudy moleskins patched at the knees and held up by a plaited greenhide belt buckled loosely round his hips, a pair of well-worn, fuzzy blucher boots, and a soft felt hat, green with age, and with no brim worth mentioning, and no crown to speak of. He swung a swag on to the platform, shouldered it, pulled out a billy and water-bag, and then went to a dog-box in the brake van.

Five minutes later he appeared on the edge of the cab platform, with an anxious-looking cattle-dog crouching against his legs, and one end of the chain in his hand. He eased down the swag against a post, turned his face to the city, tilted his hat forward, and scratched the well-developed back of his head with a little finger. He seemed undecided what track to take.

"Cab, Sir!"

The swagman turned slowly and regarded cabby with a quiet grin.

"Now, do I look as if I want a cab?"

"Well, why not? No harm, anyway—I thought you might want a cab."

Swaggy scratched his head, reflectively.

"Well," he said, "you're the first man that has thought so these ten years. What do I want with a cab?"

"To go where you're going, of course."

"Do I look knocked up?"

"I didn't say you did."

"And I didn't say you said I did.... Now, I've been on the track this five years. I've tramped two thousan' miles since last Chris'mas, and I don't see why I can't tramp the last mile. Do you think my old dog wants a cab?"

The dog shivered and whimpered; he seemed to want to get away from the crowd.

"But then, you see, you ain't going to carry that swag through the streets, are you?" asked the cabman.

"Why not? Who'll stop me! There ain't no law agin it, I b'lieve?"

"But then, you see, it don't look well, you know."

"Ah! I thought we'd get to it at last."

The traveller up-ended his bluey against his knee, gave it an affectionate pat, and then straightened himself up and looked fixedly at the cabman.

"Now, look here!" he said, sternly and impressively, "can you see anything wrong with that old swag o' mine?"

It was a stout, dumpy swag, with a red blanket outside, patched with blue, and the edge of a blue blanket showing in the inner rings at the end. The swag might have been newer; it might have been cleaner; it might have been hooped with decent straps, instead of bits of clothes-line and greenhide— but otherwise there was nothing the matter with it, as swags go.

"I've humped that old swag for years," continued the bushman; "I've carried that old swag thousands of miles—as that old dog knows—an' no one ever bothered about the look of it, or of me, or of my old dog, neither; and do you think I'm going to be ashamed of that old swag, for a cabby or anyone else? Do you think I'm going to study anybody's feelings? No one ever studied mine! I'm in two minds to summon you for using insulting language towards me!"

He lifted the swag by the twisted towel which served for a shoulder-strap, swung it into the cab, got in himself and hauled the dog after him.

"You can drive me somewhere where I can leave my swag and dog while I get some decent clothes to see a tailor in," he said to the cabman. "My old dog ain't used to cabs, you see."

Then he added, reflectively: "I drove a cab myself, once, for five years in Sydney."

STIFFNER AND JIM

(THIRDLY, BILL)

We were tramping down in Canterbury, Maoriland, at the time, swagging it—me and Bill—looking for work on the new railway line. Well, one afternoon, after a long, hot tramp, we comes to Stiffner's Hotel—between Christchurch and that other place—I forget the name of it—with throats on us like sunstruck bones, and not the price of a stick of tobacco.

We had to have a drink, anyway, so we chanced it. We walked right into the bar, handed over our swags, put up four drinks, and tried to look as if we'd just drawn our cheques and didn't care a curse for any man. We looked solvent enough, as far as swagmen go. We were dirty and haggard and ragged and tired-looking, and that was all the more reason why we might have our cheques all right.

This Stiffner was a hard customer. He'd been a spieler, fighting man, bush parson, temperance preacher, and a policeman, and a commercial traveller, and everything else that was damnable; he'd been a journalist, and an editor; he'd been a lawyer, too. He was an ugly brute to look at, and uglier to have a row with—about six-foot-six, wide in proportion, and stronger than Donald Dinnie.

He was meaner than a gold-field Chinaman, and sharper than a sewer rat: he wouldn't give his own father a feed, nor lend him a sprat—unless some safe person backed the old man's I.O.U.

We knew that we needn't expect any mercy from Stiffner; but something had to be done, so I said to Bill:

"Something's got to be done, Bill! What do you think of it?"

Bill was mostly a quiet young chap, from Sydney, except when he got drunk—which was seldom—and then he was a customer, from all round. He was cracked on the subject of spielers. He held that the population of the world was divided into two classes—one was spielers and the other was the mugs. He reckoned that he wasn't a mug. At first I thought he was a spieler, and afterwards I thought that he was a mug. He used to say that a man had to do it these times; that he was honest once and a fool, and was robbed and starved in consequences by his friends and relations; but now he intended to take all that he could get. He said that you either had to have or be had; that men were driven to be sharps, and there was no help for it.

Bill said:

"We'll have to sharpen our teeth, that's all, and chew somebody's lug."

"How?" I asked.

There was a lot of navvies at the pub, and I knew one or two by sight, so Bill says:

"You know one or two of these mugs. Bite one of their ears.

"So I took aside a chap that I knowed and bit his ear for ten bob, and gave it to Bill to mind, for I thought it would be safer with him than with me.

"Hang on to that," I says, "and don't lose it for your natural life's sake, or Stiffner'll stiffen us."

We put up about nine bob's worth of drinks that night—me and Bill—and Stiffner didn't squeal: he was too sharp. He shouted once or twice.

By-and-by I left Bill and turned in, and in the morning when I woke up there was Bill sitting alongside of me, and looking about as lively as the fighting kangaroo in London in fog time. He had a black eye and eighteen pence. He'd been taking down some of the mugs.

"Well, what's to be done now?" I asked. "Stiffner can smash us both with one hand, and if we don't pay up he'll pound our swags and cripple us. He's just the man to do it. He loves a fight even more than he hates being had."

"There's only one thing to be done, Jim," says Bill, in a tired, disinterested tone that made me mad.

"Well, what's than" I said.

"Smoke!"

"Smoke be damned," I snarled, losing my temper.

"You know dashed well that our swags are in the bar, and we can't smoke without them.

"Well, then," says Bill, "I'll toss you to see who's to face the landlord."

"Well, I'll be blessed!" I says. "I'll see you further first. You have got a front. You mugged that stuff away, and you'll have to get us out of the mess."

It made him wild to be called a mug, and we swore and growled at each other for a while; but we daren't speak loud enough to have a fight, so at last I agreed to toss up for it, and I lost.

Bill started to give me some of his points, but I shut him up quick.

"You've had your turn, and made a mess of it," I said. "For God's sake give me a show. Now, I'll go into the bar and ask for the swags, and carry them out on to the veranda, and then go back to settle up. You keep him talking all the time. You dump the two swags together, and smoke like sheol. That's all you've got to do."

I went into the bar, got the swags front the missus, carried them out on to the veranda, and then went back.

Stiffner came in.

"Good morning!"

"Good morning, sir," says Stiffner.

"It'll be a nice day, I think?"

"Yes, I think so. I suppose you are going on?"

"Yes, we'll have to make a move to-day."

Then I hooked carelessly on to the counter with one elbow, and looked dreamy-like out across the clearing, and presently I gave a sort of sigh and said: "Ah, well! I think I'll have a beer."

"Right you are! Where's your mate?"

"Oh, he's round at the back. He'll be round directly; but he ain't drinking this morning."

Stiffner laughed that nasty empty laugh of his. He thought Bill was whipping the cat.

"What's yours, boss?" I said.

"Thankee!... Here's luck!"

"Here's luck!"

The country was pretty open round there—the nearest timber was better than a mile away, and I wanted to give Bill a good start across the flat before the go-as-you-can commenced; so I talked for a while, and while we were talking I thought I might as well go the whole hog—I might as well die for a pound as a penny, if I had to die; and if I hadn't I'd have the pound to the good, anyway, so to speak. Anyhow, the risk would be about the same, or less, for I might have the spirit to run harder the more I had to run for—the more spirits I had to run for, in fact, as it turned out—so I says:

"I think I'll take one of them there flasks of whisky to last us on the road."

"Right y'are," says Stiffner. "What'll ye have—a small one or a big one?"

"Oh, a big one, I think—if I can get it into my pocket."

"It'll be a tight squeeze," he said, and he laughed.

"I'll try," I said. "Bet you two drinks I'll get it in."

"Done!" he says. "The top inside coat-pocket, and no tearing."

It was a big bottle, and all my pockets were small; but I got it into the pocket he'd betted against. It was a tight squeeze, but I got it in.

Then we both laughed, but his laugh was nastier than usual, because it was meant to be pleasant, and he'd lost two drinks; and my laugh wasn't easy—I was anxious as to which of us would laugh next.

Just then I noticed something, and an idea struck me—about the most up-to-date idea that ever struck me in my life. I noticed that Stiffner was limping on his right foot this morning, so I said to him:

"What's up with your foot?" putting my hand in my pocket. "Oh, it's a crimson nail in my boot," he said. "I thought I got the blanky thing out this morning; but I didn't."

There just happened to be an old bag of shoemaker's tools in the bar, belonging to an old cobbler who was lying dead drunk on the veranda. So I said, taking my hand out of my pocket again:

"Lend us the boot, and I'll fix it in a minute. That's my old trade."

"Oh, so you're a shoemaker," he said. "I'd never have thought it."

He laughs one of his useless laughs that wasn't wanted, and slips off the boot—he hadn't laced it up—and hands it across the bar to me. It was an ugly brute—a great thick, iron-bound, boiler-plated navvy's boot. It made me feel sore when I looked at it.

I got the bag and pretended to fix the nail; but I didn't.

"There's a couple of nails gone from the sole," I said. "I'll put 'em in if I can find any hobnails, and it'll save the sole," and I rooted in the bag and found a good long nail, and shoved it right through the sole on the sly. He'd been a bit of a sprinter in his time, and I thought it might be better for me in the near future if the spikes of his running-shoes were inside.

"There, you'll find that better, I fancy," I said, standing the boot on the bar counter, but keeping my hand on it in an absent-minded kind of way. Presently I yawned and stretched myself, and said in a careless way:

"Ah, well! How's the slate?" He scratched the back of his head and pretended to think.

"Oh, well, we'll call it thirty bob."

Perhaps he thought I'd slap down two quid.

"Well," I says, "and what will you do supposing we don't pay you?"

He looked blank for a moment. Then he fired up and gasped and choked once or twice; and then he cooled down suddenly and laughed his nastiest laugh—he was one of those men who always laugh when they're wild—and said in a nasty, quiet tone:

"You thundering, jumped-up crawlers! If you don't (something) well part up I'll take your swags and (something) well kick your gory pants so you won't be able to sit down for a month—or stand up either!"

"Well, the sooner you begin the better," I said; and I chucked the boot into a corner and bolted.

He jumped the bar counter, got his boot, and came after me. He paused to slip the boot on—but he only made one step, and then gave a howl and slung the boot off and rushed back. When I looked round again he'd got a slipper on, and was coming—and gaining on me, too. I shifted scenery pretty quick the next five minutes. But I was soon pumped. My heart began to beat against the ceiling of my head, and my lungs all choked up in my throat. When I guessed he was getting within kicking distance I glanced round so's to dodge the kick. He let out; but I shied just in time. He missed fire, and the slipper went about twenty feet up in the air and fell in a waterhole.

He was done then, for the ground was stubbly and stony. I seen Bill on ahead pegging out for the horizon, and I took after him and reached for the timber for all I was worth, for I'd seen Stiffner's missus coming with a shovel—to bury the remains, I suppose; and those two were a good match—Stiffner and his missus, I mean.

Bill looked round once, and melted into the bush pretty soon after that. When I caught up he was about done; but I grabbed my swag and we pushed on, for I told Bill that I'd seen Stiffner making for the stables when I'd last looked round; and Bill thought that we'd better get lost in the bush as soon as ever we could, and stay lost, too, for Stiffner was a man that couldn't stand being had.

The first thing that Bill said when we got safe into camp was: "I told you that we'd pull through all right. You need never be frightened when you're travelling with me. Just take my advice and leave things to me, and we'll hang out all right. Now-."

But I shut him up. He made me mad.

"Why, you—! What the sheol did you do?"

"Do?" he says. "I got away with the swags, didn't I? Where'd they be now if it wasn't for me?"

Then I sat on him pretty hard for his pretensions, and paid him out for all the patronage he'd worked off on me, and called him a mug straight, and walked round him, so to speak, and blowed, and told him never to pretend to me again that he was a battler.

Then, when I thought I'd licked him into form, I cooled down and soaped him up a bit; but I never thought that he had three climaxes and a crisis in store for me.

He took it all pretty cool; he let me have my fling, and gave me time to get breath; then he leaned languidly over on his right side, shoved his left hand down into his left trouserpocket, and brought up a boot-lace, a box of matches, and nine-and-six.

As soon as I got the focus of it I gasped:

"Where the deuce did you get that?"

"I had it all along," he said, "but I seen at the pub that you had the show to chew a lug, so I thought we'd save it—nine-and-sixpences ain't picked up every day."

Then he leaned over on his left, went down into the other pocket, and came up with a piece of tobacco and half-a-sovereign.

My eyes bulged out.

"Where the blazes did you get that from?" I yelled.

"That," he said, "was the half-quid you give me last night. Half-quids ain't to be thrown away these times; and, besides, I had a down on Stiffner, and meant to pay him out; I reckoned that if we wasn't sharp enough to take him down we hadn't any business to be supposed to be alive. Anyway, I guessed we'd do it; and so we did—and got a bottle of whisky into the bargain."

Then he leaned back, tired-like, against the log, and dredged his upper left-hand waistcoat-pocket, and brought up a sovereign wrapped in a pound note. Then he waited for me to speak; but I couldn't. I got my mouth open, but couldn't get it shut again.

"I got that out of the mugs last night, but I thought that we'd want it, and might as well keep it. Quids ain't so easily picked up, nowadays; and, besides, we need stuff more'n Stiffner does, and so—"

"And did he know you had the stuff?" I gasped.

"Oh, yes, that's the fun of it. That's what made him so excited. He was in the parlour all the time I was playing. But we might as well have a drink!

"We did. I wanted it."

Bill turned in by-and-by, and looked like a sleeping innocent in the moonlight. I sat up late, and smoked, and thought hard, and watched Bill, and turned in, and thought till near daylight, and then went to sleep, and had a nightmare about it. I dreamed I chased Stiffner forty miles to buy his pub, and that Bill turned out to be his nephew.

Bill divvied up all right, and gave me half a crown over, but I didn't travel with him long after that. He was a decent young fellow as far as chaps go, and a good mate as far as mates go; but he was too far ahead for a peaceful, easy-going chap like me. It would have worn me out in a year to keep up to him.

P.S.—The name of this should have been: 'Bill and Stiffner (thirdly, Jim)'

WHEN THE SUN WENT DOWN

Jack Drew sat on the edge of the shaft, with his foot in the loop and one hand on the rope, ready to descend. His elder brother, Tom, stood at one end of the windlass and the third mate at the other. Jack paused before swinging off, looked up at his brother, and impulsively held out his hand:

"You ain't going to let the sun go down, are you, Tom?"

But Tom kept both hands on the windlass-handle and said nothing.

"Lower away!"

They lowered him to the bottom, and Tom shouldered his pick in silence and walked off to the tent. He found the tin plate, pint-pot, and things set ready for him on the rough slab table under the bush shed. The tea was made, the cabbage and potatoes strained and placed in a billy near the fire. He found the fried bacon and steak between two plates in the camp-oven. He sat down to the table but he could not eat. He felt mean. The inexperience and hasty temper of his brother had caused the quarrel between them that morning; but then Jack admitted that, and apologized when he first tried to make it up.

Tom moved round uneasily and tried to smoke: he could not get Jack's last appeal out of his ears—"You ain't going to let the sun go down, Tom?"

Tom found himself glancing at the sun. It was less than two hours from sunset. He thought of the words of the old Hebrew—or Chinese—poet; he wasn't religious, and the authorship didn't matter. The old poet's words began to haunt him "Let not the sun go down upon your wrath—Let not the sun go down upon your wrath."

The line contains good, sound advice; for quick-tempered men are often the most sensitive, and when they let the sun go down on the aforesaid wrath that quality is likely to get them down and worry them during the night.

Tom started to go to the claim, but checked himself, and sat down and tried to draw comfort from his pipe. He understood his brother thoroughly, but his brother never understood him—that was where the trouble was. Presently he got thinking how Jack would worry about the quarrel and have no heart for his work. Perhaps he was fretting over it now, all alone by himself, down at the end of the damp, dark drive. Tom had a lot of the old woman about him, in spite of his unsociable ways and brooding temper.

He had almost made up his mind to go below again, on some excuse, when his mate shouted from the top of the shaft:

"Tom! Tom! For Christ's sake come here!"

Tom's heart gave a great thump, and he ran like a kangaroo to the shaft. All the diggers within hearing were soon on the spot. They saw at a glance what had happened. It was madness to sink without timber in such treacherous ground. The sides of the shaft were closing in. Tom sprang forward and shouted through the crevice:

"To the face, Jack! To the face, for your life!"

"The old Workings!" he cried, turning to the diggers. "Bring a fan and tools. We'll dig him out."

A few minutes later a fan was rigged over a deserted shaft close by, where fortunately the windlass had been left for bailing purposes, and men were down in the old drive. Tom knew that he and his mates had driven very close to the old workings.

He knelt in the damp clay before the face and worked like a madman; he refused to take turn about, and only dropped the pick to seize a shovel in his strong hands, and snatch back the loose clay from under his feet; he reckoned that he had six or, perhaps, eight feet to drive, and he knew that the air could not last long in the new drive—even if that had not already fallen in and crushed his brother. Great drops of perspiration stood out on Tom's forehead, and his breath began to come in choking sobs, but he still struck strong, savage blows into the clay before him, and the drive lengthened quickly. Once he paused a moment to listen, and then distinctly heard a sound as of a tool or stone being struck against the end of the new drive. Jack was safe!

Tom dug on until the clay suddenly fell away from his pick and left a hole, about the size of a plate, in the "face" before him. "Thank God!" said a hoarse, strained voice at the other side.

"All right, Jack!"

"Yes, old man; you are just in time; I've hardly got room to stand in, and I'm nearly smothered." He was crouching against the "face" of the new drive.

Tom dropped his pick and fell back against the man behind him.

"Oh, God! my back!" he cried.

Suddenly he struggled to his knees, and then fell forward on his hand and dragged himself close to the hole in the end of the drive.

"Jack!" he gasped, "Jack!"

"Right, old man; what's the matter?"

"I've hurt my heart, Jack!—Put your hand—quick!... The sun's going down."

Jack's hand came out through the hole, Tom gripped it, and then fell with his face in the damp clay.

They half carried, half dragged him from the drive, for the roof was low and they were obliged to stoop. They took him to the shaft and sent him up, lashed to the rope.

A few blows of the pick, and Jack scrambled from his prison and went to the surface, and knelt on the grass by the body of his brother. The diggers gathered round and took off their hats. And the sun went down.

THE MAN WHO FORGOT

"Well, I dunno," said Tom Marshall—known as "The Oracle"—"I've heerd o' sich cases before: they ain't commin, but—I've heerd o' sich cases before," and he screwed up the left side of his face whilst he reflectively scraped his capacious right ear with the large blade of a pocket-knife.

They were sitting at the western end of the rouseabouts' hut, enjoying the breeze that came up when the sun went down, and smoking and yarning. The "case" in question was a wretchedly forlorn-looking specimen of the swag-carrying clan whom a boundary-rider had found wandering about the adjacent plain, and had brought into the station. He was a small, scraggy man, painfully fair, with a big, baby-like head, vacant watery eyes, long thin hairy hands, that felt like pieces of damp seaweed, and an apologetic cringe-and-look-up-at-you manner. He professed to have forgotten who he was and all about himself.

The Oracle was deeply interested in this case, as indeed he was in anything else that "looked curious." He was a big, simple-minded shearer, with more heart than brains, more experience than sense, and more curiosity than either. It was a wonder that he had not profited, even indirectly, by the last characteristic. His heart was filled with a kind of reverential pity for anyone who was fortunate or unfortunate enough to possess an "affliction;" and amongst his mates had been counted a deaf man, a blind man, a poet, and a man who "had rats." Tom had dropped across them individually, when they were down in the world, and had befriended them, and studied them with great interest—especially the poet; and they thought kindly of him, and were grateful—except the individual with the rats, who reckoned Tom had an axe to grind—that he, in fact, wanted to cut his (Rat's) liver out as a bait for Darling cod—and so renounced the mateship.

It was natural, then, for The Oracle to take the present case under his wing. He used his influence with the boss to get the Mystery on "picking up," and studied him in spare time, and did his best to assist the poor hushed memory, which nothing the men could say or do seemed able to push further back than the day on which the stranger "kind o' woke up" on the plain, and found a swag beside him. The swag had been prospected and fossicked for a clue, but yielded none. The chaps were sceptical at first, and inclined to make fun of the Mystery; but Tom interfered, and intimated that if they were skunks enough to chyack or try on any of their "funny business" with a "pore afflicted chap," he (Tom) would be obliged to "perform." Most of the men there had witnessed Tom's performance, and no one seemed ambitious to take a leading part in it. They preferred to be in the audience.

"Yes," reflected The Oracle, "it's a curious case, and I dare say some of them big doctors, like Morell Mackenzie, would be glad to give a thousand or two to get holt on a case like this."

"Done," cried Mitchell, the goat of the shed. "I'll go halves!—or stay, let's form a syndicate and work the Mystery."

Some of the rouseabouts laughed, but the joke fell as flat with Tom as any other joke.

"The worst of it is," said the Mystery himself, in the whine that was natural to him, and with a timid side look up at Tom—"the worst of it is I might be a lord or duke, and don't know anything about it. I might be a rich man, with a lot of houses and money. I might be a lord."

The chaps guffawed.

"Wot'yer laughing at?" asked Mitchell. "I don't see anything unreasonable about it; he might be a lord as far as looks go. I've seen two."

"Yes," reflected Tom, ignoring Mitchell, "there's something in that; but then again, you see, you might be Jack the Ripper. Better let it slide, mate; let the dead past bury its dead. Start fresh with a clean sheet."

"But I don't even know my name, or whether I'm married or not," whined the outcast. "I might have a good wife and little ones."

"Better keep on forgetting, mate," Mitchell said, "and as for a name, that's nothing. I don't know mine, and I've had eight. There's plenty good names knocking round. I knew a man named Jim Smith that died. Take his name, it just suits you, and he ain't likely to call round for it; if he does, you can say you was born with it."

So they called him Smith, and soon began to regard him as a harmless lunatic and to take no notice of his eccentricities. Great interest was taken in the case for a time, and even Mitchell put in his oar and tried all sorts of ways to assist the Mystery in his weak, helpless, and almost pitiful endeavours to recollect who he was. A similar case happened to appear in the papers at this time, and the thing caught on to such an extent that The Oracle was moved to impart some advice from his store of wisdom.

"I wouldn't think too much over it if I was you," said he to Mitchell, "hundreds of sensible men went mad over that there Tichborne case who didn't have anything to do with it, but just through thinking on it; and you're ratty enough already, Jack. Let it alone and trust me to find out who's Smith just as soon as ever we cut out."

Meanwhile Smith ate, worked, and slept, and borrowed tobacco and forgot to return it—which was made a note of. He talked freely about his case when asked, but if he addressed anyone, it was with the air of the timid but good young man, who is fully aware of the extent and power of this world's wickedness, and stands somewhat in awe of it, but yet would beg you to favour a humble worker in the vineyard by kindly accepting a tract, and passing it on to friends after perusal.

One Saturday morning, about a fortnight before cut out, The Oracle came late to his stand, and apparently with something on his mind. Smith hadn't turned up, and the next rouseabout was doing his work, to the mutual dissatisfaction of all parties immediately concerned.

"Did you see anything of Smith?" asked Mitchell of The Oracle. "Seems to have forgot to get up this morning."

Tom looked disheartened and disappointed. "He's forgot again," said he, slowly and impressively.

"Forgot what? We know he's blessed well forgot to come to graft."

"He's forgot again," repeated Tom. "He woke up this morning and wanted to know who he was and where he was." Comments.

"Better give him best, Oracle," said Mitchell presently. "If he can't find out who he is and where he is, the boss'll soon find it out for him."

"No," said Tom, "when I take a thing in hand I see it through."

This was also characteristic of the boss-over-the-board, though in another direction. He went down to the but and inquired for Smith.

"Why ain't you at work?"

"Who am I, sir? Where am I?" whined Smith. "Can you please tell me who I am and where I am?"

The boss drew a long breath and stared blankly at the Mystery; then he erupted.

"Now, look here!" he howled, "I don't know who the gory sheol you are, except that you're a gory lunatic, and what's more, I don't care a damn. But I'll soon show you where you are! You can call up at the store and get your cheque, and soon as you blessed well like; and then take a walk, and don't forget to take your lovely swag with you."

The matter was discussed at the dinner-table. The Oracle swore that it was a cruel, mean way to treat a "pore afflicted chap," and cursed the boss. Tom's admirers cursed in sympathy, and trouble seemed threatening, when the voice of Mitchell was heard to rise in slow, deliberate tones over the clatter of cutlery and tin plates.

"I wonder," said the voice, "I wonder whether Smith forgot his cheque?"

It was ascertained that Smith hadn't.

There was some eating and thinking done. Soon Mitchell's voice was heard again, directed at The Oracle.

It said "Do you keep any vallabels about your bunk, Oracle?"

Tom looked hard at Mitchell. "Why?"

"Oh, nothin': only I think it wouldn't be a bad idea for you to look at your bunk and see whether Smith forgot."

The chaps grew awfully interested. They fixed their eyes on Tom, and he looked with feeling from one face to another; then he pushed his plate back, and slowly extracted his long legs from between the stool and the table. He climbed to his bunk, and carefully reviewed the ingredients of his swag. Smith hadn't forgot.

When The Oracle's face came round again there was in it a strange expression which a close study would have revealed to be more of anger than of sorrow, but that was not all. It was an expression such as a man might wear who is undergoing a terrible operation, without chloroform, but is determined not to let a whimper escape him. Tom didn't swear, and by that token they guessed how mad he was. 'Twas a rough shed, with a free and lurid vocabulary, but had they all sworn in chorus, with One-eyed Bogan as lead, it would not have done justice to Tom's feelings—and they realized this.

The Oracle took down his bridle from its peg, and started for the door amid a respectful and sympathetic silence, which was only partly broken once by the voice of Mitchell, which asked in an awed whisper:

"Going ter ketch yer horse, Tom?" The Oracle nodded, and passed on; he spake no word—he was too full for words.

Five minutes passed, and then the voice of Mitchell was heard again, uninterrupted by the clatter of tinware. It said in impressive tones:

"It would not be a bad idea for some of you chaps that camp in the bunks along there, to have a look at your things. Scotty's bunk is next to Tom's."

Scotty shot out of his place as if a snake had hold of his leg, starting a plank in the table and upsetting three soup plates. He reached for his bunk like a drowning man clutching at a plank, and tore out the bedding. Again, Smith hadn't forgot.

Then followed a general overhaul, and it was found in most cases that Smith had remembered. The pent-up reservoir of blasphemy burst forth.

The Oracle came up with Smith that night at the nearest shanty, and found that he had forgotten again, and in several instances, and was forgetting some more under the influence of rum and of the flattering interest taken in his case by a drunken Bachelor of Arts who happened to be at the pub. Tom came in quietly from the rear, and crooked his finger at the shanty-keeper. They went apart from the rest, and talked together a while very earnestly. Then they secretly examined Smith's swag, the core of which was composed of Tom's and his mate's valuables.

Then The Oracle stirred up Smith's recollections and departed.

Smith was about again in a couple of weeks. He was damaged somewhat physically, but his memory was no longer impaired.

HUNGERFORD

One of the hungriest cleared roads in New South Wales runs to within a couple of miles of Hungerford, and stops there; then you strike through the scrub to the town. There is no distant prospect of Hungerford—you don't see the town till you are quite close to it, and then two or three white-washed galvanized-iron roofs start out of the mulga.

They say that a past Ministry commenced to clear the road from Bourke, under the impression that Hungerford was an important place, and went on, with the blindness peculiar to governments, till they got to within two miles of the town. Then they ran short of rum and rations, and sent a man on to get them, and make inquiries. The member never came back, and two more were sent to find him—or

Hungerford. Three days later the two returned in an exhausted condition, and submitted a motion of want-of-confidence, which was lost. Then the whole House went on and was lost also. Strange to relate, that Government was never missed.

However, we found Hungerford and camped there for a day. The town is right on the Queensland border, and an interprovincial rabbit-proof fence—with rabbits on both sides of it—runs across the main street.

This fence is a standing joke with Australian rabbits—about the only joke they have out there, except the memory of Pasteur and poison and inoculation. It is amusing to go a little way out of town, about sunset, and watch them crack Noah's Ark rabbit jokes about that fence, and burrow under and play leap-frog over it till they get tired. One old buck rabbit sat up and nearly laughed his ears off at a joke of his own about that fence. He laughed so much that he couldn't get away when I reached for him. I could hardly eat him for laughing. I never saw a rabbit laugh before; but I've seen a 'possum do it.

Hungerford consists of two houses and a humpy in New South Wales, and five houses in Queensland. Characteristically enough, both the pubs are in Queensland. We got a glass of sour yeast at one and paid sixpence for it—we had asked for English ale.

The post office is in New South Wales, and the police-barracks in Bananaland. The police cannot do anything if there's a row going on across the street in New South Wales, except to send to Brisbane and have an extradition warrant applied for; and they don't do much if there's a row in Queensland. Most of the rows are across the border, where the pubs are.

At least, I believe that's how it is, though the man who told me might have been a liar. Another man said he was a liar, but then he might have been a liar himself—a third person said he was one. I heard that there was a fight over it, but the man who told me about the fight might not have been telling the truth.

One part of the town swears at Brisbane when things go wrong, and the other part curses Sydney.

The country looks as though a great ash-heap had been spread out there, and mulga scrub and firewood planted—and neglected. The country looks just as bad for a hundred miles round Hungerford, and beyond that it gets worse—a blasted, barren wilderness that doesn't even howl. If it howled it would be a relief.

I believe that Bourke and Wills found Hungerford, and it's a pity they did; but, if I ever stand by the graves of the men who first travelled through this country, when there were neither roads nor stations, nor tanks, nor bores, nor pubs, I'll—I'll take my hat off. There were brave men in the land in those days.

It is said that the explorers gave the district its name chiefly because of the hunger they found there, which has remained there ever since. I don't know where the "ford" comes in—there's nothing to ford, except in flood-time. Hungerthirst would have been better. The town is supposed to be situated on the banks of a river called the Paroo, but we saw no water there, except what passed for it in a tank. The goats and sheep and dogs and the rest of the population drink there. It is dangerous to take too much of that water in a raw state.

Except in flood-time you couldn't find the bed of the river without the aid of a spirit-level and a long straight-edge. There is a Custom-house against the fence on the northern side. A pound of tea often costs six shillings on that side, and you can get a common lead pencil for fourpence at the rival store across the street in the mother province. Also, a small loaf of sour bread sells for a shilling at the humpy aforementioned. Only about sixty per cent of the sugar will melt.

We saw one of the storekeepers give a dead-beat swagman five shillings' worth of rations to take him on into Queensland. The storekeepers often do this, and put it down on the loss side of their books. I hope the recording angel listens, and puts it down on the right side of his book.

We camped on the Queensland side of the fence, and after tea had a yarn with an old man who was minding a mixed flock of goats and sheep; and we asked him whether he thought Queensland was better than New South Wales, or the other way about.

He scratched the back of his head, and thought a while, and hesitated like a stranger who is going to do you a favour at some personal inconvenience.

At last, with the bored air of a man who has gone through the same performance too often before, he stepped deliberately up to the fence and spat over it into New South Wales. After which he got leisurely through and spat back on Queensland.

"That's what I think of the blanky colonies!" he said.

He gave us time to become sufficiently impressed; then he said:

"And if I was at the Victorian and South Australian border I'd do the same thing."

He let that soak into our minds, and added: "And the same with West Australia—and—and Tasmania." Then he went away.

The last would have been a long spit—and he forgot Maoriland.

We heard afterwards that his name was Clancy and he had that day been offered a job droving at "twenty-five shillings a week and find your own horse." Also find your own horse feed and tobacco and soap and other luxuries, at station prices. Moreover, if you lost your own horse you would have to find another, and if that died or went astray you would have to find a third—or forfeit your pay and return on foot. The boss drover agreed to provide flour and mutton—when such things were procurable.

Consequently, Clancy's unfavourable opinion of the colonies.

My mate and I sat down on our swags against the fence to talk things over. One of us was very deaf. Presently a black tracker went past and looked at us, and returned to the pub. Then a trooper in Queensland uniform came along and asked us what the trouble was about, and where we came from and were going, and where we camped. We said we were discussing private business, and he explained that he thought it was a row, and came over to see. Then he left us, and later on we saw him sitting with the rest of the population on a bench under the hotel veranda. Next morning we rolled up our swags and left Hungerford to the north-west.

A CAMP-FIRE YARN

"This girl," said Mitchell, continuing a yarn to his mate, "was about the ugliest girl I ever saw, except one, and I'll tell you about her directly. The old man had a carpenter's shop fixed up in a shed at the back of his house, and he used to work there pretty often, and sometimes I'd come over and yarn with him. One day I was sitting on the end of the bench, and the old man was working away, and Mary was standing there too, all three of us yarning—she mostly came poking round where I was if I happened to be on the premises—or at least I thought so—and we got yarning about getting married, and the old cove said he'd get married again if the old woman died.

"'You get married again!' said Mary. 'Why, father, you wouldn't get anyone to marry you—who'd have you?'

"'Well,' he said, 'I bet I'll get someone sooner than you, anyway. You don't seem to be able to get anyone, and it's pretty near time you thought of settlin' down and gettin' married. I wish someone would have you.'

"He hit her pretty hard there, but it served her right. She got as good as she gave. She looked at me and went all colours, and then she went back to her washtub.

"She was mighty quiet at tea-time—she seemed hurt a lot, and I began to feel sorry I'd laughed at the old man's joke, for she was really a good, hard-working girl, and you couldn't help liking her.

"So after tea I went out to her in the kitchen, where she was washing up, to try and cheer her up a bit. She'd scarcely speak at first, except to say 'Yes' or 'No', and kept her face turned away from me; and I could see that she'd been crying. I began to feel sorry for her and mad at the old man, and I started to comfort her. But I didn't go the right way to work about it. I told her that she mustn't take any notice of the old cove, as he didn't mean half he said. But she seemed to take it harder than ever, and at last I got so sorry for her that I told her that I'd have her if she'd have me."

"And what did she say?" asked Mitchell's mate, after a pause.

"She said she wouldn't have me at any price!"

The mate laughed, and Mitchell grinned his quiet grin.

"Well, this set me thinking," he continued. "I always knew I was a dashed ugly cove, and I began to wonder whether any girl would really have me; and I kept on it till at last I made up my mind to find out and settle the matter for good—or bad.

"There was another farmer's daughter living close by, and I met her pretty often coming home from work, and sometimes I had a yarn with her. She was plain, and no mistake: Mary was a Venus alongside of her. She had feet like a Lascar, and hands about ten sizes too large for her, and a face like that camel—only red; she walked like a camel, too. She looked like a ladder with a dress on, and she didn't know a great A from a corner cupboard.

"Well, one evening I met her at the sliprails, and presently I asked her, for a joke, if she'd marry me. Mind you, I never wanted to marry her; I was only curious to know whether any girl would have me.

"She turned away her face and seemed to hesitate, and I was just turning away and beginning to think I was a dashed hopeless case, when all of a sudden she fell up against me and said she'd be my wife.... And it wasn't her fault that she wasn't."

"What did she do?"

"Do! What didn't she do? Next day she went down to our place when I was at work, and hugged and kissed mother and the girls all round, and cried, and told mother that she'd try and be a dutiful daughter to her. Good Lord! You should have seen the old woman and the girls when I came home.

"Then she let everyone know that Bridget Page was engaged to Jack Mitchell, and told her friends that she went down on her knees every night and thanked the Lord for getting the love of a good man. Didn't the fellows chyack me, though! My sisters were raving mad about it, for their chums kept asking them how they liked their new sister, and when it was going to come off, and who'd be bridesmaids and best man, and whether they weren't surprised at their brother Jack's choice; and then I'd gammon at home that it was all true.

"At last the place got too hot for me. I got sick of dodging that girl. I sent a mate of mine to tell her that it was all a joke, and that I was already married in secret; but she didn't see it, then I cleared, and got a job in Newcastle, but had to leave there when my mates sent me the office that she was coming. I wouldn't wonder but what she is humping her swag after me now. In fact, I thought you was her in disguise when I set eyes on you first.... You needn't get mad about it; I don't mean to say that you're quite as ugly as she was, because I never saw a man that was—or a woman either. Anyway, I'll never ask a woman to marry me again unless I'm ready to marry her."

Then Mitchell's mate told a yarn.

"I knew a case once something like the one you were telling me about; the landlady of a hash-house where I was stopping in Albany told me. There was a young carpenter staying there, who'd run away from Sydney from an old maid who wanted to marry him. He'd cleared from the church door, I believe. He was scarcely more'n a boy—about nineteen—and a soft kind of a fellow, something like you, only good-looking—that is, he was passable. Well, as soon as the woman found out where he'd gone, she came after him. She turned up at the boarding-house one Saturday morning when Bobbie was at work; and the first thing she did was to rent a double room from the landlady and buy some cups and saucers to start housekeeping with. When Bobbie came home he just gave her one look and gave up the game.

"'Get your dinner, Bobbie,' she said, after she'd slobbered over him a bit, 'and then get dressed and come with me and get married!'

"She was about three times his age, and had a face like that picture of a lady over Sappho Smith's letters in the Sydney Bulletin.

"Well, Bobbie went with her like a—like a lamb; never gave a kick or tried to clear."

"Hold on," said Mitchell, "did you ever shear lambs?"

"Never mind. Let me finish the yarn. Bobbie was married; but she wouldn't let him out of her sight all that afternoon, and he had to put up with her before them all. About bedtime he sneaked out and started along the passage to his room that he shared with two or three mates. But she'd her eye on him.

"'Bobbie, Bobbie!' she says, 'Where are you going?'

"'I'm going to bed,' said Bobbie. 'Good night!'

"'Bobbie, Bobbie,' she says, sharply. 'That isn't our room; this is our room, Bobbie. Come back at once! What do you mean, Bobbie? Do you hear me, Bobbie?'

"So Bobbie came back, and went in with the scarecrow. Next morning she was first at the breakfast table, in a dressing-gown and curl papers. And when they were all sitting down Bobbie sneaked in, looking awfully sheepish, and sidled for his chair at the other end of the table. But she'd her eyes on him.

"'Bobbie, Bobbie!' she said, 'Come and kiss me, Bobbie!'" And he had to do it in front of them all.

"But I believe she made him a good wife."

HIS COUNTRY-AFTER ALL

The Blenheim coach was descending into the valley of the Avetere River—pronounced Aveterry—from the saddle of Taylor's Pass. Across the river to the right, the grey slopes and flats stretched away to the distant sea from a range of tussock hills. There was no native bush there; but there were several groves of imported timber standing wide apart—sentinel-like—seeming lonely and striking in their isolation.

"Grand country, New Zealand, eh?" said a stout man with a brown face, grey beard, and grey eyes, who sat between the driver and another passenger on the box.

"You don't call this grand country!" exclaimed the other passenger, who claimed to be, and looked like, a commercial traveller, and might have been a professional spieler—quite possibly both. "Why, it's about the poorest country in New Zealand! You ought to see some of the country in the North Island— Wairarapa and Napier districts, round about Pahiatua. I call this damn poor country."

"Well, I reckon you wouldn't, if you'd ever been in Australia—back in New South Wales. The people here don't seem to know what a grand country they've got. You say this is the worst, eh? Well, this would make an Australian cockatoo's mouth water-the worst of New Zealand would."

"I always thought Australia was all good country," mused the driver—a flax-stick. "I always thought—"

"Good country!" exclaimed the man with the grey beard, in a tone of disgust. "Why, it's only a mongrel desert, except some bits round the coast. The worst dried-up and God-forsaken country I was ever in."

There was a silence, thoughtful on the driver's part, and aggressive on that of the stranger.

"I always thought," said the driver, reflectively, after the pause—"I always thought Australia was a good country," and he placed his foot on the brake.

They let him think. The coach descended the natural terraces above the river bank, and pulled up at the pub.

"So you're a native of Australia?" said the bagman to the grey-beard, as the coach went on again.

"Well, I suppose I am. Anyway, I was born there. That's the main thing I've got against the darned country."

"How long did you stay there?"

"Till I got away," said the stranger. Then, after a think, he added, "I went away first when I was thirty-five—went to the islands. I swore I'd never go back to Australia again; but I did. I thought I had a kind of affection for old Sydney. I knocked about the blasted country for five or six years, and then I cleared out to 'Frisco. I swore I'd never go back again, and I never will."

"But surely you'll take a run over and have a look at old Sydney and those places, before you go back to America, after getting so near?"

"What the blazes do I want to have a look at the blamed country for?" snapped the stranger, who had refreshed considerably. "I've got nothing to thank Australia for—except getting out of it. It's the best country to get out of that I was ever in."

"Oh, well, I only thought you might have had some friends over there," interposed the traveller in an injured tone.

"Friends! That's another reason. I wouldn't go back there for all the friends and relations since Adam. I had more than quite enough of it while I was there. The worst and hardest years of my life were spent in Australia. I might have starved there, and did do it half my time. I worked harder and got less in my own country in five years than I ever did in any other in fifteen"—he was getting mixed—"and I've been in a few since then. No, Australia is the worst country that ever the Lord had the sense to forget. I mean to stick to the country that stuck to me, when I was starved out of my own dear native land—and that country is the United States of America. What's Australia? A big, thirsty, hungry wilderness, with one or two cities for the convenience of foreign speculators, and a few collections of humpies, called towns— also for the convenience of foreign speculators; and populated mostly by mongrel sheep, and partly by fools, who live like European slaves in the towns, and like dingoes in the bush—who drivel about 'democracy,' and yet haven't any more spunk than to graft for a few Cockney dudes that razzle-dazzle most of the time in Paris. Why, the Australians haven't even got the grit to claim enough of their own money to throw a few dams across their watercourses, and so make some of the interior fit to live in. America's bad enough, but it was never so small as that.... Bah! The curse of Australia is sheep, and the Australian war cry is Baa!"

"Well, you're the first man I ever heard talk as you've been doing about his own country," said the bagman, getting tired and impatient of being sat on all the time. "'Lives there a man with a soul so dead, who never said—to—to himself'... I forget the darned thing."

He tried to remember it. The man whose soul was dead cleared his throat for action, and the driver—for whom the bagman had shouted twice as against the stranger's once—took the opportunity to observe that he always thought a man ought to stick up for his own country.

The stranger ignored him and opened fire on the bagman. He proceeded to prove that that was all rot—that patriotism was the greatest curse on earth; that it had been the cause of all war; that it was the false, ignorant sentiment which moved men to slave, starve, and fight for the comfort of their sluggish masters; that it was the enemy of universal brotherhood, the mother of hatred, murder, and slavery, and that the world would never be any better until the deadly poison, called the sentiment of patriotism, had been "educated" out of the stomachs of the people. "Patriotism!" he exclaimed scornfully. "My country! The darned fools; the country never belonged to them, but to the speculators, the absentees, land-boomers, swindlers, gangs of thieves—the men the patriotic fools starve and fight for—their masters. Ba-a!"

The opposition collapsed.

The coach had climbed the terraces on the south side of the river, and was bowling along on a level stretch of road across the elevated flat.

"What trees are those?" asked the stranger, breaking the aggressive silence which followed his unpatriotic argument, and pointing to a grove ahead by the roadside. "They look as if they've been planted there. There ain't been a forest here surely?"

"Oh, they're some trees the Government imported," said the bagman, whose knowledge on the subject was limited. "Our own bush won't grow in this soil."

"But it looks as if anything else would—"

Here the stranger sniffed once by accident, and then several times with interest.

It was a warm morning after rain. He fixed his eyes on those trees.

They didn't look like Australian gums; they tapered to the tops, the branches were pretty regular, and the boughs hung in shipshape fashion. There was not the Australian heat to twist the branches and turn the leaves.

"Why!" exclaimed the stranger, still staring and sniffing hard. "Why, dang me if they ain't (sniff) Australian gums!"

"Yes," said the driver, flicking his horses, "they are."

"Blanky (sniff) blanky old Australian gums!" exclaimed the ex-Australian, with strange enthusiasm.

"They're not old," said the driver; "they're only young trees. But they say they don't grow like that in Australia—'count of the difference in the climate. I always thought—"

But the other did not appear to hear him; he kept staring hard at the trees they were passing. They had been planted in rows and cross-rows, and were coming on grandly.

There was a rabbit trapper's camp amongst those trees; he had made a fire to boil his billy with gum-leaves and twigs, and it was the scent of that fire which interested the exile's nose, and brought a wave of memories with it.

"Good day, mate!" he shouted suddenly to the rabbit trapper, and to the astonishment of his fellow passengers.

"Good day, mate!" The answer came back like an echo—it seemed to him—from the past.

Presently he caught sight of a few trees which had evidently been planted before the others—as an experiment, perhaps—and, somehow, one of them had grown after its own erratic native fashion—gnarled and twisted and ragged, and could not be mistaken for anything else but an Australian gum.

"A thunderin' old blue-gum!" ejaculated the traveller, regarding the tree with great interest.

He screwed his neck to get a last glimpse, and then sat silently smoking and gazing straight ahead, as if the past lay before him—and it was before him.

"Ah, well!" he said, in explanation of a long meditative silence on his part; "ah, well—them saplings—the smell of them gum-leaves set me thinking." And he thought some more.

"Well, for my part," said a tourist in the coach, presently, in a condescending tone, "I can't see much in Australia. The bally colonies are—"

"Oh, that be damned!" snarled the Australian-born—they had finished the second flask of whisky. "What do you Britishers know about Australia? She's as good as England, anyway."

"Well, I suppose you'll go straight back to the States as soon as you've done your business in Christchurch," said the bagman, when near their journey's end they had become confidential.

"Well, I dunno. I reckon I'll just take a run over to Australia first. There's an old mate of mine in business in Sydney, and I'd like to have a yarn with him."

A DAY ON A SELECTION

The scene is a small New South Wales western selection, the holder whereof is native-English. His wife is native-Irish. Time, Sunday, about 8 a.m. A used-up looking woman comes from the slab-and-bark house, turns her face towards the hillside, and shrieks:

"T-o-o-mmay!"

No response, and presently she draws a long breath and screams again:

"Tomm-a-a-y!"

A faint echo comes from far up the siding where Tommy's presence is vaguely indicated by half a dozen cows moving slowly—very slowly—down towards the cow-yard.

The woman retires. Ten minutes later she comes out again and screams:

"Tommy!

"Y-e-e-a-a-s-s!" very passionately and shrilly.

"Ain't you goin' to bring those cows down to-day?"

"Y-e-e-a-a-s-s-s!—carn't yer see I'm comin'?"

A boy is seen to run wildly along the siding and hurl a missile at a feeding cow; the cow runs forward a short distance through the trees, and then stops to graze again while the boy stirs up another milker.

An hour goes by.

The rising Australian generation is represented by a thin, lanky youth of about fifteen. He is milking. The cow-yard is next the house, and is mostly ankle-deep in slush. The boy drives a dusty, discouraged-looking cow into the bail, and pins her head there; then he gets tackle on to her right hind leg, hauls it back, and makes it fast to the fence. There are eleven cows, but not one of them can be milked out of the bail—chiefly because their teats are sore. The selector does not know what makes the teats sore, but he has an unquestioning faith in a certain ointment, recommended to him by a man who knows less about cows than he does himself, which he causes to be applied at irregular intervals—leaving the mode of application to the discretion of his son. Meanwhile the teats remain sore.

Having made the cow fast, the youngster cautiously takes hold of the least sore teat, yanks it suddenly, and dodges the cow's hock. When he gets enough milk to dip his dirty hands in, he moistens the teats, and things go on more smoothly. Now and then he relieves the monotony of his occupation by squirting at the eye of a calf which is dozing in the adjacent pen. Other times he milks into his mouth. Every time the cow kicks, a burr or a grass-seed or a bit of something else falls into the milk, and the boy drowns these things with a well-directed stream—on the principle that what's out of sight is out of mind.

Sometimes the boy sticks his head into the cow's side, hangs on by a teat, and dozes, while the bucket, mechanically gripped between his knees, sinks lower and lower till it rests on the ground. Likely as not he'll doze on until his mother's shrill voice startles him with an inquiry as to whether he intends to get that milking done to-day; other times he is roused by the plunging of the cow, or knocked over by a calf which has broken through a defective panel in the pen. In the latter case the youth gets tackle on to the calf, detaches its head from the teat with the heel of his boot, and makes it fast somewhere. Sometimes the cow breaks or loosens the leg-rope and gets her leg into the bucket and then the youth clings desperately to the pail and hopes she'll get her hoof out again without spilling the milk. Sometimes she does, more often she doesn't—it depends on the strength of the boy and the pail and on the strategy of the former. Anyway, the boy will lam the cow down with a jagged yard shovel, let her out, and bail up another.

When he considers that he has finished milking he lets the cows out with their calves and carries the milk down to the dairy, where he has a heated argument with his mother, who—judging from the quantity of milk—has reason to believe that he has slummed some of the milkers. This he indignantly denies, telling her she knows very well the cows are going dry.

The dairy is built of rotten box bark—though there is plenty of good stringy-bark within easy distance—and the structure looks as if it wants to lie down and is only prevented by three crooked props on the leaning side; more props will soon be needed in the rear for the dairy shows signs of going in that direction. The milk is set in dishes made of kerosene-tins, cut in halves, which are placed on bark shelves fitted round against the walls. The shelves are not level and the dishes are brought to a comparatively horizontal position by means of chips and bits of bark, inserted under the lower side. The milk is covered by soiled sheets of old newspapers supported on sticks laid across the dishes. This protection is necessary, because the box bark in the roof has crumbled away and left fringed holes—also because the fowls roost up there. Sometimes the paper sags, and the cream may have to be scraped off an article on dairy farming.

The selector's wife removes the newspapers, and reveals a thick, yellow layer of rich cream, plentifully peppered with dust that has drifted in somehow. She runs a forefinger round the edges of the cream to detach it from the tin, wipes her finger in her mouth, and skims. If the milk and cream are very thick she rolls the cream over like a pancake with her fingers, and lifts it out in sections. The thick milk is poured into a slop-bucket, for the pigs and calves, the dishes are "cleaned"—by the aid of a dipper full of warm water and a rag—and the wife proceeds to set the morning's milk. Tom holds up the doubtful-looking rag that serves as a strainer while his mother pours in the milk. Sometimes the boy's hands get tired and he lets some of the milk run over, and gets into trouble; but it doesn't matter much, for the straining-cloth has several sizable holes in the middle.

The door of the dairy faces the dusty road and is off its hinges and has to be propped up. The prop is missing this morning, and Tommy is accused of having been seen chasing old Poley with it at an earlier hour. He never seed the damn prop, never chased no cow with it, and wants to know what's the use of always accusing him. He further complains that he's always blamed for everything. The pole is not forthcoming, and so an old dray is backed against the door to keep it in position. There is more trouble about a cow that is lost, and hasn't been milked for two days. The boy takes the cows up to the paddock sliprails and lets the top rail down: the lower rail fits rather tightly and some exertion is required to free it, so he makes the animals jump that one. Then he "poddies"—hand-feeds—the calves which have been weaned too early. He carries the skim-milk to the yard in a bucket made out of an oil-drum—sometimes a kerosene-tin—seizes a calf by the nape of the neck with his left hand, inserts the dirty forefinger of his right into its mouth, and shoves its head down into the milk. The calf sucks, thinking it has a teat, and pretty soon it butts violently—as calves do to remind their mothers to let down the milk—and the boy's wrist gets barked against the jagged edge of the bucket. He welts that calf in the jaw, kicks it in the stomach, tries to smother it with its nose in the milk, and finally dismisses it with the assistance of the calf rope and a shovel, and gets another. His hand feels sticky and the cleaned finger makes it look as if he wore a filthy, greasy glove with the forefinger torn off.

The selector himself is standing against a fence talking to a neighbour. His arms rest on the top rail of the fence, his chin rests on his hands, his pipe rests between his fingers, and his eyes rest on a white cow that is chewing her cud on the opposite side of the fence. The neighbour's arms rest on the top rail also, his chin rests on his hands, his pipe rests between his fingers, and his eyes rest on the cow. They are talking about that cow. They have been talking about her for three hours. She is chewing her cud. Her nose is well up and forward, and her eyes are shut. She lets her lower jaw fall a little, moves it to one side, lifts it again, and brings it back into position with a springing kind of jerk that has almost a visible recoil. Then her jaws stay perfectly still for a moment, and you would think she had stopped chewing. But she hasn't. Now and again a soft, easy, smooth-going swallow passes visibly along her clean, white throat and disappears. She chews again, and by and by she loses consciousness and forgets to chew. She never opens her eyes. She is young and in good condition; she has had enough to eat, the sun is just properly warm for her, and—well, if an animal can be really happy, she ought to be.

Presently the two men drag themselves away from the fence, fill their pipes, and go to have a look at some rows of forked sticks, apparently stuck in the ground for some purpose. The selector calls these sticks fruit-trees, and he calls the place "the orchard." They fool round these wretched sticks until dinnertime, when the neighbour says he must be getting home. "Stay and have some dinner! Man alive! Stay and have some dinner!" says the selector; and so the friend stays.

It is a broiling hot day in summer, and the dinner consists of hot roast meat, hot baked potatoes, hot cabbage, hot pumpkin, hot peas, and burning-hot plum-pudding. The family drinks on an average four cups of tea each per meal. The wife takes her place at the head of the table with a broom to keep the fowls out, and at short intervals she interrupts the conversation with such exclamations as "Shoo! shoo!" "Tommy, can't you see that fowl? Drive it out!" The fowls evidently pass a lot of their time in the house. They mark the circle described by the broom, and take care to keep two or three inches beyond it. Every now and then you see a fowl on the dresser amongst the crockery, and there is great concern to get it out before it breaks something. While dinner is in progress two steers get into the wheat through a broken rail which has been spliced with stringy-bark, and a calf or two break into the vineyard. And yet this careless Australian selector, who is too shiftless to put up a decent fence, or build a decent house and who knows little or nothing about farming, would seem by his conversation to have read up all the great social and political questions of the day. Here are some fragments of conversation caught at the dinner-table. Present—the selector, the missus, the neighbour, Corney George—nicknamed "Henry George"—Tommy, Jacky, and the younger children. The spaces represent interruptions by the fowls and children:

Corney George (continuing conversation): "But Henry George says, in 'Progress and Poverty,' he says—"

Missus (to the fowls): "Shoo! Shoo!"

Corney: "He says—"

Tom: "Marther, jist speak to this Jack."

Missus (to Jack): "If you can't behave yourself, leave the table."

Tom [Corney, probably]: "He says in Progress and—"

Missus: "Shoo!"

Neighbour: "I think 'Lookin' Backwards' is more—"

Missus: "Shoo! Shoo! Tom, can't you see that fowl?"

Selector: "Now I think 'Caesar's Column' is more likely—Just look at—"

Missus: "Shoo! Shoo!"

Selector: "Just look at the French Revolution."

Corney: "Now, Henry George-"

Tom: "Marther! I seen a old-man kangaroo up on—"

Missus: "Shut up! Eat your dinner an' hold your tongue. Carn't you see someone's speakin'?"

Selector: "Just look at the French—"

Missus (to the fowls): "Shoo! Shoo!" (turning suddenly and unexpectedly on Jacky): "Take your fingers out of the sugar!—Blast yer! that I should say such a thing."

Neighbour: "But 'Lookin' Backwards"'

Missus: "There you go, Tom! Didn't I say you'd spill that tea? Go away from the table!"

Selector: "I think 'Caesar's Column' is the only natural—"

Missus: "Shoo! Shoo!" She loses patience, gets up and fetches a young rooster with the flat of the broom, sending him flying into the yard; he falls with his head towards the door and starts in again. Later on the conversation is about Deeming.

Selector: "There's no doubt the man's mad—"

Missus: "Deeming! That Windsor wretch! Why, if I was in the law I'd have him boiled alive! Don't tell me he didn't know what he was doing! Why, I'd have him—"

Corney: "But, missus, you—"

Missus (to the fowls): "Shoo! Shoo!"

THAT THERE DOG O' MINE

Macquarie the shearer had met with an accident. To tell the truth, he had been in a drunken row at a wayside shanty, from which he had escaped with three fractured ribs, a cracked head, and various minor abrasions. His dog, Tally, had been a sober but savage participator in the drunken row, and had escaped with a broken leg. Macquarie afterwards shouldered his swag and staggered and struggled along the track ten miles to the Union Town hospital. Lord knows how he did it. He didn't exactly know himself. Tally limped behind all the way, on three legs.

The doctors examined the man's injuries and were surprised at his endurance. Even doctors are surprised sometimes—though they don't always show it. Of course they would take him in, but they objected to Tally. Dogs were not allowed on the premises.

"You will have to turn that dog out," they said to the shearer, as he sat on the edge of a bed.

Macquarie said nothing.

"We cannot allow dogs about the place, my man," said the doctor in a louder tone, thinking the man was deaf.

"Tie him up in the yard then."

"No. He must go out. Dogs are not permitted on the grounds."

Macquarie rose slowly to his feet, shut his agony behind his set teeth, painfully buttoned his shirt over his hairy chest, took up his waistcoat, and staggered to the corner where the swag lay.

"What are you going to do?" they asked.

"You ain't going to let my dog stop?"

"No. It's against the rules. There are no dogs allowed on premises."

He stooped and lifted his swag, but the pain was too great, and he leaned back against the wall.

"Come, come now! man alive!" exclaimed the doctor, impatiently. "You must be mad. You know you are not in a fit state to go out. Let the wardsman help you to undress."

"No!" said Macquarie. "No. If you won't take my dog in you don't take me. He's got a broken leg and wants fixing up just—just as much as—as I do. If I'm good enough to come in, he's good enough—and—and better."

He paused awhile, breathing painfully, and then went on.

"That—that there old dog of mine has follered me faithful and true, these twelve long hard and hungry years. He's about—about the only thing that ever cared whether I lived or fell and rotted on the cursed track."

He rested again; then he continued: "That—that there dog was pupped on the track," he said, with a sad sort of a smile. "I carried him for months in a billy, and afterwards on my swag when he knocked up.... And the old slut—his mother—she'd foller along quite contented—and sniff the billy now and again— just to see if he was all right.... She follered me for God knows how many years. She follered me till she was blind—and for a year after. She follered me till she could crawl along through the dust no longer, and—and then I killed her, because I couldn't leave her behind alive!"

He rested again.

"And this here old dog," he continued, touching Tally's upturned nose with his knotted fingers, "this here old dog has follered me for—for ten years; through floods and droughts, through fair times and— and hard—mostly hard; and kept me from going mad when I had no mate nor money on the lonely track; and watched over me for weeks when I was drunk—drugged and poisoned at the cursed shanties; and saved my life more'n once, and got kicks and curses very often for thanks; and forgave me for it all; and—and fought for me. He was the only living thing that stood up for me against that crawling push of curs when they set onter me at the shanty back yonder—and he left his mark on some of 'em too; and—and so did I."

He took another spell.

Then he drew in his breath, shut his teeth hard, shouldered his swag, stepped into the doorway, and faced round again.

The dog limped out of the corner and looked up anxiously.

"That there dog," said Macquarie to the hospital staff in general, "is a better dog than I'm a man—or you too, it seems—and a better Christian. He's been a better mate to me than I ever was to any man—or any man to me. He's watched over me; kep' me from getting robbed many a time; fought for me; saved my life and took drunken kicks and curses for thanks—and forgave me. He's been a true, straight, honest, and faithful mate to me—and I ain't going to desert him now. I ain't going to kick him out in the road with a broken leg. I—Oh, my God! my back!"

He groaned and lurched forward, but they caught him, slipped off the swag, and laid him on a bed.

Half an hour later the shearer was comfortably fixed up.

"Where's my dog!" he asked, when he came to himself.

"Oh, the dog's all right," said the nurse, rather impatiently. "Don't bother. The doctor's setting his leg out in the yard."

GOING BLIND

I met him in the Full-and-Plenty Dining Rooms. It was a cheap place in the city, with good beds upstairs let at one shilling per night—"Board and residence for respectable single men, fifteen shillings per week." I was a respectable single man then. I boarded and resided there. I boarded at a greasy little table in the greasy little corner under the fluffy little staircase in the hot and greasy little dining-room or restaurant downstairs. They called it dining-rooms, but it was only one room, and them wasn't half enough room in it to work your elbows when the seven little tables and forty-nine chairs were occupied. There was not room for an ordinary-sized steward to pass up and down between the tables; but our waiter was not an ordinary-sized man—he was a living skeleton in miniature. We handed the soup, and the "roast beef one," and "roast lamb one," "corn beef and cabbage one," "veal and stuffing one," and the "veal and pickled pork," one—or two, or three, as the case might be—and the tea and coffee, and the various kinds of puddings—we handed them over each other, and dodged the drops as well as we could. The very hot and very greasy little kitchen was adjacent, and it contained the bathroom and other conveniences, behind screens of whitewashed boards.

I resided upstairs in a room where there were five beds and one wash-stand; one candle-stick, with a very short bit of soft yellow candle in it; the back of a hair-brush, with about a dozen bristles in it; and half a comb—the big-tooth end—with nine and a half teeth at irregular distances apart.

He was a typical bushman, not one of those tall, straight, wiry, brown men of the West, but from the old Selection Districts, where many drovers came from, and of the old bush school; one of those slight active little fellows whom we used to see in cabbage-tree hats, Crimean shirts, strapped trousers, and elastic-side boots—"larstins," they called them. They could dance well; sing indifferently, and mostly through their noses, the old bush songs; play the concertina horribly; and ride like—like—well, they could ride.

He seemed as if he had forgotten to grow old and die out with this old colonial school to which he belonged. They had careless and forgetful ways about them. His name was Jack Gunther, he said, and he'd come to Sydney to try to get something done to his eyes. He had a portmanteau, a carpet bag, some things in a three-bushel bag, and a tin bog. I sat beside him on his bed, and struck up an acquaintance, and he told me all about it. First he asked me would I mind shifting round to the other side, as he was rather deaf in that ear. He'd been kicked by a horse, he said, and had been a little dull o' hearing on that side ever since.

He was as good as blind. "I can see the people near me," he said, "but I can't make out their faces. I can just make out the pavement and the houses close at hand, and all the rest is a sort of white blur." He looked up: "That ceiling is a kind of white, ain't it? And this," tapping the wall and putting his nose close to it, "is a sort of green, ain't it?" The ceiling might have been whiter. The prevalent tints of the wall-paper had originally been blue and red, but it was mostly green enough now—a damp, rotten green; but I was ready to swear that the ceiling was snow and that the walls were as green as grass if it would have made him feel more comfortable. His sight began to get bad about six years before, he said; he didn't take much notice of it at first, and then he saw a quack, who made his eyes worse. He had already the manner of the blind—the touch of every finger, and even the gentleness in his speech. He had a boy down with him—a "sorter cousin of his," and the boy saw him round. "I'll have to be sending that youngster back," he said, "I think I'll send him home next week. He'll be picking up and learning too much down here."

I happened to know the district he came from, and we would sit by the hour and talk about the country, and chaps by the name of this and chaps by the name of that—drovers mostly, whom we had met or had heard of. He asked me if I'd ever heard of a chap by the name of Joe Scott—a big sandy-complexioned chap, who might be droving; he was his brother, or, at least, his half-brother, but he hadn't heard of him for years; he'd last heard of him at Blackall, in Queensland; he might have gone overland to Western Australia with Tyson's cattle to the new country.

We talked about grubbing and fencing and digging and droving and shearing—all about the bush—and it all came back to me as we talked. "I can see it all now," he said once, in an abstracted tone, seeming to fix his helpless eyes on the wall opposite. But he didn't see the dirty blind wall, nor the dingy window, nor the skimpy little bed, nor the greasy wash-stand; he saw the dark blue ridges in the sunlight, the grassy sidings and flats, the creek with clumps of she-oak here and there, the course of the willow-fringed river below, the distant peaks and ranges fading away into a lighter azure, the granite ridge in the middle distance, and the rocky rises, the stringy-bark and the apple-tree flats, the scrubs, and the sunlit plains—and all. I could see it, too—plainer than ever I did.

He had done a bit of fencing in his time, and we got talking about timber. He didn't believe in having fencing-posts with big butts; he reckoned it was a mistake. "You see," he said, "the top of the butt catches the rain water and makes the post rot quicker. I'd back posts without any butt at all to last as long or longer than posts with 'em—that's if the fence is well put up and well rammed." He had supplied fencing stuff, and fenced by contract, and—well, you can get more posts without butts out of a tree than posts with them. He also objected to charring the butts. He said it only made more work—and wasted time—the butts lasted longer without being charred.

I asked him if he'd ever got stringy-bark palings or shingles out of mountain ash, and he smiled a smile that did my heart good to see, and said he had. He had also got them out of various other kinds of trees.

We talked about soil and grass, and gold-digging, and many other things which came back to one like a revelation as we yarned.

He had been to the hospital several times. "The doctors don't say they can cure me," he said, "they say they might, be able to improve my sight and hearing, but it would take a long time—anyway, the treatment would improve my general health. They know what's the matter with my eyes," and he explained it as well as he could. "I wish I'd seen a good doctor when my eyes first began to get weak; but young chaps are always careless over things. It's harder to get cured of anything when you're done growing."

He was always hopeful and cheerful. "If the worst comes to the worst," he said, "there's things I can do where I come from. I might do a bit o' wool-sorting, for instance. I'm a pretty fair expert. Or else when they're weeding out I could help. I'd just have to sit down and they'd bring the sheep to me, and I'd feel the wool and tell them what it was—being blind improves the feeling, you know."

He had a packet of portraits, but he couldn't make them out very well now. They were sort of blurred to him, but I described them and he told me who they were. "That's a girl o' mine," he said, with reference to one—a jolly, good-looking bush girl. "I got a letter from her yesterday. I managed to scribble something, but I'll get you, if you don't mind, to write something more I want to put in on another piece of paper, and address an envelope for me."

Darkness fell quickly upon him now—or, rather, the "sort of white blur" increased and closed in. But his hearing was better, he said, and he was glad of that and still cheerful. I thought it natural that his hearing should improve as he went blind.

One day he said that he did not think he would bother going to the hospital any more. He reckoned he'd get back to where he was known. He'd stayed down too long already, and the "stuff" wouldn't stand it. He was expecting a letter that didn't come. I was away for a couple of days, and when I came back he had been shifted out of the room and had a bed in an angle of the landing on top of the staircase, with the people brushing against him and stumbling over his things all day on their way up and down. I felt indignant, thinking that—the house being full—the boss had taken advantage of the bushman's helplessness and good nature to put him there. But he said that he was quite comfortable. "I can get a whiff of air here," he said.

Going in next day I thought for a moment that I had dropped suddenly back into the past and into a bush dance, for there was a concertina going upstairs. He was sitting on the bed, with his legs crossed, and a new cheap concertina on his knee, and his eyes turned to the patch of ceiling as if it were a piece of music and he could read it. "I'm trying to knock a few tunes into my head," he said, with a brave smile, "in case the worst comes to the worst." He tried to be cheerful, but seemed worried and anxious. The letter hadn't come. I thought of the many blind musicians in Sydney, and I thought of the bushman's chance, standing at a corner swanking a cheap concertina, and I felt sorry for him.

I went out with a vague idea of seeing someone about the matter, and getting something done for the bushman—of bringing a little influence to his assistance; but I suddenly remembered that my clothes were worn out, my hat in a shocking state, my boots burst, and that I owed for a week's board and lodging, and was likely to be thrown out at any moment myself; and so I was not in a position to go where there was influence.

When I went back to the restaurant there was a long, gaunt sandy-complexioned bushman sitting by Jack's side. Jack introduced him as his brother, who had returned unexpectedly to his native district, and had followed him to Sydney. The brother was rather short with me at first, and seemed to regard the restaurant people—all of us, in fact—in the light of spielers who wouldn't hesitate to take advantage of Jack's blindness if he left him a moment; and he looked ready to knock down the first man who stumbled against Jack, or over his luggage—but that soon wore off. Jack was going to stay with Joe at the Coffee Palace for a few weeks, and then go back up-country, he told me. He was excited and happy. His brother's manner towards him was as if Jack had just lost his wife, or boy or someone very dear to him. He would not allow him to do anything for himself, nor try to—not even lace up his boot. He seemed to think that he was thoroughly helpless, and when I saw him pack up Jack's things, and help him at the table and fix his tie and collar with his great brown hands, which trembled all the time with grief and gentleness, and make Jack sit down on the bed whilst he got a cab and carried the trap down to it, and take him downstairs as if he were made of thin glass, and settle with the landlord—then I knew that Jack was all right.

We had a drink together—Joe, Jack, the cabman, and I. Joe was very careful to hand Jack the glass, and Jack made joke about it for Joe's benefit. He swore he could see a glass yet, and Joe laughed, but looked extra troubled the next moment.

I felt their grips on my hand for five minutes after we parted.

ARVIE ASPINALL'S ALARM CLOCK

In one of these years a paragraph appeared in a daily paper to the effect that a constable had discovered a little boy asleep on the steps of Grinder Bros' factory at four o'clock one rainy morning. He awakened him, and demanded an explanation.

The little fellow explained that he worked there, and was frightened of being late; he started work at six, and was apparently greatly astonished to hear that it was only four. The constable examined a small parcel which the frightened child had in his hand. It contained a clean apron and three slices of bread and treacle.

The child further explained that he woke up and thought it was late, and didn't like to wake mother and ask her the time "because she'd been washin'." He didn't look at the clock, because they "didn't have one." He volunteered no explanations as to how he expected mother to know the time, but, perhaps, like many other mites of his kind, he had unbounded faith in the infinitude of a mother's wisdom. His name was Arvie Aspinall, please sir, and he lived in Jones's Alley. Father was dead.

A few days later the same paper took great pleasure in stating, in reference to that "Touching Incident" noticed in a recent issue, that a benevolent society lady had started a subscription among her friends with the object of purchasing an alarm-clock for the little boy found asleep at Grinder Bros' workshop door.

Later on, it was mentioned, in connection with the touching incident, that the alarm-clock had been bought and delivered to the boy's mother, who appeared to be quite overcome with gratitude. It was learned, also, from another source, that the last assertion was greatly exaggerated.

The touching incident was worn out in another paragraph, which left no doubt that the benevolent society lady was none other than a charming and accomplished daughter of the House of Grinder.

It was late in the last day of the Easter Holidays, during which Arvie Aspinall had lain in bed with a bad cold. He was still what he called "croopy." It was about nine o'clock, and the business of Jones's Alley was in full swing.

"That's better, mother, I'm far better," said Arvie, "the sugar and vinegar cuts the phlegm, and the both'rin' cough gits out. It got out to such an extent for the next few minutes that he could not speak. When he recovered his breath, he said:

"Better or worse, I'll have to go to work to-morrow. Gimme the clock, mother."

"I tell you you shall not go! It will be your death."

"It's no use talking, mother; we can't starve—and—s'posin' somebody got my place! Gimme the clock, mother."

"I'll send one of the children round to say you're ill. They'll surely let you off for a day or two."

"Tain't no use; they won't wait; I know them—what does Grinder Bros care if I'm ill? Never mind, mother, I'll rise above 'em all yet. Give me the clock, mother."

She gave him the clock, and he proceeded to wind it up and set the alarm.

"There's somethin' wrong with the gong," he muttered, "it's gone wrong two nights now, but I'll chance it. I'll set the alarm at five, that'll give me time to dress and git there early. I wish I hadn't to walk so far."

He paused to read some words engraved round the dial:

Early to bed and early to rise
Makes a man healthy and wealthy and wise.

He had read the verse often before, and was much taken with the swing and rhythm of it. He had repeated it to himself, over and over again, without reference to the sense or philosophy of it. He had never dreamed of doubting anything in print—and this was engraved. But now a new light seemed to dawn upon him. He studied the sentence awhile, and then read it aloud for the second time. He turned it over in his mind again in silence.

"Mother!" he said suddenly, "I think it lies." She placed the clock on the shelf, tucked him into his little bed on the sofa, and blew out the light.

Arvie seemed to sleep, but she lay awake thinking of her troubles. Of her husband carried home dead from his work one morning; of her eldest son who only came to loaf on her when he was out of jail; of the second son, who had feathered his nest in another city, and had no use for her any longer; of the next—poor delicate little Arvie—struggling manfully to help, and wearing his young life out at Grinder Bros when he should be at school; of the five helpless younger children asleep in the next room: of her hard life—scrubbing floors from half-past five till eight, and then starting her day's work—washing!—of having to rear her children in the atmosphere of the slums, because she could not afford to move and pay a higher rent; and of the rent.

Arvie commenced to mutter in his sleep.

"Can't you get to sleep, Arvie?" she asked. "Is your throat sore? Can I get anything for you?"

"I'd like to sleep," he muttered, dreamily, "but it won't seem more'n a moment before—before—"

"Before what, Arvie?" she asked, quickly, fearing that he was becoming delirious.

"Before the alarm goes off!"

He was talking in his sleep.

She rose gently and put the alarm on two hours. "He can rest now," she whispered to herself.

Presently Arvie sat bolt upright, and said quickly, "Mother! I thought the alarm went off!" Then, without waiting for an answer, he lay down as suddenly and slept.

The rain had cleared away, and a bright, starry dome was over sea and city, over slum and villa alike; but little of it could be seen from the hovel in Jones's Alley, save a glimpse of the Southern Cross and a few stars round it. It was what ladies call a "lovely night," as seen from the house of Grinder— "Grinderville"—with its moonlit terraces and gardens sloping gently to the water, and its windows lit up for an Easter ball, and its reception-rooms thronged by its own exclusive set, and one of its charming and accomplished daughters melting a select party to tears by her pathetic recitation about a little crossing sweeper.

There was something wrong with the alarm-clock, or else Mrs Aspinall had made a mistake, for the gong sounded startlingly in the dead of night. She woke with a painful start, and lay still, expecting to hear Arvie get up; but he made no sign. She turned a white, frightened face towards the sofa where he lay— the light from the alley's solitary lamp on the pavement above shone down through the window, and she saw that he had not moved.

Why didn't the clock wake him? He was such a light sleeper! "Arvie!" she called; no answer. "Arvie!" she called again, with a strange ring of remonstrance mingling with the terror in her voice. Arvie never answered.

"Oh! my God!" she moaned.

She rose and stood by the sofa. Arvie lay on his back with his arms folded—a favourite sleeping position of his; but his eyes were wide open and staring upwards as though they would stare through ceiling and roof to the place where God ought to be.

STRAGGLERS

An oblong hut, walled with blue-grey hardwood slabs, adzed at the ends and set horizontally between the round sapling studs; high roof of the eternal galvanized iron. A big rubbish heap lies about a yard to the right of the door, which opens from the middle of one of the side walls; it might be the front or the back wall—there is nothing to fix it. Two rows of rough bunks run round three sides of the interior; and a fire-place occupies one end—the kitchen end. Sleeping, eating, gambling and cooking accommodation for thirty men in about eighteen by forty feet.

The rouseabouts and shearers use the hut in common during shearing. Down the centre of the place runs a table made of stakes driven into the ground, with cross-pieces supporting a top of half-round slabs set with the flat sides up, and affording a few level places for soup-plates; on each side are crooked, unbarked poles laid in short forks, to serve as seats. The poles are worn smoothest opposite the level places on the table. The floor is littered with rubbish—old wool-bales, newspapers, boots, worn-out shearing pants, rough bedding, etc., raked out of the bunks in impatient search for missing articles—signs of a glad and eager departure with cheques when the shed last cut out.

To the west is a dam, holding back a broad, shallow sheet of grey water, with dead trees standing in it.

Further up along this water is a brush shearing-shed, a rough framework of poles with a brush roof. This kind of shed has the advantage of being cooler than iron. It is not rain-proof, but shearers do not work in rainy weather; shearing even slightly damp sheep is considered the surest and quickest way to get the worst kind of rheumatism. The floor is covered with rubbish from the roof, and here and there lies a rusty pair of shears. A couple of dry tar-pots hang by nails in the posts. The "board" is very uneven and must be bad for sweeping. The pens are formed by round, crooked stakes driven into the ground in irregular lines, and the whole business reminds us of the "cubby-house" style of architecture of our childhood.

Opposite stands the wool-shed, built entirely of galvanized iron; a blinding object to start out of the scrub on a blazing, hot day. God forgive the man who invented galvanized iron, and the greed which introduced it into Australia: you could not get worse roofing material for a hot country.

The wool-washing, soap-boiling, and wool-pressing arrangements are further up the dam. "Government House" is a mile away, and is nothing better than a bush hut; this station belongs to a company. And the company belongs to a bank. And the banks belong to England, mostly.

Mulga scrub all round, and, in between, patches of reddish sand where the grass ought to be.

It is New Year's Eve. Half a dozen travellers are camping in the hut, having a spell. They need it, for there are twenty miles of dry lignum plain between here and the government bore to the east; and about eighteen miles of heavy, sandy, cleared road north-west to the next water in that direction. With one exception, the men do not seem hard up; at least, not as that condition is understood by the swagmen of these times. The least lucky one of the lot had three weeks' work in a shed last season, and there might probably be five pounds amongst the whole crowd. They are all shearers, or at least they say they are. Some might be only "rousers."

These men have a kind of stock hope of getting a few stragglers to shear somewhere; but their main object is to live till next shearing. In order to do this they must tramp for tucker, and trust to the regulation—and partly mythical—pint of flour, and bit of meat, or tea and sugar, and to the goodness of cooks and storekeepers and boundary-riders. You can only depend on getting tucker once at one place; then you must tramp on to the next. If you cannot get it once you must go short; but there is a lot of energy in an empty stomach. If you get an extra supply you may camp for a day and have a spell. To live you must walk. To cease walking is to die.

The Exception is an outcast amongst bush outcasts, and looks better fitted for Sydney Domain. He lies on the bottom of a galvanized-iron case, with a piece of blue blanket for a pillow. He is dressed in a blue cotton jumper, a pair of very old and ragged tweed trousers, and one boot and one slipper. He found the slipper in the last shed, and the boot in the rubbish-heap here. When his own boots gave out he walked a hundred and fifty miles with his feet roughly sewn up in pieces of sacking from an old wool-bale. No sign of a patch, or an attempt at mending anywhere about his clothes, and that is a bad sign; when a swagman leaves off mending or patching his garments, his case is about hopeless. The Exception's swag consists of the aforesaid bit of blanket rolled up and tied with pieces of rag. He has no water-bag; carries his water in a billy; and how he manages without a bag is known only to himself. He has read every scrap of print within reach, and now lies on his side, with his face to the wall and one arm thrown up over his head; the jumper is twisted back, and leaves his skin bare from hip to arm-pit. His lower face is brutal, his eyes small and shifty, and ugly straight lines run across his low forehead. He says very little, but scowls most of the time—poor devil. He might be, or at least seem, a totally different man under more favourable conditions. He is probably a free labourer.

A very sick jackaroo lies in one of the bunks. A sandy, sawney-looking Bourke native takes great interest in this wreck; watches his every movement as though he never saw a sick man before. The men lie about in the bunks, or the shade of the hut, and rest, and read all the soiled and mutilated scraps of literature they can rake out of the rubbish, and sleep, and wake up swimming in perspiration, and growl about the heat.

It is hot, and two shearers' cats—a black and a white one—sit in one of the upper bunks with their little red tongues out, panting like dogs. These cats live well during shearing, and take their chances the rest of the year—just as shed rouseabouts have to do. They seem glad to see the traveller come; he makes things more homelike. They curl and sidle affectionately round the table-legs, and the legs of the men, and purr, and carry their masts up, and regard the cooking with feline interest and approval, and look as cheerful as cats can—and as contented. God knows how many tired, dusty, and sockless ankles they rub against in their time.

Now and then a man takes his tucker-bags and goes down to the station for a bit of flour, or meat, or tea, or sugar, choosing the time when the manager is likely to be out on the run. The cook here is a "good cook," from a traveller's point of view; too good to keep his place long.

Occasionally someone gets some water in an old kerosene-tin and washes a shirt or pair of trousers, and a pair or two of socks—or foot-rags—(Prince Alfreds they call them). That is, he soaks some of the stiffness out of these articles.

Three times a day the black billies and cloudy nose-bags are placed on the table. The men eat in a casual kind of way, as though it were only a custom of theirs, a matter of form—a habit which could be left off if it were worth while.

The Exception is heard to remark to no one in particular that he'll give all he has for a square meal.

"An' ye'd get it cheap, begod!" says a big Irish shearer. "Come and have dinner with us; there's plenty there."

But the Exception only eats a few mouthfuls, and his appetite is gone; his stomach has become contracted, perhaps.

The Wreck cannot eat at all, and seems internally disturbed by the sight of others eating.

One of the men is a cook, and this morning he volunteered good-naturedly to bake bread for the rest. His mates amuse themselves by chyacking him.

"I've heard he's a dirty and slow cook," says one, addressing Eternity.

"Ah!" says the cook, "you'll be glad to come to me for a pint of flour when I'm cooking and you're on the track, some day."

Sunset. Some of the men sit at the end of the hut to get the full benefit of a breeze which comes from the west. A great bank of rain-clouds is rising in that direction, but no one says he thinks it will rain; neither does anybody think we're going to have some rain. None but the greenest jackaroo would venture that risky and foolish observation. Out here, it can look more like rain without raining, and continue to do so for a longer time, than in most other places.

The Wreck went down to the station this afternoon to get some medicine and bush medical advice. The Bourke sawney helped him to do up his swag; he did it with an awed look and manner, as though he thought it a great distinction to be allowed to touch the belongings of such a curiosity. It was afterwards generally agreed that it was a good idea for the Wreck to go to the station; he would get some physic and, a bit of tucker to take him on. "For they'll give tucker to a sick man sooner than to a chap what's all right."

The Exception is rooting about in the rubbish for the other blucher boot.

The men get a little more sociable, and "feel" each other to find out who's "Union," and talk about water, and exchange hints as to good tucker-tracks, and discuss the strike, and curse the squatter (which is all they have got to curse), and growl about Union leaders, and tell lies against each other sociably.

There are tally lies; and lies about getting tucker by trickery; and long-tramp-with-heavy-swag-and-no-water lies; and lies about getting the best of squatters and bosses-over-the-board; and droving, fighting, racing, gambling and drinking lies. Lies ad libitum; and every true Australian bushman must try his best to tell a bigger out-back lie than the last bush-liar.

Pat is not quite easy in his mind. He found an old pair of pants in the scrub this morning, and cannot decide whether they are better than his own, or, rather, whether his own are worse—if that's possible. He does not want to increase the weight of his swag unnecessarily by taking both pairs. He reckons that the pants were thrown away when the shed cut out last, but then they might have been lying out exposed to the weather for a longer period. It is rather an important question, for it is very annoying, after you've mended and patched an old pair of pants, to find, when a day or two further on the track, that they are more rotten than the pair you left behind.

There is some growling about the water here, and one of the men makes a billy of tea. The water is better cooked. Pint-pots and sugar-bags are groped out and brought to the kitchen hut, and each man fills his pannikin; the Irishman keeps a thumb on the edge of his, so as to know when the pot is full, for it is very dark, and there is no more firewood. You soon know this way, especially if you are in the habit of pressing lighted tobacco down into your pipe with the top of your thumb. The old slush-lamps are all burnt out.

Each man feels for the mouth of his sugar-bag with one hand while he keeps the bearings of his pot with the other.

The Irishman has lost his match-box, and feels for it all over the table without success. He stoops down with his hands on his knees, gets the table-top on a level with the flicker of firelight, and "moons" the object, as it were.

Time to turn in. It is very dark inside and bright moonlight without; every crack seems like a ghost peering in. Some of the men will roll up their swags on the morrow and depart; some will take another day's spell. It is all according to the tucker.

THE UNION BURIES ITS DEAD

While out boating one Sunday afternoon on a billabong across the river, we saw a young man on horseback driving some horses along the bank. He said it was a fine day, and asked if the Water was deep there. The joker of our party said it was deep enough to drown him, and he laughed and rode farther up. We didn't take much notice of him.

Next day a funeral gathered at a corner pub and asked each other in to have a drink while waiting for the hearse. They passed away some of the time dancing jigs to a piano in the bar parlour. They passed away the rest of the time skylarking and fighting.

The defunct was a young Union labourer, about twenty-five, who had been drowned the previous day while trying to swim some horses across a billabong of the Darling.

He was almost a stranger in town, and the fact of his having been a Union man accounted for the funeral. The police found some Union papers in his swag, and called at the General Labourers' Union Office for information about him. That's how we knew. The secretary had very little information to give. The departed was a "Roman," and the majority of the town were otherwise—but Unionism is stronger than creed. Liquor, however, is stronger than Unionism; and, when the hearse presently arrived, more than two-thirds of the funeral were unable to follow.

The procession numbered fifteen, fourteen souls following the broken shell of a soul. Perhaps not one of the fourteen possessed a soul any more than the corpse did—but that doesn't matter.

Four or five of the funeral, who were boarders at the pub, borrowed a trap which the landlord used to carry passengers to and from the railway station. They were strangers to us who were on foot, and we to them. We were all strangers to the corpse.

A horseman, who looked like a drover just returned from a big trip, dropped into our dusty wake and followed us a few hundred yards, dragging his packhorse behind him, but a friend made wild and demonstrative signals from a hotel veranda—hooking at the air in front with his right hand and jobbing his left thumb over his shoulder in the direction of the bar—so the drover hauled off and didn't catch up to us any more. He was a stranger to the entire show.

We walked in twos. There were three twos. It was very hot and dusty; the heat rushed in fierce dazzling rays across every iron roof and light-coloured wall that was turned to the sun. One or two pubs closed respectfully until we got past. They closed their bar doors and the patrons went in and out through some side or back entrance for a few minutes. Bushmen seldom grumble at an inconvenience of this sort, when it is caused by a funeral. They have too much respect for the dead.

On the way to the cemetery we passed three shearers sitting on the shady side of a fence. One was drunk—very drunk. The other two covered their right ears with their hats, out of respect for the departed—whoever he might have been—and one of them kicked the drunk and muttered something to him.

He straightened himself up, stared, and reached helplessly for his hat, which he shoved half off and then on again. Then he made a great effort to pull himself together—and succeeded. He stood up, braced his back against the fence, knocked off his hat, and remorsefully placed his foot on it—to keep it off his head till the funeral passed.

A tall, sentimental drover, who walked by my side, cynically quoted Byronic verses suitable to the occasion—to death—and asked with pathetic humour whether we thought the dead man's ticket would be recognized "over yonder." It was a G.L.U. ticket, and the general opinion was that it would be recognized.

Presently my friend said:

"You remember when we were in the boat yesterday, we saw a man driving some horses along the bank?"

"Yes."

He nodded at the hearse and said "Well, that's him."

I thought awhile.

"I didn't take any particular notice of him," I said. "He said something, didn't he?"

"Yes; said it was a fine day. You'd have taken more notice if you'd known that he was doomed to die in the hour, and that those were the last words he would say to any man in this world."

"To be sure," said a full voice from the rear. "If ye'd known that, ye'd have prolonged the conversation."

We plodded on across the railway line and along the hot, dusty road which ran to the cemetery, some of us talking about the accident, and lying about the narrow escapes we had had ourselves. Presently someone said:

"There's the Devil."

I looked up and saw a priest standing in the shade of the tree by the cemetery gate.

The hearse was drawn up and the tail-boards were opened. The funeral extinguished its right ear with its hat as four men lifted the coffin out and laid it over the grave. The priest—a pale, quiet young fellow—stood under the shade of a sapling which grew at the head of the grave. He took off his hat, dropped it carelessly on the ground, and proceeded to business. I noticed that one or two heathens winced slightly when the holy water was sprinkled on the coffin. The drops quickly evaporated, and the little round black spots they left were soon dusted over; but the spots showed, by contrast, the cheapness and shabbiness of the cloth with which the coffin was covered. It seemed black before; now it looked a dusky grey.

Just here man's ignorance and vanity made a farce of the funeral. A big, bull-necked publican, with heavy, blotchy features, and a supremely ignorant expression, picked up the priest's straw hat and held it about two inches over the head of his reverence during the whole of the service. The father, be it remembered, was standing in the shade. A few shoved their hats on and off uneasily, struggling between their disgust for the living and their respect for the dead. The hat had a conical crown and a brim sloping down all round like a sunshade, and the publican held it with his great red claw spread over the crown. To do the priest justice, perhaps he didn't notice the incident. A stage priest or parson in the same position might have said, "Put the hat down, my friend; is not the memory of our departed brother worth more than my complexion?" A wattle-bark layman might have expressed himself in stronger language, none the less to the point. But my priest seemed unconscious of what was going on. Besides, the publican was a great and important pillar of the church. He couldn't, as an ignorant and conceited ass, lose such a good opportunity of asserting his faithfulness and importance to his church.

The grave looked very narrow under the coffin, and I drew a breath of relief when the box slid easily down. I saw a coffin get stuck once, at Rookwood, and it had to be yanked out with difficulty, and laid on the sods at the feet of the heart-broken relations, who howled dismally while the grave-diggers widened the hole. But they don't cut contracts so fine in the West. Our grave-digger was not altogether bowelless, and, out of respect for that human quality described as "feelin's," he scraped up some light and dusty soil and threw it down to deaden the fall of the clay lumps on the coffin. He also tried to steer the first few shovelfuls gently down against the end of the grave with the back of the shovel turned outwards, but the hard dry Darling River clods rebounded and knocked all the same. It didn't matter much—nothing does. The fall of lumps of clay on a stranger's coffin doesn't sound any different from the fall of the same things on an ordinary wooden box—at least I didn't notice anything awesome or unusual in the sound; but, perhaps, one of us—the most sensitive—might have been impressed by being reminded of a burial of long ago, when the thump of every sod jolted his heart.

I have left out the wattle—because it wasn't there. I have also neglected to mention the heart-broken old mate, with his grizzled head bowed and great pearly drops streaming down his rugged cheeks. He was absent—he was probably "Out Back." For similar reasons I have omitted reference to the suspicious moisture in the eyes of a bearded bush ruffian named Bill. Bill failed to turn up, and the only moisture was that which was induced by the heat. I have left out the "sad Australian sunset" because the sun was not going down at the time. The burial took place exactly at midday.

The dead bushman's name was Jim, apparently; but they found no portraits, nor locks of hair, nor any love letters, nor anything of that kind in his swag—not even a reference to his mother; only some papers relating to Union matters. Most of us didn't know the name till we saw it on the coffin; we knew him as "that poor chap that got drowned yesterday."

"So his name's James Tyson," said my drover acquaintance, looking at the plate.

"Why! Didn't you know that before?" I asked.

"No; but I knew he was a Union man."

It turned out, afterwards, that J.T. wasn't his real name—only "the name he went by." Anyhow he was buried by it, and most of the "Great Australian Dailies" have mentioned in their brevity columns that a young man named James John Tyson was drowned in a billabong of the Darling last Sunday.

We did hear, later on, what his real name was; but if we ever chance to read it in the "Missing Friends Column," we shall not be able to give any information to heart-broken mother or sister or wife, nor to anyone who could let him hear something to his advantage—for we have already forgotten the name.

ON THE EDGE OF A PLAIN

"I'd been away from home for eight years," said Mitchell to his mate, as they dropped their swags in the mulga shade and sat down. "I hadn't written a letter—kept putting it off, and a blundering fool of a fellow that got down the day before me told the old folks that he'd heard I was dead."

Here he took a pull at his water-bag.

"When I got home they were all in mourning for me. It was night, and the girl that opened the door screamed and fainted away like a shot."

He lit his pipe.

"Mother was upstairs howling and moaning in a chair, with all the girls boo-hoo-ing round her for company. The old man was sitting in the back kitchen crying to himself."

He put his hat down on the ground, dinted in the crown, and poured some water into the hollow for his cattle-pup.

"The girls came rushing down. Mother was so pumped out that she couldn't get up. They thought at first I was a ghost, and then they all tried to get holt of me at once—nearly smothered me. Look at that pup! You want to carry a tank of water on a dry stretch when you've got a pup that drinks as much as two men."

He poured a drop more water into the top of his hat.

"Well, mother screamed and nearly fainted when she saw me. Such a picnic you never saw. They kept it up all night. I thought the old cove was gone off his chump. The old woman wouldn't let go my hand for three mortal hours. Have you got the knife?"

He cut up some more tobacco.

"All next day the house was full of neighbours, and the first to come was an old sweetheart of mine; I never thought she cared for me till then. Mother and the girls made me swear never to go away any more; and they kept watching me, and hardly let me go outside for fear I'd—"

"Get drunk?"

"No—you're smart—for fear I'd clear. At last I swore on the Bible that I'd never leave home while the old folks were alive; and then mother seemed easier in her mind."

He rolled the pup over and examined his feet. "I expect I'll have to carry him a bit—his feet are sore. Well, he's done pretty well this morning, and anyway he won't drink so much when he's carried."

"You broke your promise about leaving home," said his mate.

Mitchell stood up, stretched himself, and looked dolefully from his heavy swag to the wide, hot, shadeless cotton-bush plain ahead.

"Oh, yes," he yawned, "I stopped at home for a week, and then they began to growl because I couldn't get any work to do."

The mate guffawed and Mitchell grinned. They shouldered the swags, with the pup on top of Mitchell's, took up their billies and water-bags, turned their unshaven faces to the wide, hazy distance, and left the timber behind them.

IN A DRY SEASON

Draw a wire fence and a few ragged gums, and add some scattered sheep running away from the train. Then you'll have the bush all along the New South Wales western line from Bathurst on.

The railway towns consist of a public house and a general store, with a square tank and a school-house on piles in the nearer distance. The tank stands at the end of the school and is not many times smaller than the building itself. It is safe to call the pub "The Railway Hotel," and the store "The Railway Stores," with an "s." A couple of patient, ungroomed hacks are probably standing outside the pub, while their masters are inside having a drink—several drinks. Also it's safe to draw a sundowner sitting listlessly on a bench on the veranda, reading the Bulletin. The Railway Stores seem to exist only in the shadow of the pub, and it is impossible to conceive either as being independent of the other. There is sometimes a small, oblong weather-board building—unpainted, and generally leaning in one of the eight possible directions, and perhaps with a twist in another—which, from its half-obliterated sign, seems to have started as a rival to the Railway Stores; but the shutters are up and the place empty.

The only town I saw that differed much from the above consisted of a box-bark humpy with a clay chimney, and a woman standing at the door throwing out the wash-up water.

By way of variety, the artist might make a water-colour sketch of a fettler's tent on the line, with a billy hanging over the fire in front, and three fettlers standing round filling their pipes.

Slop sac suits, red faces, and old-fashioned, flat-brimmed hats, with wire round the brims, begin to drop into the train on the other side of Bathurst; and here and there a hat with three inches of crape round the crown, which perhaps signifies death in the family at some remote date, and perhaps doesn't. Sometimes, I believe, it only means grease under the band. I notice that when a bushman puts crape round his hat he generally leaves it there till the hat wears out, or another friend dies. In the latter case, he buys a new piece of crape. This outward sign of bereavement usually has a jolly red face beneath it. Death is about the only cheerful thing in the bush.

We crossed the Macquarie—a narrow, muddy gutter with a dog swimming across, and three goats interested.

A little farther on we saw the first sundowner. He carried a Royal Alfred, and had a billy in one hand and a stick in the other. He was dressed in a tail-coat turned yellow, a print shirt, and a pair of moleskin trousers, with big square calico patches on the knees; and his old straw hat was covered with calico. Suddenly he slipped his swag, dropped his billy, and ran forward, boldly flourishing the stick. I thought that he was mad, and was about to attack the train, but he wasn't; he was only killing a snake. I didn't have time to see whether he cooked the snake or not—perhaps he only thought of Adam.

Somebody told me that the country was very dry on the other side of Nevertire. It is. I wouldn't like to sit down on it any where. The least horrible spot in the bush, in a dry season, is where the bush isn't—where it has been cleared away and a green crop is trying to grow. They talk of settling people on the land! Better settle in it. I'd rather settle on the water; at least, until some gigantic system of irrigation is perfected in the West.

Along about Byrock we saw the first shearers. They dress like the unemployed, but differ from that body in their looks of independence. They sat on trucks and wool-bales and the fence, watching the train, and hailed Bill, and Jim, and Tom, and asked how those individuals were getting on.

Here we came across soft felt hats with straps round the crowns, and full-bearded faces under them. Also a splendid-looking black tracker in a masher uniform and a pair of Wellington boots.

One or two square-cuts and stand-up collars struggle dismally through to the bitter end. Often a member of the unemployed starts cheerfully out, with a letter from the Government Labour Bureau in his pocket, and nothing else. He has an idea that the station where he has the job will be within easy walking distance of Bourke. Perhaps he thinks there'll be a cart or a buggy waiting for him. He travels for a night and day without a bite to eat, and, on arrival, he finds that the station is eighty or a hundred miles away. Then he has to explain matters to a publican and a coach-driver. God bless the publican and the coach-driver! God forgive our social system!

Native industry was represented at one place along the line by three tiles, a chimney-pot, and a length of piping on a slab.

Somebody said to me, "Yer wanter go out back, young man, if yer wanter see the country. Yer wanter get away from the line." I don't wanter; I've been there.

You could go to the brink of eternity so far as Australia is concerned and yet meet an animated mummy of a swagman who will talk of going "out back." Out upon the out-back fiend!

About Byrock we met the bush liar in all his glory. He was dressed like—like a bush larrikin. His name was Jim. He had been to a ball where some blank had "touched" his blanky overcoat. The overcoat had a cheque for ten "quid" in the pocket. He didn't seem to feel the loss much. "Wot's ten quid?" He'd been everywhere, including the Gulf country. He still had three or four sheds to go to. He had telegrams in his pocket from half a dozen squatters and supers offering him pens on any terms. He didn't give a blank whether he took them or no. He thought at first he had the telegrams on him but found that he had left them in the pocket of the overcoat aforesaid. He had learned butchering in a day. He was a bit of a scrapper himself and talked a lot about the ring. At the last station where he shore he gave the super the father of a hiding. The super was a big chap, about six-foot-three, and had knocked out Paddy Somebody in one round. He worked with a man who shore four hundred sheep in nine hours.

Here a quiet-looking bushman in a corner of the carriage grew restless, and presently he opened his mouth and took the liar down in about three minutes.

At 5.30 we saw a long line of camels moving out across the sunset. There's something snaky about camels. They remind me of turtles and goannas.

Somebody said, "Here's Bourke."

HE'D COME BACK

The yarn was all lies, I suppose; but it wasn't bad. A city bushman told it, of course, and he told it in the travellers' hut.

"As true's God hears me I never meant to desert her in cold blood," he said. "We'd only been married about two years, and we'd got along grand together; but times was hard, and I had to jump at the first chance of a job, and leave her with her people, an' go up-country."

He paused and fumbled with his pipe until all ears were brought to bear on him.

"She was a beauty, and no mistake; she was far too good for me—I often wondered how she came to have a chap like me."

He paused again, and the others thought over it—and wondered too, perhaps.

The joker opened his lips to speak, but altered his mind about it.

"Well, I travelled up into Queensland, and worked back into Victoria 'n' South Australia, an' I wrote home pretty reg'lar and sent what money I could. Last I got down on to the south-western coast of South Australia—an' there I got mixed up with another woman—you know what that means, boys?"

Sympathetic silence.

"Well, this went on for two years, and then the other woman drove me to drink. You know what a woman can do when the devil's in her?"

Sound between a sigh and a groan from Lally Thompson. "My oath," he said, sadly.

"You should have made it three years, Jack," interposed the joker; "you said two years before." But he was suppressed.

"Well, I got free of them both, at last—drink and the woman, I mean; but it took another—it took a couple of years to pull myself straight—"

Here the joker opened his mouth again, but was warmly requested to shut it.

"Then, chaps, I got thinking. My conscience began to hurt me, and—and hurt worse every day. It nearly drove me to drink again. Ah, boys, a man—if he is a man—can't expect to wrong a woman and escape scot-free in the end." (Sigh from Lally Thompson.) "It's the one thing that always comes home to a man, sooner or later—you know what that means, boys."

Lally Thompson: "My oath!"

The joker: "Dry up yer crimson oath! What do you know about women?"

Cries of "Order!"

"Well," continued the story-teller, "I got thinking. I heard that my wife had broken her heart when I left her, and that made matters worse. I began to feel very bad about it. I felt mean. I felt disgusted with myself. I pictured my poor, ill-treated, little wife and children in misery and poverty, and my conscience wouldn't let me rest night or day"—(Lally Thompson seemed greatly moved)—"so at last I made up my mind to be a man, and make—what's the word?"

"Reparation," suggested the joker.

"Yes, so I slaved like a nigger for a year or so, got a few pounds together and went to find my wife. I found out that she was living in a cottage in Burwood, Sydney, and struggling through the winter on what she'd saved from the money her father left her.

"I got a shave and dressed up quiet and decent. I was older-looking and more subdued like, and I'd got pretty grey in those few years that I'd been making a fool of myself; and, some how, I felt rather glad about it, because I reckoned she'd notice it first thing—she was always quick at noticing things—and forgive me all the quicker. Well, I waylaid the school kids that evening, and found out mine—a little boy and a girl—and fine youngsters they were. The girl took after her mother, and the youngster was the dead spit o' me. I gave 'em half a crows each and told them to tell their mother that someone would come when the sun went down."

Bogan Bill nodded approvingly.

"So at sundown I went and knocked at the door. It opened and there stood my little wife looking prettier than ever—only careworn."

Long, impressive pause.

"Well, Jack, what did she do?" asked Bogan.

"She didn't do nothing."

"Well, Jack, and what did she say?"

Jack sighed and straightened himself up: "She said—she said—'Well, so you've come back.'"

"Painful silence.

"Well, Jack, and what did you say?"

"I said yes."

"Well, and so you had!" said Tom Moonlight.

"It wasn't that, Tom," said Jack sadly and wearily—"It was the way she said it!"

Lally Thompson rubbed his eyes: "And what did you do, Jack?" he asked gently.

"I stayed for a year, and then I deserted her again—but meant it that time."

"Ah, well! It's time to turn in."

"I'll get down among the cockies along the Lachlan, or some of these rivers," said Mitchell, throwing down his swag beneath a big tree. "A man stands a better show down there. It's a mistake to come out back. I knocked around a good deal down there among the farms. Could always get plenty of tucker, and a job if I wanted it. One cocky I worked for wanted me to stay with him for good. Sorry I didn't. I'd have been better off now. I was treated more like one of the family, and there was a couple of good-looking daughters. One of them was clean gone on me. There are some grand girls down that way. I always got on well with the girls, because I could play the fiddle and sing a bit. They'll be glad to see me when I get back there again, I know. I'll be all right—no more bother about tucker. I'll just let things slide as soon as I spot the house. I'll bet my boots the kettle will be boiling, and everything in the house will be on the table before I'm there twenty minutes. And the girls will be running to meet the old cocky when he comes riding home at night, and they'll let down the sliprails, and ask him to guess 'who's up at our place?' Yes, I'll find a job with some old cocky, with a good-looking daughter or two. I'll get on ploughing if I can; that's the sort of work I like; best graft about a farm.

"By and by the cocky'll have a few sheep he wants shorn, and one day he'll say to me, 'Jack, if you hear of a shearer knockin' round let me know—I've got a few sheep I want shore.'

"'How many have you got?' I'll say.

"'Oh, about fifteen hundred.'

"'And what d'you think of giving?'

"'Well, about twenty-five bob a hundred, but if a shearer sticks out for thirty, send him up to talk with me. I want to get 'em shore as soon as possible.'

"'It's all right,' I'll say, 'you needn't bother; I'll shear your sheep.'

"'Why,' he'll say, 'can you shear?'

"'Shear? Of course I can! I shore before you were born.' It won't matter if he's twice as old as me.

"So I'll shear his sheep and make a few pounds, and he'll be glad and all the more eager to keep me on, so's to always have someone to shear his sheep. But by and by I'll get tired of stopping in the one place and want to be on the move, so I'll tell him I'm going to leave.

"'Why, what do you want to go for?' he'll say, surprised, 'ain't you satisfied?'

"'Oh, yes, I'm satisfied, but I want a change.'

"'Oh, don't go,' he'll say; 'stop and we'll call it twenty-five bob a week.'

"But I'll tell him I'm off—wouldn't stay for a hundred when I'd made up my mind; so, when he sees he can't persuade me he'll get a bit stiff and say:

"'Well, what about that there girl? Are you goin' to go away and leave her like that?'

"'Why, what d'yer mean?' I'll say. 'Leave her like what?' I won't pretend to know what he's driving at.

"'Oh!' he'll say, 'you know very well what I mean. The question is: Are you going to marry the girl or not?'

"I'll see that things are gettin' a little warm and that I'm in a corner, so I'll say:

"'Why, I never thought about it. This is pretty sudden and out of the common, isn't it? I don't mind marrying the girl if she'll have me. Why! I haven't asked her yet!'

"'Well, look here,' he'll say, 'if you agree to marry the girl—and I'll make you marry her, any road—I'll give you that there farm over there and a couple of hundred to start on.'

"So, I'll marry her and settle down and be a cocky myself and if you ever happen to be knocking round there hard up, you needn't go short of tucker a week or two; but don't come knocking round the house when I'm not at home."

STEELMAN

Steelman was a hard case. If you were married, and settled down, and were so unfortunate as to have known Steelman in other days, he would, if in your neighbourhood and dead-beat, be sure to look you up. He would find you anywhere, no matter what precautions you might take. If he came to your house, he would stay to tea without invitation, and if he stayed to tea, he would ask you to "fix up a shake-down on the floor, old man," and put him up for the night; and, if he stopped all night, he'd remain—well, until something better turned up.

There was no shaking off Steelman. He had a way about him which would often make it appear as if you had invited him to stay, and pressed him against his roving inclination, and were glad to have him round for company, while he remained only out of pure goodwill to you. He didn't like to offend an old friend by refusing his invitation.

Steelman knew his men.

The married victim generally had neither the courage nor the ability to turn him out. He was cheerfully blind and deaf to all hints, and if the exasperated missus said anything to him straight, he would look shocked, and reply, as likely as not:

"Why, my good woman, you must be mad! I'm your husband's guest!"

And if she wouldn't cook for him, he'd cook for himself. There was no choking him off. Few people care to call the police in a case like this; and besides, as before remarked, Steelman knew his men. The only way to escape from him was to move—but then, as likely as not, he'd help pack up and come along with his portmanteau right on top of the last load of furniture, and drive you and your wife to the verge of madness by the calm style in which he proceeded to superintend the hanging of your pictures.

Once he quartered himself like this on an old schoolmate of his, named Brown, who had got married and steady and settled down. Brown tried all ways to get rid of Steelman, but he couldn't do it. One day Brown said to Steelman:

"Look here, Steely, old man, I'm very sorry, but I'm afraid we won't be able to accommodate you any longer—to make you comfortable, I mean. You see, a sister of the missus is coming down on a visit for a month or two, and we ain't got anywhere to put her, except in your room. I wish the missus's relations to blazes! I didn't marry the whole blessed family; but it seems I've got to keep them."

Pause—very awkward and painful for poor Brown. Discouraging silence from Steelman. Brown rested his elbows on his knees, and, with a pathetic and appealing movement of his hand across his forehead, he continued desperately:

"I'm very sorry, you see, old man—you know I'd like you to stay—I want you to stay.... It isn't my fault—it's the missus's doings. I've done my best with her, but I can't help it. I've been more like a master in my own house—more comfortable—and I've been better treated since I've had you to back me up.... I'll feel mighty lonely, anyway, when ycu're gone.... But... you know... as soon as her sister goes... you know.... "

Here poor Brown broke down—very sorry he had spoken at all; but Steely came to the rescue with a ray of light.

"What's the matter with the little room at the back?" he asked.

"Oh, we couldn't think of putting you there," said Brown, with a last effort; "it's not fined up; you wouldn't be comfortable, and, besides, it's damp, and you'd catch your death of cold. It was never meant for anything but a wash-house. I'm sorry I didn't get another room built on to the house."

"Bosh!" interrupted Steelman, cheerfully. "Catch a cold! Here I've been knocking about the country for the last five years—sleeping out in all weathers—and do you think a little damp is going to hurt me? Pooh! What do you take me for? Don't you bother your head about it any more, old man; I'll fix up the lumber-room for myself, all right; and all you've got to do is to let me know when the sister-in-law business is coming on, and I'll shift out of my room in time for the missus to get it ready for her. Here, have you got a bob on you? I'll go out and get some beer. A drop'll do you good."

"Well, if you can make yourself comfortable, I'll be only too glad for you to stay," said Brown, wearily.

"You'd better invite some woman you know to come on a visit, and pass her off as your sister," said Brown to his wife, while Steelman was gone for the beer. "I've made a mess of it."

Mrs Brown said, "I knew you would."

Steelman knew his men.

But at last Brown reckoned that he could stand it no longer. The thought of it made him so wild that he couldn't work. He took a day off to get thoroughly worked up in, came home that night full to the chin of indignation and Dunedin beer, and tried to kick Steelman out. And Steelman gave him a hiding.

Next morning Steelman was sitting beside Brown's bed with a saucer of vinegar, some brown paper, a raw beef-steak, and a bottle of soda.

"Well, what have you got to say for yourself now, Brown?" he said, sternly. "Ain't you jolly well ashamed of yourself to come home in the beastly state you did last night, and insult a guest in your house, to say nothing of an old friend—and perhaps the best friend you ever had, if you only knew it? Anybody else would have given you in charge and got you three months for the assault. You ought to have some consideration for your wife and children, and your own character—even if you haven't any for your old mate's feelings. Here, drink this, and let me fix you up a bit; the missus has got the breakfast waiting."

DRIFTED BACK

The stranger walked into the corner grocery with the air of one who had come back after many years to see someone who would be glad to see him. He shed his swag and stood it by the wall with great deliberation; then he rested his elbow on the counter, stroked his beard, and grinned quizzically at the shopman, who smiled back presently in a puzzled way.

"Good afternoon," said the grocer.

"Good afternoon."

Pause.

"Nice day," said the grocer.

Pause.

"Anything I can do for you?"

"Yes; tell the old man there's a chap wants to speak to him for a minute."

"Old man? What old man?"

"Hake, of course—old Ben Hake! Ain't he in?"

The grocer smiled.

"Hake ain't here now. I'm here."

"How's that?"

"Why, he sold out to me ten years ago."

"Well, I suppose I'll find him somewhere about town?"

"I don't think you will. He left Australia when he sold out. He's—he's dead now."

"Dead! Old Ben Hake?"

"Yes. You knew him, then?"

The stranger seemed to have lost a great deal of his assurance. He turned his side to the counter, hooked his elbow on it, and gazed out through the door along Sunset Track.

"You can give me half a pound of nailrod," he said, in a quiet tone—"I s'pose young Hake is in town?"

"No; the whole family went away. I think there's one of the sons in business in Sydney now."

"I s'pose the M'Lachlans are here yet?"

"No; they are not. The old people died about five years ago; the sons are in Queensland, I think; and both the girls are married and in Sydney."

"Ah, well!... I see you've got the railway here now."

"Oh, yes! Six years."

"Times is changed a lot."

"They are."

"I s'pose—I s'pose you can tell me where I'll find old Jimmy Nowlett?"

"Jimmy Nowlett? Jimmy Nowlett? I never heard of the name. What was he?"

"Oh, he was a bullock-driver. Used to carry from the mountains before the railway was made."

"Before my time, perhaps. There's no one of that name round here now."

"Ah, well!... I don't suppose you knew the Duggans?"

"Yes, I did. The old man's dead, too, and the family's gone away—Lord knows where. They weren't much loss, to all accounts. The sons got into trouble, I b'lieve—went to the bad. They had a bad name here."

"Did they? Well, they had good hearts—at least, old Malachi Duggan and the eldest son had.... You can give me a couple of pounds of sugar."

"Right. I suppose it's a long time since you were here last?"

"Fifteen years."

"Indeed!"

"Yes. I don't s'pose I remind you of anyone you know around here?"

"N—no!" said the grocer with a smile. "I can't say you do."

"Ah, well! I s'pose I'll find the Wilds still living in the same place?"

"The Wilds? Well, no. The old man is dead, too, and—"

"And—and where's Jim? He ain't dead?"

"No; he's married and settled down in Sydney."

Long pause.

"Can you—" said the stranger, hesitatingly; "did you—I suppose you knew Mary—Mary Wild?"

"Mary?" said the grocer, smilingly. "That was my wife's maiden name. Would you like to see her?"

"No, no! She mightn't remember me!"

He reached hastily for his swag, and shouldered it.

"Well, I must be gettin' on."

"I s'pose you'll camp here over Christmas?"

"No; there's nothing to stop here for—I'll push on. I did intend to have a Christmas here—in fact, I came a long way out of my road a-purpose.... I meant to have just one more Christmas with old Ben Hake an' the rest of the boys—but I didn't know as they'd moved on so far west. The old bush school is dyin' out."

There was a smile in his eyes, but his bearded lips twitched a little.

"Things is changed. The old houses is pretty much the same, an' the old signs want touchin' up and paintin' jest as bad as ever; an' there's that old palin' fence that me an' Ben Hake an' Jimmy Nowlett put up twenty year ago. I've tramped and travelled long ways since then. But things is changed—at least, people is.... Well, I must be goin'. There's nothing to keep me here. I'll push on and get into my track again. It's cooler travellin' in the night."

"Yes, it's been pretty hot to-day."

"Yes, it has. Well, s'long."

"Good day. Merry Christmas!"

"Eh? What? Oh, yes! Same to you! S'long!"

"Good day!" He drifted out and away along Sunset Track.

REMAILED

There is an old custom prevalent in Australasia—and other parts, too, perhaps, for that matter—which, we think, deserves to be written up. It might not be an "honoured" custom from a newspaper manager's or proprietor's point of view, or from the point of view (if any) occupied by the shareholders on the subject; but, nevertheless, it is a time-honoured and a good old custom. Perhaps, for several reasons, it was more prevalent among diggers than with the comparatively settled bushmen of to-day—the poor, hopeless, wandering swaggy doesn't count in the matter, for he has neither the wherewithal nor the opportunity to honour the old custom; also his movements are too sadly uncertain to permit of his being honoured by it. We refer to the remailing of newspapers and journals from one mate to another.

Bill gets his paper and reads it through conscientiously from beginning to end by candle or slush-lamp as he lies on his back in the hut or tent with his pipe in his mouth; or, better still, on a Sunday afternoon as he reclines on the grass in the shade, in all the glory and comfort of a clean pair of moleskins and socks and a clean shirt. And when he has finished reading the paper—if it is not immediately bespoke—he turns it right side out, folds it, and puts it away where he'll know where to find it. The paper is generally bespoke in the following manner:

"Let's have a look at that paper after you, Bill, when yer done with it," says Jack.

And Bill says:

"I just promised it to Bob. You can get it after him."

And, when it is finally lent, Bill says:

"Don't forget to give that paper back to me when yer done with it. Don't let any of those other blanks get holt of it, or the chances are I won't set eyes on it again."

But the other blanks get it in their turn after being referred to Bill. "You must ask Bill," says Jack to the next blank, "I got it from him." And when Bill gets his paper back finally—which is often only after much bush grumbling, accusation, recrimination, and denial—he severely and carefully re-arranges theme pages, folds the paper, and sticks it away up over a rafter, or behind a post or batten, or under his pillow where it will safe. He wants that paper to send to Jim.

Bill is but an indifferent hand at folding, and knows little or nothing about wrappers. He folds and re-folds the paper several times and in various ways, but the first result is often the best, and is finally adopted. The parcel looks more ugly than neat; but Bill puts a weight upon it so that it won't fly open, and looks round for a piece of string to tie it with. Sometimes he ties it firmly round the middle, sometimes at both ends; at other times he runs the string down inside the folds and ties it that way, or both ways, or all the ways, so as to be sure it won't come undone—which it doesn't as a rule. If he can't find a piece of string long enough, he ties two bits together, and submits the result to a rather severe test; and if the string is too thin, or he has to use thread, he doubles it. Then he worries round to find out who has got the ink, or whether anyone has seen anything of the pen; and when he gets them, he writes the address with painful exactitude on the margin of the paper, sometimes in two or three places. He has to think a moment before he writes; and perhaps he'll scratch the back of his head afterwards with an inky finger, and regard the address with a sort of mild, passive surprise. His old mate Jim was always plain Jim to him, and nothing else; but, in order to reach Jim, this paper has to be addressed to—

MR JAMES MITCHELL,
c/o J. W. Dowell, Esq.,
Munnigrub Station—

and so on. "Mitchell" seems strange—Bill couldn't think of it for the moment—and so does "James."

And, a week or so later, over on Coolgardie, or away up in northern Queensland, or bush-felling down in Maoriland, Jim takes a stroll up to the post office after tea on mail night. He doesn't expect any letters, but there might be a paper from Bill. Bill generally sends him a newspaper. They seldom write to each other, these old mates.

There were points, of course, upon which Bill and Jim couldn't agree—subjects upon which they argued long and loud and often in the old days; and it sometimes happens that Bill across an article or a paragraph which agrees with and, so to speak, barracks for a pet theory of his as against one held by Jim; and Bill marks it with a chuckle and four crosses at the corners—and an extra one at each side perhaps—and sends it on to Jim; he reckons it'll rather corner old Jim. The crosses are not over ornamental nor artistic, but very distinct; Jim sees them from the reverse side of the sheet first, maybe, and turns it over with interest to see what it is. He grins a good-humoured grin as he reads—poor old Bill is just as thick-headed and obstinate as ever—just as far gone on his old fad. It's rather rough on Jim, because he's too far off to argue; but, if he's very earnest on the subject, he'll sit down and write, using all his old arguments to prove that the man who wrote that rot was a fool. This is one of the few things that will make them write to each other. Or else Jim will wait till he comes across a paragraph in another paper which barracks for his side of the argument, and, in his opinion; rather knocks the stuffing out of Bill's man; then he marks it with more and bigger crosses and a grin, and sends it along to Bill. They are both democrats—these old mates generally are—and at times one comes across a stirring article or poem, and marks it with approval and sends it along. Or it may be a good joke, or the notice of the death of an old mate. What a wave of feeling and memories a little par can take through the land!

Jim is a sinner and a scoffer, and Bill is an earnest, thorough, respectable old freethinker, and consequently they often get a War Cry or a tract sent inside their exchanges—somebody puts it in for a joke.

Long years ago—long years ago Bill and Jim were sweet on a rose of the bush—or a lily of the goldfields—call her Lily King. Both courted her at the same time, and quarrelled over her—fought over her, perhaps—and were parted by her for years. But that's all bygones. Perhaps she loved Bill, perhaps she loved Jim—perhaps both; or, maybe, she wasn't sure which. Perhaps she loved neither, and was only stringing them on. Anyway, she didn't marry either the one or the other. She married another man—call him Jim Smith. And so, in after years, Bill comes across a paragraph in a local paper, something like the following:

On July 10th, at her residence, Eureka Cottage, Ballarat-street, Tally Town, the wife of James Smith of twins (boy and girl); all three doing well.

And Bill marks it with a loud chuckle and big crosses, and sends it along to Jim. Then Bill sits and thinks and smokes, and thinks till the fire goes out, and quite forgets all about putting that necessary patch on his pants.

And away down on Auckland gum-fields, perhaps, Jim reads the par with a grin; then grows serious, and sits and scrapes his gum by the flickering firelight in a mechanical manner, and—thinks. His thoughts are far away in the back years—faint and far, far and faint. For the old, lingering, banished pain returns and hurts a man's heart like the false wife who comes back again, falls on her knees before him, and holds up her trembling arms and pleads with swimming, upturned eyes, which are eloquent with the love she felt too late.

It is supposed to be something to have your work published in an English magazine, to have it published in book form, to be flattered by critics and reprinted throughout the country press, or even to be cut up well and severely. But, after all, now we come to think of it, we would almost as soon see a piece of ours marked with big inky crosses in the soiled and crumpled rag that Bill or Jim gets sent him by an old mate of his—the paper that goes thousands of miles scrawled all over with smudgy addresses and tied with a piece of string.

MITCHELL DOESN'T BELIEVE IN THE SACK

"If ever I do get a job again," said Mitchell, "I'll stick to it while there's a hand's turn of work to do, and put a few pounds together. I won't be the fool I always was. If I'd had sense a couple of years ago, I wouldn't be tramping through this damned sand and mulga now. I'll get a job on a station, or at some toff's house, knocking about the stables and garden, and I'll make up my mind to settle down to graft for four or five years."

"But supposing you git the sack?" said his mate.

"I won't take it. Only for taking the sack I wouldn't be hard up to-day. The boss might come round and say:

'I won't want you after this week, Mitchell. I haven't got any more work for you to do. Come up and see me at the office presently.'

"So I'll go up and get my money; but I'll be pottering round as usual on Monday, and come up to the kitchen for my breakfast. Some time in the day the boss'll be knocking round and see me.

"'Why, Mitchell,' he'll say, 'I thought you was gone.'

"'I didn't say I was going,' I'll say. 'Who told you that—or what made you think so?'

"'I thought I told you on Saturday that I wouldn't want you any more,' he'll say, a bit short. 'I haven't got enough work to keep a man going; I told you that; I thought you understood. Didn't I give you the sack on Saturday?'

"'It's no use;' I'll say, 'that sort of thing's played out. I've been had too often that way; I've been sacked once too often. Taking the sack's been the cause of all my trouble; I don't believe in it. If I'd never taken the sack I'd have been a rich man to-day; it might be all very well for horses, but it doesn't suit me; it doesn't hurt you, but it hurts me. I made up my mind that when I got a place to suit me, I'd stick in it. I'm comfortable here and satisfied, and you've had no cause to find fault with me. It's no use you trying to sack me, because I won't take it. I've been there before, and you might as well try to catch an old bird with chaff.'

"'Well, I won't pay you, and you'd better be off,' he'll say, trying not to grin.

"'Never mind the money,' I'll say, 'the bit of tucker won't cost you anything, and I'll find something to do round the house till you have some more work. I won't ask you for anything, and, surely to God I'll find enough to do to pay for my grub!'

"So I'll potter round and take things easy and call up at the kitchen as usual at meal times, and by and by the boss'll think to himself: 'Well, if I've got to feed this chap I might as well get some work out of him.'

"So he'll find me, something regular to do—a bit of fencing, or carpentering, or painting, or something, and then I'll begin to call up for my stuff again, as usual."

SHOOTING THE MOON

We lay in camp in the fringe of the mulga, and watched the big, red, smoky, rising moon out on the edge of the misty plain, and smoked and thought together sociably. Our nose-bags were nice and heavy, and we still had about a pound of nail-rod between us.

The moon reminded my mate, Jack Mitchell, of something—anything reminded him of something, in fact.

"Did you ever notice," said Jack, in a lazy tone, just as if he didn't want to tell a yarn—"Did you ever notice that people always shoot the moon when there's no moon? Have you got the matches?"

He lit up; he was always lighting up when he was reminded of something.

"This reminds me—Have you got the knife? My pipe's stuffed up."

He dug it out, loaded afresh, and lit up again.

"I remember once, at a pub I was staying at, I had to leave without saying good-bye to the landlord. I didn't know him very well at that time.

"My room was upstairs at the back, with the window opening on to the backyard. I always carried a bit of clothes-line in my swag or portmanteau those times. I travelled along with a portmanteau those times. I carried the rope in case of accident, or in case of fire, to lower my things out of the window—or hang myself, maybe, if things got too bad. No, now I come to think of it, I carried a revolver for that, and it was the only thing I never pawned."

"To hang yourself with?" asked the mate.

"Yes—you're very smart," snapped Mitchell; "never mind—. This reminds me that I got a chap at a pub to pawn my last suit, while I stopped inside and waited for an old mate to send me a pound; but I kept the shooter, and if he hadn't sent it I'd have been the late John Mitchell long ago."

"And sometimes you lower'd out when there wasn't a fire."

"Yes, that will pass; you're improving in the funny business. But about the yarn. There was two beds in my room at the pub, where I had to go away without shouting for the boss, and, as it happened, there was a strange chap sleeping in the other bed that night, and, just as I raised the window and was going to lower my bag out, he woke up.

"'Now, look here,' I said, shaking my fist at him, like that, 'if you say a word, I'll stoush yer!'

"'Well,' he said, 'well, you needn't be in such a sweat to jump down a man's throat. I've got my swag under the bed, and I was just going to ask you for the loan of the rope when you're done with it.'

"Well, we chummed. His name was Tom—Tom—something, I forget the other name, but it doesn't matter. Have you got the matches?"

He wasted three matches, and continued—

"There was a lot of old galvanized iron lying about under the window, and I was frightened the swag would make a noise; anyway, I'd have to drop the rope, and that was sure to make a noise. So we agreed for one of us to go down and land the swag. If we were seen going down without the swags it didn't matter, for we could say we wanted to go out in the yard for something."

"If you had the swag you might pretend you were walking in your sleep," I suggested, for the want of something funnier to say.

"Bosh," said Jack, "and get woke up with a black eye. Bushies don't generally carry their swags out of pubs in their sleep, or walk neither; it's only city swells who do that. Where's the blessed matches?

"Well, Tom agreed to go, and presently I saw a shadow under the window, and lowered away.

"'All right?' I asked in a whisper.

"'All right!" whispered the shadow.

"I lowered the other swag.

"'All right?'

"'All right!' said the shadow, and just then the moon came out.

"'All right!' says the shadow.

"But it wasn't all right. It was the landlord himself!

"It seems he got up and went out to the back in the night, and just happened to be coming in when my mate Tom was sneaking out of the back door. He saw Tom, and Tom saw him, and smoked through a hole in the palings into the scrub. The boss looked up at the window, and dropped to it. I went down, funky enough, I can tell you, and faced him. He said:

"'Look here, mate, why didn't you come straight to me, and tell me how you was fixed, instead of sneaking round the trouble in that fashion? There's no occasion for it.'

"I felt mean at once, but I said: 'Well, you see, we didn't know you, boss.'

"'So it seems. Well, I didn't think of that. Anyway, call up your mate and come and have a drink; we'll talk over it afterwards.' So I called Tom. 'Come on,' I shouted. 'It's all right.'

"And the boss kept us a couple of days, and then gave us as much tucker as we could carry, and a drop of stuff and a few bob to go on the track again with."

"Well, he was white, any road."

"Yes. I knew him well after that, and only heard one man say a word against him."

"And did you stoush him?"

"No; I was going to, but Tom wouldn't let me. He said he was frightened I might make a mess of it, and he did it himself."

"Did what? Make a mess of it?"

"He made a mess of the other man that slandered that publican. I'd be funny if I was you. Where's the matches?"

"And could Tom fight?"

"Yes. Tom could fight."

"Did you travel long with him after that?"

"Ten years."

"And where is he now?"

"Dead—Give us the matches."

HIS FATHER'S MATE

It was Golden Gully still, but golden in name only, unless indeed the yellow mullock heaps or the bloom of the wattle-trees on the hillside gave it a claim to the title. But the gold was gone from the gully, and the diggers were gone, too, after the manner of Timon's friends when his wealth deserted him. Golden Gully was a dreary place, dreary even for an abandoned goldfield. The poor, tortured earth, with its wounds all bare, seemed to make a mute appeal to the surrounding bush to come up and hide it, and, as if in answer to its appeal, the shrub and saplings were beginning to close in from the foot of the range. The wilderness was reclaiming its own again.

The two dark, sullen hills that stood on each side were clothed from tip to hollow with dark scrub and scraggy box-trees; but above the highest row of shafts on one side ran a line of wattle-trees in full bloom.

The top of the western hill was shaped somewhat like a saddle, and standing high above the eucalypti on the point corresponding with the pommel were three tall pines. These lonely trees, seen for many miles around, had caught the yellow rays of many a setting sun long before the white man wandered over the ranges.

The predominant note of the scene was a painful sense of listening, that never seemed to lose its tension—a listening as though for the sounds of digger life, sounds that had gone and left a void that was accentuated by the signs of a former presence. The main army of diggers had long ago vanished to new rushes, leaving only its stragglers and deserters behind. These were men who were too poor to drag families about, men who were old and feeble, and men who had lost their faith in fortune. They had dropped unnoticed out of the ranks; and remained to scratch out a living among the abandoned claims.

Golden Gully had its little community of fossickers who lived in a clearing called Spencer's Flat on one side and Pounding Flat on the other, but they lent no life to the scene; they only haunted it. A stranger might have thought the field entirely deserted until he came on a coat and a billy at the foot of saplings amongst the holes, and heard, in the shallow ground underneath, the thud of a pick, which told of some fossicker below rooting out what little wash remained.

One afternoon towards Christmas, a windlass was erected over an old shaft of considerable depth at the foot of the gully. A greenhide bucket attached to a rope on the windlass was lying next morning near the mouth of the shaft, and beside it, on a clear-swept patch, was a little mound of cool wet wash-dirt.

A clump of saplings near at hand threw a shade over part of the mullock heap, and in this shade, seated on an old coat, was a small boy of eleven or twelve years, writing on a slate.

He had fair hair, blue eyes, and a thin old-fashioned face—a face that would scarcely alter as he grew to manhood. His costume consisted of a pair of moleskin trousers, a cotton shirt, and one suspender. He held the slate rigidly with a corner of its frame pressed close against his ribs, whilst his head hung to one side, so close to the slate that his straggling hair almost touched it. He was regarding his work fixedly out of the corners of his eyes, whilst he painfully copied down the head line, spelling it in a different way each time. In this laborious task he appeared to be greatly assisted by a tongue that lolled out of the corner of his mouth and made an occasional revolution round it, leaving a circle of temporarily clean face. His small clay-covered toes also entered into the spirit of the thing, and helped him not a little by their energetic wriggling. He paused occasionally to draw the back of his small brown arm across his mouth.

Little Isley Mason, or, as he was called, "His Father's Mate," had always been a favourite with the diggers and fossickers from the days when he used to slip out first thing in the morning and take a run across the frosty flat in his shirt. Long Bob Sawkins would often tell how Isley came home one morning from his run in the long, wet grass as naked as he was born, with the information that he had lost his shirt.

Later on, when most of the diggers had gone, and Isley's mother was dead, he was to be seen about the place with bare, sunbrowned arms and legs, a pick and shovel, and a gold dish about two-thirds of his height in diameter, with which he used to go "a-speckin'" and "fossickin'" amongst the old mullock heaps. Long Bob was Isley's special crony, and he would often go out of his way to lay the boy outer bits o' wash and likely spots, lamely excusing his long yarns with the child by the explanation that it was "amusin' to draw Isley out."

Isley had been sitting writing for some time when a deep voice called out from below:

"Isley!"

"Yes, father."

"Send down the bucket."

"Right."

Isley put down his slate, and going to the shaft dropped the bucket down as far as the slack rope reached; then, placing one hand on the bole of the windlass and holding the other against it underneath, he let it slip round between his palms until the bucket reached bottom. A sound of shovelling was heard for a few moments, and presently the voice cried, "Wind away, sonny."

"Thet ain't half enough," said the boy, peering down. "Don't be frightened to pile it in, father. I kin wind up a lot more'n thet."

A little more scraping, and the boy braced his feet well upon the little mound of clay which he had raised under the handle of the windlass to make up for his deficiency in stature.

"Now then, Isley!"

Isley wound slowly but sturdily, and soon the bucket of "wash" appeared above the surface; then he took it in short lifts and deposited it with the rest of the wash-dirt.

"Isley!" called his father again.

"Yes, father."

"Have you done that writing lesson yet?"

"Very near."

"Then send down the slate next time for some sums."

"All right."

The boy resumed his seat, fixed the corner of the slate well into his ribs, humped his back, and commenced another wavering line.

Tom Mason was known on the place as a silent, hard worker. He was a man of about sixty, tall, and dark bearded. There was nothing uncommon about his face, except, perhaps, that it hardened, as the face of a man might harden who had suffered a long succession of griefs and disappointments. He lived in little hut under a peppermint tree at the far edge of Pounding Flat. His wife had died there about six years before, and new rushes broke out and he was well able to go, he never left Golden Gully.

Mason was kneeling in front of the "face" digging away by the light of a tallow candle stuck in the side. The floor of the drive was very wet, and his trousers were heavy and cold with clay and water; but the old digger was used to this sort of thing. His pick was not bringing out much to-day, however, for he seemed abstracted and would occasionally pause in his work, while his thoughts wandered far away from the narrow streak of wash-dirt in the "face."

He was digging out pictures from a past life. They were not pleasant ones, for his face was stony and white in the dim glow of the candle.

Thud, thud, thud—the blows became slower and more irregular as the fossicker's mind wandered off into the past. The sides of the drive seemed to vanish slowly away, and the "face" retreated far out beyond a horizon that was hazy in the glow of the southern ocean. He was standing on the deck of a ship and by his side stood a brother. They were sailing southward to the Land of Promise that was shining there in all its golden glory! The sails pressed forward in the bracing wind, and the clipper ship raced along with its burden of the wildest dreamers ever borne in a vessel's hull! Up over long blue ocean ridges, down into long blue ocean gullies; on to lands so new, and yet so old, where above the sunny glow of the southern skies blazed the shining names of Ballarat! and Bendigo! The deck seemed to lurch, and the fossicker fell forward against the face of the drive. The shock recalled him, and he lifted his pick once more.

But the blows slacken again as another vision rises before him. It is Ballarat now. He is working in a shallow claim at Eureka, his brother by his side. The brother looks pale and ill, for he has been up all night dancing and drinking. Out behind them is the line of blue hills; in front is the famous Bakery Hill, and down to the left Golden Point. Two mounted troopers are riding up over Specimen Hill. What do they want?

They take the brother away, handcuffed. Manslaughter last night. Cause—drink and jealousy.

The vision is gone again. Thud, thud, goes the pick; it counts the years that follow—one, two, three, four, up to twenty, and then it stops for the next scene—a selection on the banks of a bright river in New South Wales. The little homestead is surrounded by vines and fruit-trees. Many swarms of bees work under the shade of the trees, and a crop of wheat is nearly ripe on the hillside.

A man and a boy are engaged in clearing a paddock just below the homestead. They are father and son; the son, a boy of about seventeen, is the image of his father.

Horses' feet again! Here comes Nemesis in mounted troopers' uniform.

The mail was stuck up last night about five miles away, and a refractory passenger shot. The son had been out 'possum shooting' all night with some friends.

The troopers take the son away handcuffed: "Robbery under arms."

The father was taking out a stump when the troopers came. His foot is still resting on the spade, which is half driven home. He watches the troopers take the boy up to the house, and then, driving the spade to its full depth, he turns up another sod. The troopers reach the door of the homestead; but still he digs steadily, and does not seem to hear his wife's cry of despair. The troopers search the boy's room and bring out some clothing in two bundles; but still the father digs. They have saddled up one of the farm horses and made the boy mount. The father digs. They ride off along the ridge with the boy between them. The father never lifts his eyes; the hole widens round the stump; he digs away till the brave little wife comes and takes him gently by the arm. He half rouses himself and follows her to the house like an obedient dog.

Trial and disgrace follow, and then other misfortunes, pleuro among the cattle, drought, and poverty.

Thud, thud, thud again! But it is not the sound of the fossicker's pick—it is the fall of sods on his wife's coffin.

It is a little bush cemetery, and he stands stonily watching them fill up her grave. She died of a broken heart and shame. "I can't bear disgrace! I can't bear disgrace!" she had moaned all these six weary years—for the poor are often proud.

But he lives on, for it takes a lot to break a man's heart. He holds up his head and toils on for the sake of a child that is left, and that child is—Isley.

And now the fossicker seems to see a vision of the future. He seems to be standing somewhere, an old, old man, with a younger one at his side; the younger one has Isley's face. Horses' feet again! Ah, God! Nemesis once more in troopers' uniform!

The fossicker falls on his knees in the mud and clay at the bottom of the drive, and prays Heaven to take his last child ere Nemesis comes for him.

Long Bob Sawkins had been known on the diggings as "Bob the Devil." His profile at least from one side, certainly did recall that of the sarcastic Mephistopheles; but the other side, like his true character, was by no means a devil's. His physiognomy had been much damaged, and one eye removed by the premature explosion of a blast in some old Ballarat mine. The blind eye was covered with a green patch, which gave a sardonic appearance to the remaining features.

He was a stupid, heavy, good-natured Englishman. He stuttered a little, and had a peculiar habit of wedging the monosyllable "why" into his conversation at times when it served no other purpose than to fill up the pauses caused by his stuttering; but this by no means assisted him in his speech, for he often stuttered over the "why" itself.

The sun was getting low down, and its yellow rays reached far up among the saplings of Golden Gully when Bob appeared coming down by the path that ran under the western hill. He was dressed in the usual costume-cotton shirt, moleskin trousers, faded hat and waistcoat, and blucher boots. He carried a pick over his shoulder, the handle of which was run through the heft of a short shovel that hung down behind, and he had a big dish under his arm. He paused opposite the shaft with the windlass, and hailed the boy in his usual form of salutation.

"Look, see here Isley!"

"What is it, Bob?"

"I seed a young—why—magpie up in the scrub, and yer oughter be able to catch it."

"Can't leave the shaft; father's b'low."

"How did yer father know there was any—why—wash in the old shaft?"

"Seed old Corney in town Saturday, 'n he said thur was enough to make it worth while bailin' out. Bin bailin' all the mornin'."

Bob came over, and letting his tools down with a clatter he hitched up the knees of his moleskins and sat down on one heel.

"What are yer—why—doin' on the slate, Isley?" said he, taking out an old clay pipe and lighting it.

"Sums," said Isley.

Bob puffed away at his pipe a moment.

"'Tain't no use!" he said, sitting down on the clay and drawing his knees up. "Edication's a failyer."

"Listen at 'im!" exclaimed the boy. "D'yer mean ter say it ain't no use learnin' readin' and writin' and sums?"

"Isley!"

"Right, father."

The boy went to the windlass and let the bucket down. Bob offered to help him wind up, but Isley, proud of showing his strength to his friend, insisted on winding by himself.

"You'll be—why—a strong man some day, Isley," said Bob, landing the bucket.

"Oh, I could wind up a lot more'n father puts in. Look how I greased the handles! It works like butter now," and the boy sent the handles spinning round with a jerk to illustrate his meaning.

"Why did they call yer Isley for?" queried Bob, as they resumed their seats. "It ain't yer real name, is it?"

"No, my name's Harry. A digger useter say I was a isle in the ocean to father 'n mother, 'n then I was nicknamed Isle, 'n then Isley."

"You hed a—why—brother once, didn't yer?"

"Yes, but thet was afore I was borned. He died, at least mother used ter say she didn't know if he was dead; but father says he's dead as fur's he's concerned."

"And your father hed a brother, too. Did yer ever—why—hear of him?"

"Yes, I heard father talkin' about it wonst to mother. I think father's brother got into some row in a bar where a man was killed."

"And was yer—why—father—why—fond of him?"

"I heard father say that he was wonst, but thet was all past."

Bob smoked in silence for a while, and seemed to look at some dark clouds that were drifting along like a funeral out in the west. Presently he said half aloud something that sounded like "All, all—why—past."

"Eh?" said Isley.

"Oh, it's—why, why—nothin'," answered Bob, rousing himself. "Is that a paper in yer father's coat-pocket, Isley?"

"Yes," said the boy, taking it out.

Bob took the paper and stared hard at it for a moment or so.

"There's something about the new goldfields there," said Bob, putting his finger on a tailor's advertisement. "I wish you'd—why—read it to me, Isley; I can't see the small print they uses nowadays."

"No, thet's not it," said the boy, taking the paper, "it's something about—"

"Isley!"

"'Old on, Bob, father wants me."

The boy ran to the shaft, rested his hands and forehead against the bole of the windlass, and leant over to hear what his father was saying.

Without a moment's warning the treacherous bole slipped round; a small body bounded a couple of times against the sides of the shaft and fell at Mason's feet, where it lay motionless!

"Mason!"

"Ay?"

"Put him in the bucket and lash him to the rope with your belt!"

A few moments, and—

"Now, Bob!"

Bob's trembling hands would scarcely grasp the handle, but he managed to wind somehow.

Presently the form of the child appeared, motionless and covered with clay and water. Mason was climbing up by the steps in the side of the shaft.

Bob tenderly unlashed the boy and laid him under the saplings on the grass; then he wiped some of the clay and blood away from the child's forehead, and dashed over him some muddy water.

Presently Isley gave a gasp and opened his eyes.

"Are yer—why—hurt much, Isley?" asked Bob.

"Ba-back's bruk, Bob!"

"Not so bad as that, old man."

"Where's father?"

"Coming up."

Silence awhile, and then—

"Father! father! be quick, father!"

Mason reached the surface and came and knelt by the other side of the boy.

"I'll, I'll—why—run fur some brandy," said Bob.

"No use, Bob," said Isley. "I'm all bruk up."

"Don't yer feel better, sonny?"

"No—I'm—goin' to—die, Bob."

"Don't say it, Isley," groaned Bob.

A short silence, and then the boy's body suddenly twisted with pain. But it was soon over. He lay still awhile, and then said quietly:

"Good-bye, Bob!"

Bob made a vain attempt to speak. "Isley!" he said,"—"

The child turned and stretched out his hands to the silent, stony-faced man on the other side.

"Father—father, I'm goin'!"

A shuddering groan broke from Mason's lips, and then all was quiet.

Bob had taken off his hat to wipe his, forehead, and his face, in spite of its disfigurement, was strangely like the face of the stone-like man opposite.

For a moment they looked at one another across the body of the child, and then Bob said quietly:

"He never knowed."

"What does it matter?" said Mason gruffly; and, taking up the dead child, he walked towards the hut.

It was a very sad little group that gathered outside Mason's but next morning. Martin's wife had been there all the morning cleaning up and doing what she could. One of the women had torn up her husband's only white shirt for a shroud, and they had made the little body look clean and even beautiful in the wretched little hut.

One after another the fossickers took off their hats and entered, stooping through the low door. Mason sat silently at the foot of the bunk with his head supported by his hand, and watched the men with a strange, abstracted air.

Bob had ransacked the camp in search of some boards for a coffin.

"It will be the last I'll be able to—why—do for him," he said.

At last he came to Mrs Martin in despair. That lady took him into the dining-room, and pointed to a large pine table, of which she was very proud.

"Knock that table to pieces," she said.

Taking off the few things that were lying on it, Bob turned it over and began to knock the top off.

When he had finished the coffin one of the fossicker's wives said it looked too bare, and she ripped up her black riding-skirt, and made Bob tack the cloth over the coffin.

There was only one vehicle available in the place, and that was Martin's old dray; so about two o'clock Pat Martin attached his old horse Dublin to the shafts with sundry bits of harness and plenty of old rope, and dragged Dublin, dray and all, across to Mason's hut.

The little coffin was carried out, and two gin-cases were placed by its side in the dray to serve as seats for Mrs Martin and Mrs Grimshaw, who mounted in tearful silence.

Pat Martin felt for his pipe, but remembered himself and mounted on the shaft. Mason fastened up the door of the hut with a padlock. A couple of blows on one of his sharp points roused Dublin from his reverie. With a lurch to the right and another to the left he started, and presently the little funeral disappeared down the road that led to the "town" and its cemetery.

About six months afterwards Bob Sawkins went on a short journey, and returned with a tall, bearded young man. He and Bob arrived after dark, and went straight to Mason's hut. There was a light inside, but when Bob knocked there was no answer.

"Go in; don't be afraid,'" he said to his companion.

The stranger pushed open the creaking door, and stood bareheaded just inside the doorway.

A billy was boiling unheeded on the fire. Mason sat at the table with his face buried in his arms.

"Father!"

There was no answer, but the flickering of the firelight made the stranger think he could detect an impatient shrug in Mason's shoulders.

For a moment the stranger paused irresolute, and then stepping up to the table he laid his hand on Mason's arm, and said gently:

"Father! Do you want another mate?"

But the sleeper did not—at least, not in this world.

AN ECHO FROM THE OLD BARK SCHOOL

It was the first Monday after the holidays. The children had taken their seats in the Old Bark School, and the master called out the roll as usual:

"Arvie Aspinall."... "'Es, sir."

"David Cooper."... "Yes, sir."

"John Heegard."... "Yezzer."

"Joseph Swallow."... "Yesser."

"James Bullock."... "Present."

"Frederick Swallow."... "Y'sir."

"James Nowlett."... . (Chorus of "Absent.")

"William Atkins."... (Chorus of "Absent.")

"Daniel Lyons."... "Perresent, sor-r-r."

Dan was a young immigrant, just out from the sod, and rolled his "r's" like a cock-dove. His brogue was rich enough to make an Irishman laugh.

Bill was "wagging it." His own especial chum was of the opinion that Bill was sick. The master's opinion did not coincide, so he penned a note to William's parents, to be delivered by the model boy of the school.

"Bertha Lambert."... "Yes, 'air."

"May Carey."... "Pesin', sair."

"Rose Cooper."... "Yes, sir."

"Janet Wild."... "Y-y-yes, s-sir."

"Mary Wild."...

A solemn hush fell upon the school, and presently Janet Wild threw her arms out on the desk before her, let her face fall on them, and sobbed heart-brokenly. The master saw his mistake too late; he gave his head a little half-affirmative, half-negative movement, in that pathetic old way of his; rested his head on one hand, gazed sadly at the name, and sighed.

But the galoot of the school spoilt the pathos of it all, for, during the awed silence which followed the calling of the girl's name, he suddenly brightened up—the first time he was ever observed to do so during school hours—and said, briskly and cheerfully "Dead—sir!"

He hadn't been able to answer a question correctly for several days.

"Children," said the master gravely and sadly, "children, this is the first time I ever had to put 'D' to the name of one of my scholars. Poor Mary! she was one of my first pupils—came the first morning the school was opened. Children, I want you to be a little quieter to-day during play-hour, out of respect for the name of your dead schoolmate whom it has pleased the Almighty to take in her youth."

"Please, sir," asked the galoot, evidently encouraged by his fancied success, "please, sir, what does 'D' stand for?"

"Damn you for a hass!" snarled Jim Bullock between his teeth, giving the galoot a vicious dig in the side with his elbow.

THE SHEARING OF THE COOK'S DOG

The dog was a little conservative mongrel poodle, with long dirty white hair all over him—longest and most over his eyes, which glistened through it like black beads. Also he seemed to have a bad liver. He always looked as if he was suffering from a sense of injury, past or to come. It did come. He used to follow the shearers up to the shed after breakfast every morning, but he couldn't have done this for love—there was none lost between him and the men. He wasn't an affectionate dog; it wasn't his style. He would sit close against the shed for an hour or two, and hump himself, and sulk, and look sick, and snarl whenever the "Sheep-Ho" dog passed, or a man took notice of him. Then he'd go home. What he wanted at the shed at all was only known to himself; no one asked him to come. Perhaps he came to collect evidence against us. The cook called him "my darg," and the men called the cook "Curry and Rice," with "old" before it mostly.

Rice was a little, dumpy, fat man, with a round, smooth, good-humoured face, a bald head, feet wide apart, and a big blue cotton apron. He had been a ship's cook. He didn't look so much out of place in the hut as the hut did round him. To a man with a vivid imagination, if he regarded the cook dreamily for a while, the floor might seem to roll gently like the deck of a ship, and mast, rigging, and cuddy rise mistily in the background. Curry might have dreamed of the cook's galley at times, but he never mentioned it. He ought to have been at sea, or comfortably dead and stowed away under ground, instead of cooking for a mob of unredeemed rouseabouts in an uncivilized shed in the scrub, six hundred miles from the ocean.

They chyacked the cook occasionally, and grumbled—or pretended to grumble—about their tucker, and then he'd make a roughly pathetic speech, with many references to his age, and the hardness of his work, and the smallness of his wages, and the inconsiderateness of the men. Then the joker of the shed would sympathize with the cook with his tongue and one side of his face—and joke with the other.

One day in the shed, during smoke-ho the devil whispered to a shearer named Geordie that it would be a lark to shear the cook's dog—the Evil One having previously arranged that the dog should be there, sitting close to Geordie's pen, and that the shearer should have a fine lamb comb on his machine. The idea was communicated through Geordie to his mates, and met with entire and general approval; and for five or ten minutes the air was kept alive by shouting and laughter of the men, and the protestations of the dog. When the shearer touched skin, he yelled "Tar!" and when he finished he shouted "Wool away!" at the top of his voice, and his mates echoed him with a will. A picker-up gathered the fleece with a great show of labour and care, and tabled it, to the well-ventilated disgust of old Scotty, the wool-roller. When they let the dog go he struck for home—a clean-shaven poodle, except for a ferocious moustache and a tuft at the end of his tail.

The cook's assistant said that he'd have given a five-pound note for a portrait of Curry-and-Rice when that poodle came back from the shed. The cook was naturally very indignant; he was surprised at first—then he got mad. He had the whole afternoon to get worked up in, and at tea-time he went for the men properly.

"Wotter yer growlin' about?" asked one. "Wot's the matter with yer, anyway?"

"I don't know nothing about yer dog!" protested a rouseabout; "wotyer gettin' on to me for?"

"Wotter they bin doin' to the cook now?" inquired a ring leader innocently, as he sprawled into his place at the table. "Can't yer let Curry alone? Wot d'yer want to be chyackin' him for? Give it a rest."

"Well, look here, chaps," observed Geordie, in a determined tone, "I call it a shame, that's what I call it. Why couldn't you leave an old man's dog alone? It was a mean, dirty trick to do, and I suppose you thought it funny. You ought to be ashamed of yourselves, the whole lot of you, for a drafted mob of crawlers. If I'd been there it wouldn't have been done; and I wouldn't blame Curry if he was to poison the whole convicted push."

General lowering of faces and pulling of hats down over eyes, and great working of knives and forks; also sounds like men trying not to laugh.

"Why couldn't you play a trick on another man's darg?" said Curry. "It's no use tellin' me. I can see it all as plain as if I was on the board—all of you runnin' an' shoutin' an' cheerin' an' laughin', and all over shearin' and ill-usin' a poor little darg! Why couldn't you play a trick on another man's darg?... It doesn't matter much—I'm nearly done cookie' here now.... Only that I've got a family to think of I wouldn't 'a' stayed so long. I've got to be up at five every mornin', an' don't get to bed till ten at night, cookin' an' bakin' an' cleanin' for you an' waitin' on you. First one lot in from the wool-wash, an' then one lot in from the shed, an' another lot in, an' at all hours an' times, an' all wantin' their meals kept hot, an' then they ain't satisfied. And now you must go an' play a dirty trick on my darg! Why couldn't you have a lark with some other man's darg!"

Geordie bowed his head and ate as though he had a cud, like a cow, and could chew at leisure. He seemed ashamed, as indeed we all were—secretly. Poor old Curry's oft-repeated appeal, "Why couldn't you play a trick with another man's dog?" seemed to have something pathetic about it. The men didn't notice that it lacked philanthropy and logic, and probably the cook didn't notice it either, else he wouldn't have harped on it. Geordie lowered his face, and just then, as luck or the devil would have it, he caught sight of the dog. Then he exploded.

The cook usually forgot all about it in an hour, and then, if you asked him what the chaps had been doing, he'd say, "Oh, nothing! nothing! Only their larks!" But this time he didn't; he was narked for three days, and the chaps marvelled much and were sorry, and treated him with great respect and consideration. They hadn't thought he'd take it so hard—the dog shearing business—else they wouldn't have done it. They were a little puzzled too, and getting a trifle angry, and would shortly be prepared to take the place of the injured party, and make things unpleasant for the cook. However, he brightened up towards the end of the week, and then it all came out.

"I wouldn't 'a' minded so much," he said, standing by the table with a dipper in one hand, a bucket in the other, and a smile on his face. "I wouldn't 'a' minded so much only they'll think me a flash man in Bourke with that theer darg trimmed up like that!"

"DOSSING OUT" AND "CAMPING"

At least two hundred poor beggars were counted sleeping out on the pavements of the main streets of Sydney the other night—grotesque bundles of rags lying under the verandas of the old Fruit Markets and York Street shops, with their heads to the wall and their feet to the gutter. It was raining and cold that night, and the unemployed had been driven in from Hyde Park and the bleak Domain—from dripping trees, damp seats, and drenched grass—from the rain, and cold, and the wind. Some had sheets of old newspapers to cover them-and some hadn't. Two were mates, and they divided a Herald between them. One had a sheet of brown paper, and another (lucky man!) had a bag—the only bag there. They all shrank as far into their rags as possible—and tried to sleep. The rats seemed to take them for rubbish, too, and only scampered away when one of the outcasts moved uneasily, or coughed, or groaned—or when a policeman came along.

One or two rose occasionally and rooted in the dust-boxes on the pavement outside the shops—but they didn't seem to get anything. They were feeling "peckish," no doubt, and wanted to see if they could get something to eat before the corporation carts came along. So did the rats.

Some men can't sleep very well on an empty stomach—at least, not at first; but it mostly comes with practice. They often sleep for ever in London. Not in Sydney as yet—so we say.

Now and then one of our outcasts would stretch his cramped limbs to ease them—but the cold soon made him huddle again. The pavement must have been hard on the men's "points," too; they couldn't dig holes nor make soft places for their hips, as you can in camp out back. And then, again, the stones had nasty edges and awkward slopes, for the pavements were very uneven.

The Law came along now and then, and had a careless glance at the unemployed in bed. They didn't look like sleeping beauties. The Law appeared to regard them as so much rubbish that ought not to have been placed there, and for the presence of which somebody ought to be prosecuted by the Inspector of Nuisances. At least, that was the expression the policeman had on his face.

And so Australian workmen lay at two o'clock in the morning in the streets of Sydney, and tried to get a little sleep before the traffic came along and took their bed.

The idea of sleeping out might be nothing to bushmen—not even an idea; but "dossing out" in the city and "camping" in the bush are two very different things. In the bush you can light a fire, boil your billy, and make some tea—if you have any; also fry a chop (there are no sheep running round in the city). You can have a clean meal, take off your shirt and wash it, and wash yourself—if there's water enough—and feel fresh and clean. You can whistle and sing by the camp-fire, and make poetry, and breathe fresh air, and watch the everlasting stars that keep the mateless traveller from going mad as he lies in his lonely camp on the plains. Your privacy is even more perfect than if you had a suite of rooms at the Australia; you are at the mercy of no policeman; there's no one to watch you but God—and He won't move you on. God watches the "dossers-out," too, in the city, but He doesn't keep them from being moved on or run in.

With the city unemployed the case is entirely different. The city outcast cannot light a fire and boil a billy—even if he has one—he'd be run in at once for attempting to commit arson, or create a riot, or on suspicion of being a person of unsound mind. If he took off his shirt to wash it, or went in for a swim, he'd be had up for indecently exposing his bones—and perhaps he'd get flogged. He cannot whistle or sing on his pavement bed at night, for, if he did, he'd be violently arrested by two great policemen for riotous conduct. He doesn't see many stars, and he's generally too hungry to make poetry. He only sleeps on the pavement on sufferance, and when the policeman finds the small hours hang heavily on him, he can root up the unemployed with his big foot and move him on—or arrest him for being around with the intention to commit a felony; and, when the wretched "dosser" rises in the morning, he cannot shoulder his swag and take the track—he must cadge a breakfast at some back gate or restaurant, and then sit in the park or walk round and round, the same old hopeless round, all day. There's no prison like the city for a poor man.

Nearly every man the traveller meets in the bush is about as dirty and ragged as himself, and just about as hard up; but in the city nearly every man the poor unemployed meets is a dude, or at least, well dressed, and the unemployed feels dirty and mean and degraded by the contrast—and despised.

And he can't help feeling like a criminal. It may be imagination, but every policeman seems to regard him with suspicion, and this is terrible to a sensitive man.

We once had the key of the street for a night. We don't know how much tobacco we smoked, how many seats we sat on, or how many miles we walked before morning. But we do know that we felt like a felon, and that every policeman seemed to regard us with a suspicious eye; and at last we began to squint furtively at every trap we met, which, perhaps, made him more suspicious, till finally we felt bad enough to be run in and to get six months' hard.

Three winters ago a man, whose name doesn't matter, had a small office near Elizabeth Street, Sydney. He was an hotel broker, debt collector, commission agent, canvasser, and so on, in a small way—a very small way—but his heart was big. He had a partner. They batched in the office, and did their cooking over a gas lamp. Now, every day the man-whose-name-doesn't-matter would carefully collect the scraps of food, add a slice or two of bread and butter, wrap it all up in a piece of newspaper, and, after dark, step out and leave the parcel on a ledge of the stonework outside the building in the street. Every morning it would be gone. A shadow came along in the night and took it. This went on for many months, till at last one night the man-whose-name-doesn't-matter forgot to put the parcel out, and didn't think of it till he was in bed. It worried him, so that at last he had to get up and put the scraps outside. It was midnight. He felt curious to see the shadow, so he waited until it came along. It wasn't his long-lost brother, but it was an old mate of his.

Let us finish with a sketch:

The scene was Circular Quay, outside the Messageries sheds. The usual number of bundles of misery— covered more or less with dirty sheets of newspaper—lay along the wall under the ghastly glare of the electric light. Time—shortly after midnight. From among the bundles an old man sat up. He cautiously drew off his pants, and then stood close to the wall, in his shirt, tenderly examining the seat of the trousers. Presently he shook them out, folded them with great care, wrapped them in a scrap of newspaper, and laid them down where his head was to be. He had thin, hairy legs and a long grey beard. From a bundle of rags he extracted another pair of pants, which were all patches and tatters, and into which he engineered his way with great caution. Then he sat down, arranged the paper over his knees, laid his old ragged grey head back on his precious Sunday-go-meetings-and-slept.

ACROSS THE STRAITS

We crossed Cook's Straits from Wellington in one of those rusty little iron tanks that go up and down and across there for twenty or thirty years and never get wrecked—for no other reason, apparently, than that they have every possible excuse to go ashore or go down on those stormy coasts. The age, construction, or condition of these boats, and the south-easters, and the construction of the coastline, are all decidedly in favour of their going down; the fares are high and the accommodation is small and dirty. It is always the same where there is no competition.

A year or two ago, when a company was running boats between Australia and New Zealand without competition, the steerage fare was three pound direct single, and two pound ten shillings between Auckland and Wellington. The potatoes were black and green and soggy, the beef like bits scraped off the inside of a hide which had lain out for a day or so, the cabbage was cabbage leaves, the tea muddy. The whole business took away our appetite regularly three times a day, and there wasn't enough to go round, even if it had been good—enough tucker, we mean; there was enough appetite to go round three or four times, but it was driven away by disgust until after meals. If we had not, under cover of darkness, broached a deck cargo of oranges, lemons, and pineapples, and thereby run the risk of being run in on arrival, there would have been starvation, disease, and death on that boat before the end—perhaps mutiny.

You can go across now for one pound, and get something to eat on the road; but the travelling public will go on patronizing the latest reducer of fares until the poorer company gets starved out and fares go up again—then the travelling public will have to pay three or four times as much as they do now, and go hungry on the voyage; all of which ought to go to prove that the travelling public is as big a fool as the general public.

We can't help thinking that the captains and crews of our primitive little coastal steamers take the chances so often that they in time get used to it, and, being used to it, have no longer any misgivings or anxiety in rough weather concerning a watery grave, but feel as perfectly safe as if they were in church with their wives or sisters—only more comfortable—and go on feeling so until the worn-out machinery breaks down and lets the old tub run ashore, or knocks a hole in her side, or the side itself rusts through at last and lets the water in, or the last straw in the shape of an extra ton of brine tumbles on board, and the John Smith (Newcastle), goes down with a swoosh before the cook has time to leave off peeling his potatoes and take to prayer.

These cheerful—and, maybe, unjust—reflections are perhaps in consequence of our having lost half a sovereign to start with. We arrived at the booking-office with two minutes to spare, two sticks of Juno tobacco, a spare wooden pipe—in case we lost the other—a letter to a friend's friend down south, a pound note (Bank of New Zealand), and two half-crowns, with which to try our fortunes in the South Island. We also had a few things in a portmanteau and two blankets in a three-bushel bag, but they didn't amount to much. The clerk put down the ticket with the half-sovereign on top of it, and we wrapped the latter in the former and ran for the wharf. On the way we snatched the ticket out to see the name of the boat we were going by, in order to find it, and it was then, we suppose, that the semi-quid got lost.

Did you ever lose a sovereign or a half-sovereign under similar circumstances? You think of it casually and feel for it carelessly at first, to be sure that it's there all right; then, after going through your pockets three or four times with rapidly growing uneasiness, you lose your head a little and dredge for that coin hurriedly and with painful anxiety. Then you force yourself to be calm, and proceed to search yourself systematically, in a methodical manner. At this stage, if you have time, it's a good plan to sit down and think out when and where you last had that half-sovereign, and where you have been since, and which way you came from there, and what you took out of your pocket, and where, and whether you might have given it in mistake for sixpence at that pub where you rushed in to have a beer—and then you calculate the chances against getting it back again. The last of these reflections is apt to be painful, and the painfulness is complicated and increased when there happen to have been several pubs and a like number of hurried farewell beers in the recent past.

And for months after that you cannot get rid of the idea that that half-sov. might be about your clothes somewhere. It haunts you. You turn your pockets out, and feel the lining of your coat and vest inch by inch, and examine your letter papers—everything you happen to have had in your pocket that day— over and over again, and by and by you peer in envelopes and unfold papers that you didn't have in your pocket at all, but might have had. And when the novelty of the first search has worn off, and the fit takes you, you make another search. Even after many months have passed away, some day—or night—when you are hard up for tobacco and a drink, you suddenly think of that late lamented half-sov., and are moved by adverse circumstances to look through your old clothes in a sort of forlorn hope, or to give good luck a sort of chance to surprise you—the only chance that you can give it.

By the way, seven-and-six of that half-quid should have gone to the landlord of the hotel where we stayed last, and somehow, in spite of this enlightened age, the loss of it seemed a judgment; and seeing that the boat was old and primitive, and there was every sign of a three days' sou'-easter, we sincerely hoped that judgment was complete—that supreme wrath had been appeased by the fine of ten bob without adding any Jonah business to it.

This reminds us that we once found a lost half-sovereign in the bowl of a spare pipe six months after it was lost. We wish it had stayed there and turned up to-night. But, although when you are in great danger—say, adrift in an open boat—tales of providential escapes and rescues may interest and comfort you, you can't get any comfort out of anecdotes concerning the turning up of lost quids when you have just lost one yourself. All you want is to find it.

It bothers you even not to be able to account for a bob. You always like to know that you have had something for your money, if only a long beer. You would sooner know that you fooled your money away on a spree, and made yourself sick than lost it out of an extra hole in your pocket, and kept well.

We left Wellington with a feeling of pained regret, a fellow-wanderer by our side telling us how he had once lost "fi-pun-note"—and about two-thirds of the city unemployed on the wharf looking for that half-sovereign. Well, we hope that some poor devil found it; although, to tell the truth, we would then have by far preferred to have found it ourselves.

A sailor said that the Moa was a good sea-boat, and, although she was small and old, he was never afraid of her. He'd sooner travel in her than in some of those big cheap ocean liners with more sand in them than iron or steel—You, know the rest. Further on, in a conversation concerning the age of these coasters, he said that they'd last fully thirty years if well painted and looked after. He said that this one was seldom painted, and never painted properly; and then, seemingly in direct contradiction to his previously expressed confidence in the safety and seaworthiness of the Moa, he said that he could poke a stick through her anywhere. We asked him not to do it.

It came on to splash, and we went below to reflect, and search once more for that half-sovereign. The cabin was small and close, and dimly lighted, and evil smelling, and shaped like the butt end of a coffin. It might not have smelt so bad if we hadn't lost that half-sovereign. There was a party of those gipsy-like Assyrians—two families apparently—the women and children lying very sick about the lower bunks; and a big, good-humoured-looking young Maori propped between the end of the table and the wall, playing a concertina. The sick people were too sick, and the concertina seemed too much in sympathy with them, and the lost half-quid haunted us more than ever down there; so we started to climb out.

The first thing that struck us was the jagged top edge of that iron hood-like arrangement over the gangway. The top half only of the scuttle was open. There was nothing to be seen except a fog of spray and a Newfoundland dog sea-sick under the lee of something. The next thing that struck us was a tub of salt water, which came like a cannon ball and broke against the hood affair, and spattered on deck like a crockery shop. We climbed down again backwards, and sat on the floor with emphasis, in consequence of stepping down a last step that wasn't there, and cracked the back of our heads against the edge of the table. The Maori helped us up, and we had a drink with him at the expense of one of the half-casers mentioned in the beginning of this sketch. Then the Maori shouted, then we, then the Maori again, then we again; and then we thought, "Dash it, what's a half-sovereign? We'll fall on our feet all right."

We went up Queen Charlotte's Sound, a long crooked arm of the sea between big, rugged, black-looking hills. There was a sort of lighthouse down near the entrance, and they said an old Maori woman kept it. There were some whitish things on the sides of the hills, which we at first took for cattle, and then for goats. They were sheep. Someone said that that country was only fit to carry sheep. It must have been bad, then, judging from some of the country in Australia which is only fit to carry sheep. Country that wouldn't carry goats would carry sheep, we think. Sheep are about the hardiest animals on the face of this planet—barring crocodiles.

You may rip a sheep open whilst watching for the boss's boots or yarning to a pen-mate, and then when you have stuffed the works back into the animal, and put a stitch in the slit, and poked it somewhere with a tar-stick (it doesn't matter much where) the jumbuck will be all right and just as lively as ever, and turn up next shearing without the ghost of a scratch on its skin.

We reached Picton, a small collection of twinkling lights in a dark pocket, apparently at the top of a sound. We climbed up on to the wharf, got through between two railway trucks, and asked a policeman where we were, and where the telegraph office was. There were several pretty girls in the office, laughing and chyacking the counter clerks, which jarred upon the feelings of this poor orphan wanderer in strange lands. We gloomily took a telegram form, and wired to a friend in North Island, using the following words: "Wire quid; stumped."

Then we crossed the street to a pub and asked for a roof and they told us to go up to No. 8. We went up, struck a match, lit the candle, put our bag in a corner, cleared the looking-glass off the toilet table, got some paper and a pencil out of our portmanteau, and sat down and wrote this sketch.

The candle is going out.

"SOME DAY"

The two travellers had yarned late in their camp, and the moon was getting low down through the mulga. Mitchell's mate had just finished a rather racy yarn, but it seemed to fall flat on Mitchell—he was in a sentimental mood. He smoked a while, and thought, and then said:

"Ah! there was one little girl that I was properly struck on. She came to our place on a visit to my sister. I think she was the best little girl that ever lived, and about the prettiest. She was just eighteen, and didn't come up to my shoulder; the biggest blue eyes you ever saw, and she had hair that reached down to her knees, and so thick you couldn't span it with your two hands—brown and glossy—and her skin with like lilies and roses. Of course, I never thought she'd look at a rough, ugly, ignorant brute like me, and I used to keep out of her way and act a little stiff towards her; I didn't want the others to think I was gone on her, because I knew they'd laugh at me, and maybe she'd laugh at me more than all. She would come and talk to me, and sit near me at table; but I thought that that was on account of her good nature, and she pitied me because I was such a rough, awkward chap. I was gone on that girl, and no joking; and I felt quite proud to think she was a countrywoman of mine. But I wouldn't let her know that, for I felt sure she'd only laugh.

"Well, things went on till I got the offer of two or three years' work on a station up near the border, and I had to go, for I was hard up; besides, I wanted to get away. Stopping round where she was only made me miserable.

"The night I left they were all down at the station to see me off—including the girl I was gone on. When the train was ready to start she was standing away by herself on the dark end of the platform, and my sister kept nudging me and winking, and fooling about, but I didn't know what she was driving at. At last she said:

"'Go and speak to her, you noodle; go and say good-bye to Edie.'

"So I went up to where she was, and, when the others turned their backs—

"'Well, good-bye, Miss Brown,' I said, holding out my hand; 'I don't suppose I'll ever see you again, for Lord knows when I'll be back. Thank you for coming to see me off.'

"Just then she turned her face to the light, and I saw she was crying. She was trembling all over. Suddenly she said, 'Jack! Jack!' just like that, and held up her arms like this."

Mitchell was speaking in a tone of voice that didn't belong to him, and his mate looked up. Mitchell's face was solemn, and his eyes were fixed on the fire.

"I suppose you gave her a good hug then, and a kiss?" asked the mate.

"I s'pose so," snapped Mitchell. "There is some things a man doesn't want to joke about.... Well, I think we'll shove on one of the billies, and have a drink of tea before we turn in."

"I suppose," said Mitchell's mate, as they drank their tea, "I suppose you'll go back and marry her some day?"

"Some day! That's it; it looks like it, doesn't it? We all say, 'Some day.' I used to say it ten years ago, and look at me now. I've been knocking round for five years, and the last two years constant on the track, and no show of getting off it unless I go for good, and what have I got for it? I look like going home and getting married, without a penny in my pocket or a rag to my back scarcely, and no show of getting them. I swore I'd never go back home without a cheque, and, what's more, I never will; but the cheque days are past. Look at that boot! If we were down among the settled districts we'd be called tramps and beggars; and what's the difference? I've been a fool, I know, but I've paid for it; and now there's nothing for it but to tramp, tramp, tramp for your tucker, and keep tramping till you get old and careless and dirty, and older, and more careless and dirtier, and you get used to the dust and sand, and heat, and flies, and mosquitoes, just as a bullock does, and lose ambition and hope, and get contented with this animal life, like a dog, and till your swag seems part of yourself, and you'd be lost and uneasy and light-shouldered without it, and you don't care a damn if you'll ever get work again, or live like a Christian; and you go on like this till the spirit of a bullock takes the place of the heart of a man. Who cares? If we hadn't found the track yesterday we might have lain and rotted in that lignum, and no one been any the wiser—or sorrier—who knows? Somebody might have found us in the end, but it mightn't have been worth his while to go out of his way and report us. Damn the world, say I!"

He smoked for a while in savage silence; then he knocked the ashes out of his pipe, felt for his tobacco with a sigh, and said:

"Well, I am a bit out of sorts to-night. I've been thinking.... I think we'd best turn in, old man; we've got a long, dry stretch before us to-morrow."

They rolled out their swags on the sand, lay down, and wrapped themselves in their blankets. Mitchell covered his face with a piece of calico, because the moonlight and wind kept him awake.

"BRUMMY USEN"

We caught up with an old swagman crossing the plain, and tramped along with him till we came to good shade to have a smoke in. We had got yarning about men getting lost in the bush or going away and being reported dead.

"Yes," said the old 'whaler', as he dropped his swag in the shade, sat down on it, and felt for his smoking tackle, "there's scarcely an old bushman alive—or dead, for the matter of that—who hasn't been dead a few times in his life—or reported dead, which amounts to the same thing for a while. In my time there was as many live men in the bush who was supposed to be dead as there was dead men who was supposed to be alive—though it's the other way about now—what with so many jackaroos tramping about out back and getting lost in the dry country that they don't know anything about, and dying within a few yards of water sometimes. But even now, whenever I hear that an old bush mate of mine is dead, I don't fret about it or put a black band round my hat, because I know he'll be pretty sure to turn up sometimes, pretty bad with the booze, and want to borrow half a crown.

"I've been dead a few times myself, and found out afterwards that my friends was so sorry about it, and that I was such a good sort of a chap after all, when I was dead that—that I was sorry I didn't stop dead. You see, I was one of them chaps that's better treated by their friends and better thought of when—when they're dead.

"Ah, well! Never mind.... Talking of killing bushmen before their time reminds me of some cases I knew. They mostly happened among the western spurs of the ranges. There was a bullock-driver named Billy Nowlett. He had a small selection, where he kept his family, and used to carry from the railway terminus to the stations up-country. One time he went up with a load and was not heard of for such a long time that his missus got mighty uneasy; and then she got a letter from a publican up Coonamble way to say that Billy was dead. Someone wrote, for the widow, to ask about the wagon and the bullocks, but the shanty-keeper wrote that Billy had drunk them before he died, and that he'd also to say that he'd drunk the money he got for the carrying; and the publican enclosed a five-pound note for the widow—which was considered very kind of him.

"Well, the widow struggled along and managed without her husband just the same as she had always struggled along and managed with him—a little better, perhaps. An old digger used to drop in of evenings and sit by the widow's fire, and yarn, and sympathize, and smoke, and think; and just as he began to yarn a lot less, and smoke and think a lot more, Billy Nowlett himself turned up with a load of rations for a sheep station. He'd been down by the other road, and the letter he'd wrote to his missus had gone astray. Billy wasn't surprised to hear that he was dead—he'd been killed before—but he was surprised about the five quid.

"You see, it must have been another bullock-driver that died. There was an old shanty-keeper up Coonamble way, so Billy said, that used to always mistake him for another bullocky and mistake the other bullocky for him—couldn't tell the one from the other no way—and he used to have bills against Billy that the other bullock-driver'd run up, and bills against the other that Billy'd run up, and generally got things mixed up in various ways, till Billy wished that one of 'em was dead. And the funniest part of the business was that Billy wasn't no more like the other man than chalk is like cheese. You'll often drop across some colour-blind old codger that can't tell the difference between two people that ain't got a bit of likeness between 'em.

"Then there was young Joe Swallow. He was found dead under a burned-down tree in Dead Man's Gully—'dead past all recognition,' they said—and he was buried there, and by and by his ghost began to haunt the gully: at least, all the schoolkids seen it, and there was scarcely a grown-up person who didn't know another person who'd seen the ghost—and the other person was always a sober chap that wouldn't bother about telling a lie. But just as the ghost was beginning to settle down to work in the gully, Joe himself turned up, and then the folks began to reckon that it was another man was killed there, and that the ghost belonged to the other man; and some of them began to recollect that they'd thought all along that the ghost wasn't Joe's ghost—even when they thought that it was really Joe that was killed there.

"Then, again, there was the case of Brummy Usen—Hughison I think they spelled it—the bushranger; he was shot by old Mr S—, of E—, while trying to stick the old gentleman up. There's something about it in a book called 'Robbery Under Arms', though the names is all altered—and some other time I'll tell you all about the digging of the body up for the inquest and burying it again. This Brummy used to work for a publican in a sawmill that the publican had; and this publican and his daughter identified the body by a woman holding up a branch tattooed on the right arm. I'll tell you all about that another time. This girl remembered how she used to watch this tattooed woman going up and down on Brummy's arm when he was working in the saw-pit—going up and down and up and down, like this, while Brummy was working his end of the saw. So the bushranger was inquested and justifiable-homicided as Brummy Usen, and buried again in his dust and blood stains and monkey-jacket.

"All the same it wasn't him; for the real Brummy turned up later on; but he couldn't make the people believe he wasn't dead. They was mostly English country people from Kent and Yorkshire and those places; and the most self-opinionated and obstinate people that ever lived when they got a thing into their heads; and they got it into their heads that Brummy Usen was shot while trying to bail up old Mr S— and was dead and buried.

"But the wife of the publican that had the saw-pit knew him; he went to her, and she recognized him at once; she'd got it into her head from the first that it wasn't Brummy that was shot, and she stuck to it— she was just as self-opinionated as the neighbours, and many a barney she had with them about it. She would argue about it till the day she died, and then she said with her dying breath: 'It wasn't Brummy Usen.' No more it was—he was a different kind of man; he hadn't spunk enough to be a bushranger, and it was a better man that was buried for him; it was a different kind of woman, holding up a different kind of branch, that was tattooed on Brummy's arm. But, you see, Brummy'd always kept himself pretty much to himself, and no one knew him very well; and, besides, most of them were pretty drunk at the inquest—except the girl, and she was too scared to know what she was saying—they had to be so because the corpse was in such a bad state.

"Well, Brummy hung around for a time, and tried to prove that he wasn't an impostor, but no one wouldn't believe him. He wanted to get some wages that was owing to him.

"He tried the police, but they were just as obstinate as the rest; and, beside, they had their dignity to hold up. 'If I ain't Brummy,' he'd say, 'who are I?' But they answered that he knew best. So he did.

"At last he said that it didn't matter much, any road; and so he went away—Lord knows where—to begin life again, I s'pose."

The traveller smoked awhile reflectively; then he quietly rolled up his right sleeve and scratched his arm.

And on that arm we saw the tattooed figure of a woman, holding up a branch.

We tramped on by his side again towards the station-thinking very hard and not feeling very comfortable.

He must have been an awful old liar, now we come to think of it.

SECOND SERIES

THE DROVER'S WIFE

The two-roomed house is built of round timber, slabs, and stringy-bark, and floored with split slabs. A big bark kitchen standing at one end is larger than the house itself, veranda included.

Bush all round—bush with no horizon, for the country is flat. No ranges in the distance. The bush consists of stunted, rotten native apple-trees. No undergrowth. Nothing to relieve the eye save the darker green of a few she-oaks which are sighing above the narrow, almost waterless creek. Nineteen miles to the nearest sign of civilization—a shanty on the main road.

The drover, an ex-squatter, is away with sheep. His wife and children are left here alone.

Four ragged, dried-up-looking children are playing about the house. Suddenly one of them yells: "Snake! Mother, here's a snake!"

The gaunt, sun-browned bushwoman dashes from the kitchen, snatches her baby from the ground, holds it on her left hip, and reaches for a stick.

"Where is it?"

"Here! gone into the wood-heap!" yells the eldest boy—a sharp-faced urchin of eleven. "Stop there, mother! I'll have him. Stand back! I'll have the beggar!"

"Tommy, come here, or you'll be bit. Come here at once when I tell you, you little wretch!"

The youngster comes reluctantly, carrying a stick bigger than himself. Then he yells, triumphantly:

"There it goes—under the house!" and darts away with club uplifted. At the same time the big, black, yellow-eyed dog-of-all-breeds, who has shown the wildest interest in the proceedings, breaks his chain and rushes after that snake. He is a moment late, however, and his nose reaches the crack in the slabs just as the end of its tail disappears. Almost at the same moment the boy's club comes down and skins the aforesaid nose. Alligator takes small notice of this, and proceeds to undermine the building; but he is subdued after a struggle and chained up. They cannot afford to lose him.

The drover's wife makes the children stand together near the dog-house while she watches for the snake. She gets two small dishes of milk and sets them down near the wall to tempt it to come out; but an hour goes by and it does not show itself.

It is near sunset, and a thunderstorm is coming. The children must be brought inside. She will not take them into the house, for she knows the snake is there, and may at any moment come up through a crack in the rough slab floor; so she carries several armfuls of firewood into the kitchen, and then takes the children there. The kitchen has no floor—or, rather, an earthen one—called a "ground floor" in this part of the bush. There is a large, roughly-made table in the centre of the place. She brings the children in, and makes them get on this table. They are two boys and two girls—mere babies. She gives them some supper, and then, before it gets dark, she goes into the house, and snatches up some pillows and bedclothes—expecting to see or lay her hand on the snake any minute. She makes a bed on the kitchen table for the children, and sits down beside it to watch all night.

She has an eye on the corner, and a green sapling club laid in readiness on the dresser by her side; also her sewing basket and a copy of the Young Ladies' Journal. She has brought the dog into the room.

Tommy turns in, under protest, but says he'll lie awake all night and smash that blinded snake.

His mother asks him how many times she has told him not to swear.

He has his club with him under the bedclothes, and Jacky protests:

"Mummy! Tommy's skinnin' me alive wif his club. Make him take it out."

Tommy: "Shet up, you little—! D'yer want to be bit with the snake?"

Jacky shuts up.

"If yer bit," says Tommy, after a pause, "you'll swell up, an' smell, an' turn red an' green an' blue all over till yer bust. Won't he, mother?"

"Now then, don't frighten the child. Go to sleep," she says.

The two younger children go to sleep, and now and then Jacky complains of being "skeezed." More room is made for him. Presently Tommy says: "Mother! listen to them (adjective) little possums. I'd like to screw their blanky necks."

And Jacky protests drowsily.

"But they don't hurt us, the little blanks!".

Mother: "There, I told you you'd teach Jacky to swear." But the remark makes her smile. Jacky goes to sleep. Presently Tommy asks:

"Mother! Do you think they'll ever extricate the (adjective) kangaroo?"

"Lord! How am I to know, child? Go to sleep."

"Will you wake me if the snake comes out?"

"Yes. Go to sleep."

Near midnight. The children are all asleep and she sits there still, sewing and reading by turns. From time to time she glances round the floor and wall-plate, and, whenever she hears a noise, she reaches for the stick. The thunderstorm comes on, and the wind, rushing through the cracks in the slab wall, threatens to blow out her candle. She places it on a sheltered part of the dresser and fixes up a newspaper to protect it. At every flash of lightning, the cracks between the slabs gleam like polished silver. The thunder rolls, and the rain comes down in torrents.

Alligator lies at full length on the floor, with his eyes turned towards the partition. She knows by this that the snake is there. There are large cracks in that wall opening under the floor of the dwelling-house.

She is not a coward, but recent events have shaken her nerves. A little son of her brother-in-law was lately bitten by a snake, and died. Besides, she has not heard from her husband for six months, and is anxious about him.

He was a drover, and started squatting here when they were married. The drought of 18— ruined him. He had to sacrifice the remnant of his flock and go droving again. He intends to move his family into the nearest town when he comes back, and, in the meantime, his brother, who keeps a shanty on the main road, comes over about once a month with provisions. The wife has still a couple of cows, one horse, and a few sheep. The brother-in-law kills one of the latter occasionally, gives her what she needs of it, and takes the rest in return for other provisions. She is used to being left alone. She once lived like this for eighteen months. As a girl she built the usual castles in the air; but all her girlish hopes and aspirations have long been dead. She finds all the excitement and recreation she needs in the Young Ladies' Journal, and Heaven help her! takes a pleasure in the fashion-plates.

Her husband is an Australian, and so is she. He is careless, but a good enough husband. If he had the means he would take her to the city and keep her there like a princess. They are used to being apart, or at least she is. "No use fretting," she says. He may forget sometimes that he is married; but if he has a good cheque when he comes back he will give most of it to her. When he had money he took her to the city several times—hired a railway sleeping compartment, and put up at the best hotels. He also bought her a buggy, but they had to sacrifice that along with the rest.

The last two children were born in the bush—one while her husband was bringing a drunken doctor, by force, to attend to her. She was alone on this occasion, and very weak. She had been ill with a fever. She prayed to God to send her assistance. God sent Black Mary—the "whitest" gin in all the land. Or, at least, God sent King Jimmy first, and he sent Black Mary. He put his black face round the door post, took in the situation at a glance, and said cheerfully: "All right, missus—I bring my old woman, she down alonga creek."

One of the children died while she was here alone. She rode nineteen miles for assistance, carrying the dead child.

It must be near one or two o'clock. The fire is burning low. Alligator lies with his head resting on his paws, and watches the wall. He is not a very beautiful dog, and the light shows numerous old wounds where the hair will not grow. He is afraid of nothing on the face of the earth or under it. He will tackle a bullock as readily as he will tackle a flea. He hates all other dogs—except kangaroo-dogs—and has a marked dislike to friends or relations of the family. They seldom call, however. He sometimes makes friends with strangers. He hates snakes and has killed many, but he will be bitten some day and die; most snake-dogs end that way.

Now and then the bushwoman lays down her work and watches, and listens, and thinks. She thinks of things in her own life, for there is little else to think about.

The rain will make the grass grow, and this reminds her how she fought a bush-fire once while her husband was away. The grass was long, and very dry, and the fire threatened to burn her out. She put on an old pair of her husband's trousers and beat out the flames with a green bough, till great drops of sooty perspiration stood out on her forehead and ran in streaks down her blackened arms. The sight of his mother in trousers greatly amused Tommy, who worked like a little hero by her side, but the terrified baby howled lustily for his "mummy." The fire would have mastered her but for four excited bushmen who arrived in the nick of time. It was a mixed-up affair all round; when she went to take up the baby he screamed and struggled convulsively, thinking it was a "blackman;" and Alligator, trusting more to the child's sense than his own instinct, charged furiously, and (being old and slightly deaf) did not in his excitement at first recognize his mistress's voice, but continued to hang on to the moleskins until choked off by Tommy with a saddle-strap. The dog's sorrow for his blunder, and his anxiety to let it be known that it was all a mistake, was as evident as his ragged tail and a twelve-inch grin could make it. It was a glorious time for the boys; a day to look back to, and talk about, and laugh over for many years.

She thinks how she fought a flood during her husband's absence. She stood for hours in the drenching downpour, and dug an overflow gutter to save the dam across the creek. But she could not save it. There are things that a bushwoman can not do. Next morning the dam was broken, and her heart was nearly broken too, for she thought how her husband would feel when he came home and saw the result of years of labour swept away. She cried then.

She also fought the pleuro-pneumonia—dosed and bled the few remaining cattle, and wept again when her two best cows died.

Again, she fought a mad bullock that besieged the house for a day. She made bullets and fired at him through cracks in the slabs with an old shot-gun. He was dead in the morning. She skinned him and got seventeen-and-sixpence for the hide.

She also fights the crows and eagles that have designs on her chickens. Her plan of campaign is very original. The children cry "Crows, mother!" and she rushes out and aims a broomstick at the birds as though it were a gun, and says "Bung!" The crows leave in a hurry; they are cunning, but a woman's cunning is greater.

Occasionally a bushman in the horrors, or a villainous-looking sundowner, comes and nearly scares the life out of her. She generally tells the suspicious-looking stranger that her husband and two sons are at work below the dam, or over at the yard, for he always cunningly inquires for the boss.

Only last week a gallows-faced swagman—having satisfied himself that there were no men on the place—threw his swag down on the veranda, and demanded tucker. She gave him something to eat; then he expressed his intention of staying for the night. It was sundown then. She got a batten from the sofa, loosened the dog, and confronted the stranger, holding the batten in one hand and the dog's collar with the other. "Now you go!" she said. He looked at her and at the dog, said "All right, mum," in a cringing tone, and left. She was a determined-looking woman, and Alligator's yellow eyes glared unpleasantly—besides, the dog's chawing-up apparatus greatly resembled that of the reptile he was named after.

She has few pleasures to think of as she sits here alone by the fire, on guard against a snake. All days are much the same to her; but on Sunday afternoon she dresses herself, tidies the children, smartens up baby, and goes for a lonely walk along the bush-track, pushing an old perambulator in front of her. She does this every Sunday. She takes as much care to make herself and the children look smart as she would if she were going to do the block in the city. There is nothing to see, however, and not a soul to meet. You might walk for twenty miles along this track without being able to fix a point in your mind, unless you are a bushman. This is because of the everlasting, maddening sameness of the stunted trees—that monotony which makes a man long to break away and travel as far as trains can go, and sail as far as ship can sail—and farther.

But this bushwoman is used to the loneliness of it. As a girl-wife she hated it, but now she would feel strange away from it.

She is glad when her husband returns, but she does not gush or make a fuss about it. She gets him something good to eat, and tidies up the children.

She seems contented with her lot. She loves her children, but has no time to show it. She seems harsh to them. Her surroundings are not favourable to the development of the "womanly" or sentimental side of nature.

It must be near morning now; but the clock is in the dwellinghouse. Her candle is nearly done; she forgot that she was out of candles. Some more wood must be got to keep the fire up, and so she shuts the dog inside and hurries round to the woodheap. The rain has cleared off. She seizes a stick, pulls it out, and— crash! the whole pile collapses.

Yesterday she bargained with a stray blackfellow to bring her some wood, and while he was at work she went in search of a missing cow. She was absent an hour or so, and the native black made good use of his time. On her return she was so astonished to see a good heap of wood by the chimney, that she gave him an extra fig of tobacco, and praised him for not being lazy. He thanked her, and left with head erect and chest well out. He was the last of his tribe and a King; but he had built that wood-heap hollow.

She is hurt now, and tears spring to her eyes as she sits down again by the table. She takes up a handkerchief to wipe the tears away, but pokes her eyes with her bare fingers instead. The handkerchief is full of holes, and she finds that she has put her thumb through one, and her forefinger through another.

This makes her laugh, to the surprise of the dog. She has a keen, very keen, sense of the ridiculous; and some time or other she will amuse bushmen with the story.

She had been amused before like that. One day she sat down "to have a good cry," as she said—and the old cat rubbed against her dress and "cried too." Then she had to laugh.

It must be near daylight now. The room is very close and hot because of the fire. Alligator still watches the wall from time to time. Suddenly he becomes greatly interested; he draws himself a few inches nearer the partition, and a thrill runs through his body. The hair on the back of his neck begins to bristle, and the battle-light is in his yellow eyes. She knows what this means, and lays her hand on the stick. The lower end of one of the partition slabs has a large crack on both sides. An evil pair of small, bright bead-like eyes glisten at one of these holes. The snake—a black one—comes slowly out, about a foot, and moves its head up and down. The dog lies still, and the woman sits as one fascinated. The snake comes out a foot farther. She lifts her stick, and the reptile, as though suddenly aware of danger, sticks his head in through the crack on the other side of the slab, and hurries to get his tail round after him. Alligator springs, and his jaws come together with a snap. He misses, for his nose is large, and the snake's body close down in the angle formed by the slabs and the floor. He snaps again as the tail comes round. He has the snake now, and tugs it out eighteen inches. Thud, thud comes the woman's club on the ground. Alligator pulls again. Thud, thud. Alligator gives another pull and he has the snake out—a black brute, five feet long. The head rises to dart about, but the dog has the enemy close to the neck. He is a big, heavy dog, but quick as a terrier. He shakes the snake as though he felt the original curse in common with mankind. The eldest boy wakes up, seizes his stick, and tries to get out of bed, but his mother forces him back with a grip of iron. Thud, thud—the snake's back is broken in several places. Thud, thud—its head is crushed, and Alligator's nose skinned again.

She lifts the mangled reptile on the point of her stick, carries it to the fire, and throws it in; then piles on the wood and watches the snake burn. The boy and dog watch too. She lays her hand on the dog's head, and all the fierce, angry light dies out of his yellow eyes. The younger children are quieted, and presently go to sleep. The dirty-legged boy stands for a moment in his shirt, watching the fire. Presently he looks up at her, sees the tears in her eyes, and, throwing his arms round her neck exclaims:

"Mother, I won't never go drovin'; blarst me if I do!" And she hugs him to her worn-out breast and kisses him; and they sit thus together while the sickly daylight breaks over the bush.

STEELMAN'S PUPIL

Steelman was a hard case, but some said that Smith was harder. Steelman was big and good-looking, and good-natured in his way; he was a spieler, pure and simple, but did things in humorous style. Smith was small and weedy, of the sneak variety; he had a whining tone and a cringing manner. He seemed to be always so afraid you were going to hit him that he would make you want to hit him on that account alone.

Steelman "had" you in a fashion that would make your friends laugh. Smith would "have" you in a way which made you feel mad at the bare recollection of having been taken in by so contemptible a little sneak.

They battled round together in the North Island of Maoriland for a couple of years.

One day Steelman said to Smith:

"Look here, Smithy, you don't know you're born yet. I'm going to take you in hand and teach you."

And he did. If Smith wouldn't do as Steelman told him, or wasn't successful in cadging, or mugged any game they had in hand, Steelman would threaten to stoush him; and, if the warning proved ineffectual after the second or third time, he would stoush him.

One day, on the track, they came to a place where an old Scottish couple kept a general store and shanty. They camped alongside the road, and Smith was just starting up to the house to beg supplies when Steelman cried:

"Here!—hold on. Now where do you think you're going to?"

"Why, I'm going to try and chew the old party's lug, of course. We'll be out of tucker in a couple of days," said Smith.

Steelman sat down on a stump in a hopeless, discouraged sort of way.

"It's no use," he said, regarding Smith with mingled reproach and disgust. "It's no use. I might as well give it best. I can see that it's only waste of time trying to learn you anything. Will I ever be able to knock some gumption into your thick skull? After all the time and trouble and pains I've took with your education, you hain't got any more sense than to go and mug a business like that! When will you learn sense? Hey? After all, I—Smith, you're a born mug!"

He always called Smith a "mug" when he was particularly wild at him, for it hurt Smith more than anything else. "There's only two classes in the world, spielers and mugs—and you're a mug, Smith."

"What have I done, anyway?" asked Smith helplessly. "That's all I want to know."

Steelman wearily rested his brow on his hand.

"That will do, Smith," he said listlessly; "don't say another word, old man; it'll only make my head worse; don't talk. You might, at the very least, have a little consideration for my feelings—even if you haven't for your own interests." He paused and regarded Smith sadly. "Well, I'll give you another show. I'll stage the business for you."

He made Smith doff his coat and get into his worst pair of trousers—and they were bad enough; they were hopelessly "gone" beyond the extreme limit of bush decency. He made Smith put on a rag of a felt hat and a pair of "'lastic-sides" which had fallen off a tramp and lain baking and rotting by turns on a rubbish heap; they had to be tied on Smith with bits of rag and string. He drew dark shadows round Smith's eyes, and burning spots on his cheek-bones with some greasepaints he used when they travelled as "The Great Steelman and Smith Combination Star Dramatic Co." He damped Smith's hair to make it dark and lank, and his face more corpse-like by comparison—in short, he made him up to look like a man who had long passed the very last stage of consumption, and had been artificially kept alive in the interests of science.

"Now you're ready," said Steelman to Smith. "You left your whare the day before yesterday and started to walk to the hospital at Palmerston. An old mate picked you up dying on the road, brought you round, and carried you on his back most of the way here. You firmly believe that Providence had something to do with the sending of that old mate along at that time and place above all others. Your mate also was hard up; he was going to a job—the first show for work he'd had in nine months—but he gave it up to see you through; he'd give up his life rather than desert a mate in trouble. You only want a couple of shillings or a bit of tucker to help you on to Palmerston. You know you've got to die, and you only want to live long enough to get word to your poor old mother, and die on a bed.

"Remember, they're Scotch up at that house. You understand the Scotch barrack pretty well by now—if you don't it ain't my fault. You were born in Aberdeen, but came out too young to remember much about the town. Your father's dead. You ran away to sea and came out in the Bobbie Burns to Sydney. Your poor old mother's in Aberdeen now—Bruce or Wallace Wynd will do. Your mother might be dead now—poor old soul!—any way, you'll never see her again. You wish you'd never run away from home. You wish you'd been a better son to your poor old mother; you wish you'd written to her and answered her last letter. You only want to live long enough to write home and ask for forgiveness and a blessing before you die. If you had a drop of spirits of some sort to brace you up you might get along the road better. (Put this delicately.) Get the whine out of your voice and breathe with a wheeze—like this; get up the nearest approach to a deathrattle that you can. Move as if you were badly hurt in your wind—like this. (If you don't do it better'n that, I'll stoush you.) Make your face a bit longer and keep your lips dry—don't lick them, you damned fool!-breathe on them; make 'em dry as chips. That's the only decent pair of breeks you've got, and the only shoon. You're a Presbyterian—not a U.P., the Auld Kirk. Your mate would have come up to the house only—well, you'll have to use the stuffing in your head a bit; you can't expect me to do all the brain work. Remember it's consumption you've got—galloping consumption; you know all the symptoms—pain on top of your right lung, bad cough, and night sweats. Something tells you that you won't see the new year—it's a week off Christmas now. And if you come back without anything, I'll blessed soon put you out of your misery."

Smith came back with about four pounds of shortbread and as much various tucker as they could conveniently carry; a pretty good suit of cast-off tweeds; a new pair of 'lastic-sides from the store stock; two bottles of patent medicine and a black bottle half-full of home-made consumption-cure; also a letter to a hospital-committee man, and three shillings to help him on his way to Palmerston. He also got about half a mile of sympathy, religious consolation, and medical advice which he didn't remember.

"Now," he said, triumphantly, "am I a mug or not?"

Steelman kindly ignored the question. "I did have a better opinion of the Scotch," he said, contemptuously.

Steelman got on at an hotel as billiard-marker and decoy, and in six months he managed that pub. Smith, who'd been away on his own account, turned up in the town one day clean broke, and in a deplorable state. He heard of Steelman's luck, and thought he was "all right," so went to his old friend.

Cold type—or any other kind of type—couldn't do justice to Steelman's disgust. To think that this was the reward of all the time and trouble he'd spent on Smith's education! However, when he cooled down, he said:

"Smith, you're a young man yet, and it's never too late to mend. There is still time for reformation. I can't help you now; it would only demoralize you altogether. To think, after the way I trained you, you can't battle round any better'n this! I always thought you were an irreclaimable mug, but I expected better things of you towards the end. I thought I'd make something of you. It's enough to dishearten any man and disgust him with the world. Why! you ought to be a rich man now with the chances and training you had! To think—but I won't talk of that; it has made me ill. I suppose I'll have to give you something, if it's only to get rid of the sight of you. Here's a quid, and I'm a mug for giving it to you. It'll do you more harm than good; and it ain't a friendly thing nor the right thing for me—who always had your welfare at heart—to give it to you under the circumstances. Now, get away out of my sight, and don't come near me till you've reformed. If you do, I'll have to stoush you out of regard for my own health and feelings."

But Steelman came down in the world again and picked up Smith on the road, and they battled round together for another year or so; and at last they were in Wellington—Steelman "flush" and stopping at an hotel, and Smith stumped, as usual, and staying with a friend. One night they were drinking together at the hotel, at the expense of some mugs whom Steelman was "educating." It was raining hard. When Smith was going home, he said:

"Look here, Steely, old man. Listen to the rain! I'll get wringing wet going home. You might as well lend me your overcoat to-night. You won't want it, and I won't hurt it."

And, Steelman's heart being warmed by his successes, he lent the overcoat.

Smith went and pawned it, got glorious on the proceeds, and took the pawn-ticket to Steelman next day.

Smith had reformed.

AN UNFINISHED LOVE STORY

Brook let down the heavy, awkward sliprails, and the gaunt cattle stumbled through, with aggravating deliberation, and scattered slowly among the native apple-trees along the sidling. First there came an old easygoing red poley cow, then a dusty white cow; then two shaggy, half-grown calves—who seemed already to have lost all interest in existence—and after them a couple of "babies," sleek, glossy, and cheerful; then three more tired-looking cows, with ragged udders and hollow sides; then a lanky barren heifer—red, of course—with half-blind eyes and one crooked horn—she was noted for her great agility in jumping two-rail fences, and she was known to the selector as "Queen Elizabeth;" and behind her came a young cream-coloured milker—a mighty proud and contented young mother—painfully and patiently dragging her first calf, which was hanging obstinately to a teat, with its head beneath her hind legs. Last of all there came the inevitable red steer, who scratched the dust and let a stupid "bwoo-ur-r-rr" out of him as he snuffed at the rails.

Brook had shifted the rails there often before—fifteen years ago—perhaps the selfsame rails, for stringy-bark lasts long; and the action brought the past near to him—nearer than he wished. He did not like to think of that hungry, wretched selection existence; he felt more contempt than pity for the old-fashioned, unhappy boy, who used to let down the rails there, and drive the cattle through.

He had spent those fifteen years in cities, and had come here, prompted more by curiosity than anything else, to have a quiet holiday. His father was dead; his other relations had moved away, leaving a tenant on the old selection.

Brook rested his elbow on the top rail of an adjacent panel and watched the cattle pass, and thought until Lizzie—the tenant's niece—shoved the red steer through and stood gravely regarding him (Brook, and not the steer); then he shifted his back to the fence and looked at her. He had not much to look at: a short, plain, thin girl of nineteen, with rather vacant grey eyes, dark ringlets, and freckles; she had no complexion to speak of; she wore an ill-fitting print frock, and a pair of men's 'lastic-sides several sizes too large for her. She was "studying for a school-teacher;" that was the height of the ambition of local youth. Brook was studying her.

He turned away to put up the rails. The lower rail went into its place all right, but the top one had got jammed, and it stuck as though it was spiked. He worked the rail up and down and to and fro, took it under his arm and tugged it; but he might as well have pulled at one of the posts. Then he lifted the loose end as high as he could, and let it fall—jumping back out of the way at the same time; this loosened it, but when he lifted it again it slid so easily and far into its socket that the other end came out and fell, barking Brook's knee. He swore a little, then tackled the rail again; he had the same trouble as before with the other end, but succeeded at last. Then he turned away, rubbing his knee.

Lizzie hadn't smiled, not once; she watched him gravely all the while.

"Did you hurt your knee?" she asked, without emotion.

"No. The rail did."

She reflected solemnly for a while, and then asked him if it felt sore.

He replied rather briefly in the negative.

"They were always nasty, awkward rails to put up," she remarked, after some more reflection.

Brook agreed, and then they turned their faces towards the homestead. Half-way down the sidling was a clump of saplings, with a big log lying amongst them. Here Brook paused. "We'll sit down for a while and have a rest," said he. "Sit down, Lizzie."

She obeyed with the greatest of gravity. Nothing was said for awhile. She sat with her hands folded in her lap, gazing thoughtfully at the ridge, which was growing dim. It looked better when it was dim, and so did the rest of the scenery. There was no beauty lost when darkness hid the scenery altogether. Brook wondered what the girl was thinking about. The silence between them did not seem awkward, somehow; but it didn't suit him just then, and so presently he broke it.

"Well, I must go to-morrow."

"Must you?"

"Yes."

She thought awhile, and then she asked him if he was glad to go.

"Well, I don't know. Are you sorry, Lizzie?"

She thought a good long while, and then she said she was.

He moved closer to the girl, and suddenly slipped his arm round her waist. She did not seem agitated; she still gazed dreamily at the line of ridges, but her head inclined slightly towards him.

"Lizzie, did you ever love anyone?"—then anticipating the usual reply—"except, of course, your father and mother, and all that sort of thing." Then, abruptly: "I mean did you ever have a sweetheart?"

She reflected, so as to be sure; then she said she hadn't. Long pause, and he, the city man, breathed hard—not the girl. Suddenly he moved nervously, and said:

"Lizzie—Lizzie! Do you know what love means?"

She pondered over this for some minutes, as a result of which she said she thought that she did.

"Lizzie! Do you think you can love me?"

She didn't seem able to find an answer to that. So he caught her to him in both arms, and kissed her hard and long on the mouth. She was agitated now—he had some complexion now; she struggled to her feet, trembling.

"We must go now," she said quickly. "They will be waiting for tea."

He stood up before her, and held her there by both hands.

"There is plenty of time. Lizzie—"

"Mis-ter Br-o-o-k-er! Li-i-z-zee-e-e! Come ter yer tea-e-e!" yelled a boy from the house.

"We must really go now."

"Oh, they can wait a minute. Lizzie, don't be frightened"—bending his head—"Lizzie, put your arms round my neck and kiss me—now. Do as I tell you, Lizzie—they cannot see us," and he drew her behind a bush. "Now, Lizzie."

She obeyed just as a frightened child might.

"We must go now," she panted, breathless from such an embrace.

"Lizzie, you will come for a walk with me after tea?"

"I don't know—I can't promise. I don't think it would be right. Aunt mightn't like me to."

"Never mind aunt. I'll fix her. We'll go for a walk over to the school-teacher's place. It will be bright moonlight."

"I don't like to promise. My father and mother might not—"

"Why, what are you frightened of? What harm is there in it?" Then, softly, "Promise, Lizzie."

"Promise, Lizzie."

She was hesitating.

"Promise, Lizzie. I'm going away to-morrow—might never see you again. You will come, Lizzie? It will be our last talk together. Promise, Lizzie.... Oh, then, if you don't like to, I won't press you.... Will you come, or no?"

"Ye-es."

"One more, and I'll take you home."

It was nearly dark.

Brook was moved to get up early next morning and give the girl a hand with the cows. There were two rickety bails in the yard. He had not forgotten how to milk, but the occupation gave him no pleasure—it brought the past near again.

Now and then he would turn his face, rest his head against the side of the cow, and watch Lizzie at her work; and each time she would, as though in obedience to an influence she could not resist, turn her face to him—having noted the pause in his milking. There was a wonder in her expression—as if something had come into her life which she could not realize—curiosity in his.

When the spare pail was full, he would follow her with it to the little bark dairy; and she held out the cloth which served as a strainer whilst he poured the milk in, and, as the last drops went through, their mouths would come together.

He carried the slop-buckets to the pigsty for her, and helped to poddy (hand feed) a young calf. He had to grip the calf by the nape of the neck, insert a forefinger in its mouth, and force its nose down into an oil-drum full of skim milk. The calf sucked, thinking it had a teat; and so it was taught to drink. But calves have a habit, born of instinct, of butting the udders with their noses, by way of reminding their mothers to let down the milk; and so this calf butted at times, splashing sour milk over Brook, and barking his wrist against the sharp edge of the drum. Then he would swear a little, and Lizzie would smile sadly and gravely.

Brook did not go away that day, nor the next, but he took the coach on the third day thereafter. He and Lizzie found a quiet corner to say good-bye in. She showed some emotion for the first time, or, perhaps, the second—maybe the third time—in that week of her life. They had been out together in the moonlight every evening. (Brook had been fifteen years in cities.) They had scarcely looked at each other that morning—and scarcely spoken.

He looked back as the coach started and saw her sitting inside the big kitchen window. She waved her hand—hopelessly it seemed. She had rolled up her sleeve, and to Brook the arm seemed strangely white and fair above the line of sunburn round the wrist. He hadn't noticed it before. Her face seemed fairer too, but, perhaps, it was only the effect of light and shade round that window.

He looked back again, as the coach turned the corner of the fence, and was just in time to see her bury her face in her hands with a passionate gesture which did not seem natural to her.

Brook reached the city next evening, and, "after hours," he staggered in through a side entrance to the lighted parlour of a private bar.

They say that Lizzie broke her heart that year, but, then, the world does not believe in such things nowadays.

BOARD AND RESIDENCE

One o'clock on Saturday. The unemployed's one o'clock on Saturday! Nothing more can be done this week, so you drag yourself wearily and despairingly "home," with the cheerful prospect of a penniless Saturday afternoon and evening and the long horrible Australian-city Sunday to drag through. One of the landlady's clutch—and she is an old hen—opens the door, exclaims:

"Oh, Mr Careless!" and grins. You wait an anxious minute, to postpone the disappointment which you feel by instinct is coming, and then ask hopelessly whether there are any letters for you.

"No, there's nothing for you, Mr Careless." Then in answer to the unspoken question, "The postman's been, but there's nothing for you."

You hang up your hat in the stuffy little passage, and start upstairs, when, "Oh, Mr Careless, mother wants to know if you've had yer dinner."

You haven't, but you say you have. You are empty enough inside, but the emptiness is filled up, as it were, with the wrong sort of hungry vacancy—gnawing anxiety. You haven't any stomach for the warm, tasteless mess which has been "kep' 'ot" for you in a cold stove. You feel just physically tired enough to go to your room, lie down on the bed, and snatch twenty minutes' rest from that terrible unemployed restlessness which, you know, is sure to drag you to your feet to pace the room or tramp the pavement even before your bodily weariness has nearly left you. So you start up the narrow, stuffy little flight of steps call the "stairs." Three small doors open from the landing—a square place of about four feet by four. The first door is yours; it is open, and—

Decided odour of bedroom dust and fluff, damped and kneaded with cold soap-suds. Rear view of a girl covered with a damp, draggled, dirt-coloured skirt, which gapes at the waistband from the "body," disclosing a good glimpse of soiled stays (ribs burst), and yawns behind over a decidedly dirty white petticoat, the slit of which last, as she reaches forward and backs out convulsively, half opens and then comes together in an unsatisfactory, startling, tantalizing way, and allows a hint of a red flannel under-something. The frayed ends of the skirt lie across a hopelessly-burst pair of elastic-sides which rest on their inner edges—toes out—and jerk about in a seemingly undecided manner. She is damping and working up the natural layer on the floor with a piece of old flannel petticoat dipped occasionally in a bucket which stands by her side, containing about a quart of muddy water. She looks round and exclaims, "Oh, did you want to come in, Mr Careless?" Then she says she'll be done in a minute; furthermore she remarks that if you want to come in you won't be in her road. You don't—you go down to the dining-room—parlour—sitting-room—nursery—and stretch yourself on the sofa in the face of the painfully-evident disapproval of the landlady.

You have been here, say, three months, and are only about two weeks behind. The landlady still says, "Good morning, Mr Careless," or "Good evening, Mr Careless," but there is an unpleasant accent on the "Mr," and a still more unpleasantly pronounced stress on the "morning" or "evening." While your money lasted you paid up well and regularly—sometimes in advance—and dined out most of the time; but that doesn't count now.

Ten minutes pass, and then the landlady's disapproval becomes manifest and aggressive. One of the little girls, a sharp-faced little larrikiness, who always wears a furtive grin of cunning—it seems as though it were born with her, and is perhaps more a misfortune than a fault—comes in and says please she wants to tidy up.

So you get up and take your hat and go out again to look for a place to rest in—to try not to think.

You wish you could get away up-country. You also wish you were dead.

The landlady, Mrs Jones, is a widow, or grass-widow, Welsh, of course, and clannish; flat face, watery grey eyes, shallow, selfish, ignorant, and a hypocrite unconsciously—by instinct.

But the worst of it is that Mrs Jones takes advantage of the situation to corner you in the passage when you want to get out, or when you come in tired, and talk. It amounts to about this: She has been fourteen years in this street, taking in boarders; everybody knows her; everybody knows Mrs Jones; her poor husband died six years ago (God rest his soul); she finds it hard to get a living these times; work, work, morning, noon, and night (talk, talk, talk, more likely). "Do you know Mr Duff of the Labour Bureau?" He has known her family for years; a very nice gentleman—a very nice gentleman indeed; he often stops at the gate to have a yarn with her on his way to the office (he must be hard up for a yarn). She doesn't know hardly nobody in this street; she never gossips; it takes her all her time to get a living; she can't be bothered with neighbours; it's always best to keep to yourself and keep neighbours at a distance. Would you believe it, Mr Careless, she has been two years in this house and hasn't said above a dozen words to the woman next door; she'd just know her by sight if she saw her; as for the other woman she wouldn't know her from a crow. Mr Blank and Mrs Blank could tell you the same.... She always had gentlemen staying with her; she never had no cause to complain of one of them except once; they always treated her fair and honest. Here follows story about the exception; he, I gathered, was a journalist, and she could never depend on him. He seemed, from her statements, to have been decidedly erratic in his movements, mode of life and choice of climes. He evidently caused her a great deal of trouble and anxiety, and I felt a kind of sneaking sympathy for his memory. One young fellow stayed with her five years; he was, etc. She couldn't be hard on any young fellow that gets out of work; of course if he can't get it he can't pay; she can't get blood out of a stone; she couldn't turn him out in the street. "I've got sons of my own, Mr Careless, I've got sons of my own."... She is sure she always does her best to make her boarders comfortable, and if they want anything they've only got to ask for it. The kettle is always on the stove if you want a cup of tea, and if you come home late at night and want a bit of supper you've only got to go to the safe (which of us would dare?). She never locks it, she never did.... And then she begins about her wonderful kids, and it goes on hour after hour. Lord! it's enough to drive a man mad.

We were recommended to this place on the day of our arrival by a young dealer in the furniture line, whose name was Moses—and he looked like it, but we didn't think of that at the time. He had Mrs Jones's card in his window, and he left the shop in charge of his missus and came round with us at once. He assured us that we couldn't do better than stay with her. He said she was a most respectable lady, and all her boarders were decent young fellows-gentlemen; she kept everything scrupulously clean, and kept the best table in town, and she'd do for us (washing included) for eighteen shillings per week; she generally took the first week in advance. We asked him to have a beer—for the want of somebody else to ask—and after that he said that Mrs Jones was a kind, motherly body, and understood young fellows; and that we'd be even more comfortable than in our own home; that we'd be allowed to do as we liked—she wasn't particular; she wouldn't mind it a bit if we came home late once in a way—she was used to that, in fact; she liked to see young fellows enjoying themselves. We afterwards found out that he got so much on every boarder he captured. We also found out—after paying in advance—that her gentlemen generally sent out their white things to be done; she only did the coloured things, so we had to pay a couple of bob extra a week to have our "biled" rags and collars sent out and done; and after the first week they bore sad evidence of having been done on the premises by one of the frowsy daughters. But we paid all the same. And, good Lord! if she keeps the best table in town, we are curious to see the worst. When you go down to breakfast you find on the table in front of your chair a cold plate, with a black something—God knows what it looks like—in the centre of it. It eats like something scraped off the inside of a hide and burnt; and with this you have a cup of warm grey slush called a "cup of tea." Dinner: A slice of alleged roast beef or boiled mutton, of no particular colour or taste; three new spuds, of which the largest is about the size of an ordinary hen's egg, the smallest that of a bantam's, and the middle one in between, and which eat soggy and have no taste to speak of, save that they are a trifle bitter; a dab of unhealthy-looking green something, which might be either cabbage leaves or turnip-tops, and a glass of water. The whole mess is lukewarm, including the water—it would all be better cold. Tea: A thin slice of the aforesaid alleged roast or mutton, and the pick of about six thin slices of stale bread—evidently cut the day before yesterday. This is the way Mrs Jones "does" for us for eighteen shillings a week. The bread gave out at tea-time this evening, and a mild financial boarder tapped his plate with his knife, and sent the bread plate out to be replenished. It came back with one slice on it.

The mild financial boarder, with desperate courage, is telling the landlady that he'll have to shift next week—it is too far to go to work, he cannot always get down in time; he is very sorry he has to go, he says; he is very comfortable here, but it can't be helped; anyway, as soon as he can get work nearer, he'll come back at once; also (oh, what cowards men are when women are concerned), he says he wishes she could shift and take a house down at the other end of the town. She says (at least here are some fragments of her gabble which we caught and shorthanded): "Well, I'm very sorry to lose you, Mr Sampson, very sorry indeed; but of course if you must go, you must. Of course you can't be expected to walk that distance every morning, and you mustn't be getting to work late, and losing your place... Of course we could get breakfast an hour earlier if... well, as I said before, I'm sorry to lose you and, indeed... You won't forget to come and see us... glad to see you at any time... Well, any way, if you ever want to come back, you know, your bed will be always ready for you, and you'll be treated just the same, and made just as comfortable—you won't forget that" (he says he won't); "and you won't forget to come to dinner sometimes" (he says he won't); "and, of course... You know I always try... Don't forget to drop in sometimes... Well, anyway, if you ever do happen to hear of a decent young fellow who wants a good, clean, comfortable home, you'll be sure to send him to me, will you?" (He says he will.) "Well, of course, Mr Sampson, etc., etc., etc., and-so-on, and-so-on, and-so-on, and-so-on,..." It's enough to give a man rats.

He escapes, and we regard his departure very much as a gang of hopeless convicts might regard the unexpected liberation of one of their number.

This is the sort of life that gives a man a God-Almighty longing to break away and take to the bush.

HIS COLONIAL OATH

I lately met an old schoolmate of mine up-country. He was much changed. He was tall and lank, and had the most hideous bristly red beard I ever saw. He was working on his father's farm. He shook hands, looked anywhere but in my face—and said nothing. Presently I remarked at a venture "So poor old Mr B., the schoolmaster, is dead."

"My oath!" he replied.

"He was a good old sort."

"My oath!"

"Time goes by pretty quick, doesn't it?"

His oath (colonial).

"Poor old Mr B. died awfully sudden, didn't he?"

He looked up the hill, and said: "My oath!"

Then he added: "My blooming oath!"

I thought, perhaps, my city rig or manner embarrassed him, so I stuck my hands in my pockets, spat, and said, to set him at his ease: "It's blanky hot to-day. I don't know how you blanky blanks stand such blank weather! It's blanky well hot enough to roast a crimson carnal bullock; ain't it?" Then I took out a cake of tobacco, bit off a quarter, and pretended to chew. He replied:

"My oath!"

The conversation flagged here. But presently, to my great surprise, he came to the rescue with:

"He finished me, yer know."

"Finished? How? Who?"

He looked down towards the river, thought (if he did think) and said: "Finished me edyercation, yer know."

"Oh! you mean Mr B.?"

"My oath—he finished me first-rate."

"He turned out a good many scholars, didn't he?"

"My oath! I'm thinkin' about going down to the trainin' school."'

"You ought to—I would if I were you."

"My oath!"

"Those were good old times," I hazarded, "you remember the old bark school?"

He looked away across the sidling, and was evidently getting uneasy. He shifted about, and said:

"Well, I must be goin'."

"I suppose you're pretty busy now?"

"My oath! So long."

"Well, good-bye. We must have a yarn some day."

"My oath!"

He got away as quickly as he could.

I wonder whether he was changed after all—or, was it I? A man does seem to get out of touch with the bush after living in cities for eight or ten years.

A VISIT OF CONDOLENCE

"Does Arvie live here, old woman?"

"Why?"

"Strike me dead! carn't yer answer a civil queschin?"

"How dare you talk to me like that, you young larrikin! Be off! or I'll send for a policeman."

"Blarst the cops! D'yer think I cares for 'em? Fur two pins I'd fetch a push an' smash yer ole shanty about yer ears—y'ole cow! I only arsked if Arvie lived here! Holy Mosis! carn't a feller ask a civil queschin?"

"What do you want with Arvie? Do you know him?"

"My oath! Don't he work at Grinder Brothers? I only come out of my way to do him a good turn; an' now I'm sorry I come—damned if I ain't—to be barracked like this, an' shoved down my own throat. (Pause) I want to tell Arvie that if he don't come ter work termorrer, another bloke'll collar his job. I wouldn't like to see a cove collar a cove's job an' not tell a bloke about it. What's up with Arvie, anyhow? Is he sick?"

"Arvie is dead!"

"Christ! (Pause) Garn! What-yer-giv'n-us? Tell Arvie Bill Anderson wants-ter see him."

"My God! haven't I got enough trouble without a young wretch like you coming to torment me? For God's sake go away and leave me alone! I'm telling you the truth, my my poor boy died of influenza last night."

"My oath!"

The ragged young rip gave a long, low whistle, glanced up and down Jones's Alley, spat out some tobacco-juice, and said "Swelp me Gord! I'm sorry, mum. I didn't know. How was I to know you wasn't havin' me?"

He withdrew one hand from his pocket and scratched the back of his head, tilting his hat as far forward as it had previously been to the rear, and just then the dilapidated side of his right boot attracted his attention. He turned the foot on one side, and squinted at the sole; then he raised the foot to his left knee, caught the ankle in a very dirty hand, and regarded the sole-leather critically, as though calculating how long it would last. After which he spat desperately at the pavement, and said:

"Kin I see him?"

He followed her up the crooked little staircase with a who's-afraid kind of swagger, but he took his hat off on entering the room.

He glanced round, and seemed to take stock of the signs of poverty—so familiar to his class—and then directed his gaze to where the body lay on the sofa with its pauper coffin already by its side. He looked at the coffin with the critical eye of a tradesman, then he looked at Arvie, and then at the coffin again, as if calculating whether the body would fit.

The mother uncovered the white, pinched face of the dead boy, and Bill came and stood by the sofa. He carelessly drew his right hand from his pocket, and laid the palm on Arvie's ice-cold forehead.

"Poor little cove!" Bill muttered, half to himself; and then, as though ashamed of his weakness, he said:

"There wasn't no post mortem, was there?"

"No," she answered; "a doctor saw him the day before—there was no post mortem."

"I thought there wasn't none," said Bill, "because a man that's been post mortemed always looks as if he'd been hurt. My father looked right enough at first—just as if he was restin'—but after they'd had him opened he looked as if he'd been hurt. No one else could see it, but I could. How old was Arvie?"

"Eleven."'

"I'm twelve—goin' on for thirteen. Arvie's father's dead, ain't he?"

"Yes."

"So's mine. Died at his work, didn't he?"

"Yes."

"So'd mine. Arvie told me his father died of something with his heart!"

"Yes."

"So'd mine; ain't it rum? You scrub offices an' wash, don't yer?"

"Yes."

"So does my mother. You find it pretty hard to get a livin', don't yer, these times?"

"My God, yes! God only knows what I'll do now my poor boy's gone. I generally get up at half-past five to scrub out some offices, and when that's done I've got to start my day's work, washing. And then I find it hard to make both ends meet."

"So does my mother. I suppose you took on bad when yer husband was brought home?"

"Ah, my God! Yes. I'll never forget it till my dying day. My poor husband had been out of work for weeks, and he only got the job two days before he died. I suppose it gave your mother a great shock?"

"My oath! One of the fellows that carried father home said: 'Yer husband's dead, mum,' he says; 'he dropped off all of a suddint,' and mother said, 'My God! my God!' just like that, and went off."

"Poor soul! poor soul! And—now my Arvie's gone. Whatever will me and the children do? Whatever will I do? Whatever will I do? My God! I wish I was under the turf."

"Cheer up, mum!" said Bill. "It's no use frettin' over what's done."

He wiped some tobacco-juice off his lips with the back of his hand, and regarded the stains reflectively for a minute or so. Then he looked at Arvie again.

"You should ha' tried cod liver oil," said Bill.

"No. He needed rest and plenty of good food."

"He wasn't very strong."

"No, he was not, poor boy."

"I thought he wasn't. They treated him bad at Grinder Brothers: they didn't give him a show to learn nothing; kept him at the same work all the time, and he didn't have cheek enough to arsk the boss for a rise, lest he'd be sacked. He couldn't fight, an' the boys used to tease him; they'd wait outside the shop to have a lark with Arvie. I'd like to see 'em do it to me. He couldn't fight; but then, of course, he wasn't strong. They don't bother me while I'm strong enough to heave a rock; but then, of course, it wasn't Arvie's fault. I s'pose he had pluck enough, if he hadn't the strength." And Bill regarded the corpse with a fatherly and lenient eye.

"My God!" she cried, "if I'd known this, I'd sooner have starved than have my poor boy's life tormented out of him in such a place. He never complained. My poor, brave-hearted child! He never complained! Poor little Arvie! Poor little Arvie!"

"He never told yer?"

"No—never a word."

"My oath! You don't say so! P'raps he didn't want to let you know he couldn't hold his own; but that wasn't his fault, I s'pose. Y'see, he wasn't strong."

An old print hanging over the bed attracted his attention, and he regarded it with critical interest for awhile:

"We've got a pickcher like that at home. We lived in Jones's Alley wunst—in that house over there. How d'yer like livin' in Jones's Alley?"

"I don't like it at all. I don't like having to bring my children up where there are so many bad houses; but I can't afford to go somewhere else and pay higher rent."

"Well, there is a good many night-shops round here. But then," he added, reflectively, "you'll find them everywheres. An', besides, the kids git sharp, an' pick up a good deal in an alley like this; 'twon't do 'em no harm; it's no use kids bein' green if they wanter get on in a city. You ain't been in Sydney all yer life, have yer?"

"No. We came from the bush, about five years ago. My poor husband thought he could do better in the city. I was brought up in the bush."'

"I thought yer was. Well, men are sick fools. I'm thinking about gittin' a billet up-country, myself, soon. Where's he goin' ter be buried?"

"At Rookwood, to-morrow."

"I carn't come. I've got ter work. Is the Guvmint goin' to bury him?"

"Yes."

Bill looked at the body with increased respect. "Kin I do anythin' for you? Now, don't be frightened to arsk!"

"No. Thank you very much, all the same."

"Well, I must be goin'; thank yer fur yer trouble, mum."

"No trouble, my boy—mind the step."

"It is gone. I'll bring a piece of board round some night and mend it for you, if you like; I'm learnin' the carpenterin'; I kin nearly make a door. Tell yer what, I'll send the old woman round to-night to fix up Arvie and lend yer a hand."

"No, thank you. I suppose your mother's got work and trouble enough; I'll manage."

"I'll send her round, anyway; she's a bit rough, but she's got a soft gizzard; an' there's nothin' she enjoys better than fixin' up a body. Good-bye, mum."

"Good-bye, my child."

He paused at the door, and said:

"I'm sorry, mum. Swelp me God! I'm sorry. S'long, an' thank yer."

An awe-stricken child stood on the step, staring at Bill with great brimming eyes. He patted it on the head and said "Keep yer pecker up, young 'un!"

IN A WET SEASON

It was raining—"general rain."

The train left Bourke, and then there began the long, long agony of scrub and wire fence, with here and there a natural clearing, which seemed even more dismal than the funereal "timber" itself. The only thing which might seem in keeping with one of these soddened flats would be the ghost of a funeral—a city funeral with plain hearse and string of cabs—going very slowly across from the scrub on one side to the scrub on the other. Sky like a wet, grey blanket; plains like dead seas, save for the tufts of coarse grass sticking up out of the water; scrub indescribably dismal—everything damp, dark, and unspeakably dreary.

Somewhere along here we saw a swagman's camp—a square of calico stretched across a horizontal stick, some rags steaming on another stick in front of a fire, and two billies to the leeward of the blaze. We knew by instinct that there was a piece of beef in the larger one. Small, hopeless-looking man standing with his back to the fire, with his hands behind him, watching the train; also, a damp, sorry-looking dingo warming itself and shivering by the fire. The rain had held up for a while. We saw two or three similar camps further on, forming a temporary suburb of Byrock.

The population was on the platform in old overcoats and damp, soft felt hats; one trooper in a waterproof. The population looked cheerfully and patiently dismal. The local push had evidently turned up to see off some fair enslavers from the city, who had been up-country for the cheque season, now over. They got into another carriage. We were glad when the bell rang.

The rain recommenced. We saw another swagman about a mile on struggling away from the town, through mud and water. He did not seem to have heart enough to bother about trying to avoid the worst mud-holes. There was a low-spirited dingo at his heels, whose sole object in life was seemingly to keep his front paws in his master's last footprint. The traveller's body was bent well forward from the hips up; his long arms—about six inches through his coat sleeves—hung by his sides like the arms of a dummy, with a billy at the end of one and a bag at the end of the other; but his head was thrown back against the top end of the swag, his hat-brim rolled up in front, and we saw a ghastly, beardless face which turned neither to the right nor the left as the train passed him.

After a long while we closed our book, and looking through the window, saw a hawker's turn-out which was too sorrowful for description.

We looked out again while the train was going slowly, and saw a teamster's camp: three or four wagons covered with tarpaulins which hung down in the mud all round and suggested death. A long, narrow man, in a long, narrow, shoddy overcoat and a damp felt hat, was walking quickly along the road past the camp. A sort of cattle-dog glided silently and swiftly out from under a wagon, "heeled" the man, and slithered back without explaining. Here the scene vanished.

We remember stopping—for an age it seemed—at half a dozen straggling shanties on a flat of mud and water. There was a rotten weather-board pub, with a low, dripping veranda, and three wretchedly forlorn horses hanging, in the rain, to a post outside. We saw no more, but we knew that there were several apologies for men hanging about the rickety bar inside—or round the parlour fire. Streams of cold, clay-coloured water ran in all directions, cutting fresh gutters, and raising a yeasty froth whenever the water fell a few inches. As we left, we saw a big man in an overcoat riding across a culvert; the tails of the coat spread over the horse's rump, and almost hid it. In fancy still we saw him—hanging up his weary, hungry little horse in the rain, and swaggering into the bar; and we almost heard someone say, in a drawling tone: "'Ello, Tom! 'Ow are yer poppin' up?"'

The train stopped (for about a year) within a mile of the next station. Trucking-yards in the foreground, like any other trucking-yard along the line; they looked drearier than usual, because the rain had darkened the posts and rails. Small plain beyond, covered with water and tufts of grass. The inevitable, God-forgotten "timber," black in the distance; dull, grey sky and misty rain over all. A small, dark-looking flock of sheep was crawling slowly in across the flat from the unknown, with three men on horse-back zigzagging patiently behind. The horses just moved—that was all. One man wore an oilskin, one an old tweed overcoat, and the third had a three-bushel bag over his head and shoulders.

Had we returned an hour later, we should have seen the sheep huddled together in a corner of the yard, and the three horses hanging up outside the local shanty.

We stayed at Nyngan—which place we refrain from sketching—for a few hours, because the five trucks of cattle of which we were in charge were shunted there, to be taken on by a very subsequent goods train. The Government allows one man to every five trucks in a cattle-train. We shall pay our fare next time, even if we have not a shilling left over and above. We had haunted local influence at Comanavadrink for two long, anxious, heart-breaking weeks ere we got the pass; and we had put up with all the indignities, the humiliation—in short, had suffered all that poor devils suffer whilst besieging Local Influence. We only thought of escaping from the bush.

The pass said that we were John Smith, drover, and that we were available for return by ordinary passenger-train within two days, we think—or words in that direction. Which didn't interest us. We might have given the pass away to an unemployed in Orange, who wanted to go out back, and who begged for it with tears in his eyes; but we didn't like to injure a poor fool who never injured us—who was an entire stranger to us. He didn't know what Out Back meant.

Local Influence had given us a kind of note of introduction to be delivered to the cattle-agent at the yards that morning; but the agent was not there—only two of his satellites, a Cockney colonial-experience man, and a scrub-town clerk, both of whom we kindly ignore. We got on without the note, and at Orange we amused ourself by reading it. It said:

"Dear Old Man—Please send this beggar on; and I hope he'll be landed safely at Orange—or—or wherever the cattle go—yours,—"

We had been led to believe that the bullocks were going to Sydney. We took no further interest in those cattle.

After Nyngan the bush grew darker and drearier; and the plains more like ghastly oceans; and here and there the "dominant note of Australian scenery" was accentuated, as it were, by naked, white, ring-barked trees standing in the water and haunting the ghostly surroundings.

We spent that night in a passenger compartment of a van which had been originally attached to old No. 1 engine. There was only one damp cushion in the whole concern. We lent that to a lady who travelled for a few hours in the other half of the next compartment. The seats were about nine inches wide and sloped in at a sharp angle to the bare matchboard wall, with a bead on the outer edge; and as the cracks had become well caulked with the grease and dirt of generations, they held several gallons of water each. We scuttled one, rolled ourself in a rug, and tried to sleep; but all night long overcoated and comfortered bushmen would get in, let down all the windows, and then get out again at the next station. Then we would wake up frozen and shut the windows.

We dozed off again, and woke at daylight, and recognized the ridgy gum-country between Dubbo and Orange. It didn't look any drearier than the country further west—because it couldn't. There is scarcely a part of the country out west which looks less inviting or more horrible than any other part.

The weather cleared, and we had sunlight for Orange, Bathurst, the Blue Mountains, and Sydney. They deserve it; also as much rain as they need.

"RATS"

"Why, there's two of them, and they're having a fight! Come on."'

It seemed a strange place for a fight—that hot, lonely, cotton-bush plain. And yet not more than half a mile ahead there were apparently two men struggling together on the track.

The three travellers postponed their smoke-ho and hurried on. They were shearers—a little man and a big man, known respectively as "Sunlight" and "Macquarie," and a tall, thin, young jackeroo whom they called "Milky."

"I wonder where the other man sprang from? I didn't see him before," said Sunlight.

"He muster bin layin' down in the bushes," said Macquarie. "They're goin' at it proper, too. Come on! Hurry up and see the fun!"

They hurried on.

"It's a funny-lookin' feller, the other feller," panted Milky. "He don't seem to have no head. Look! he's down—they're both down! They must ha' clinched on the ground. No! they're up an' at it again.... Why, good Lord! I think the other's a woman!"

"My oath! so it is!" yelled Sunlight. "Look! the brute's got her down again! He's kickin' her. Come on, chaps; come on, or he'll do for her!"

They dropped swags, water-bags and all, and raced forward; but presently Sunlight, who had the best eyes, slackened his pace and dropped behind. His mates glanced back at his face, saw a peculiar expression there, looked ahead again, and then dropped into a walk.

They reached the scene of the trouble, and there stood a little withered old man by the track, with his arms folded close up under his chin; he was dressed mostly in calico patches; and half a dozen corks, suspended on bits of string from the brim of his hat, dangled before his bleared optics to scare away the flies. He was scowling malignantly at a stout, dumpy swag which lay in the middle of the track.

"Well, old Rats, what's the trouble?" asked Sunlight.

"Oh, nothing, nothing," answered the old man, without looking round. "I fell out with my swag, that's all. He knocked me down, but I've settled him."

"But look here," said Sunlight, winking at his mates, "we saw you jump on him when he was down. That ain't fair, you know."

"But you didn't see it all," cried Rats, getting excited. "He hit me down first! And look here, I'll fight him again for nothing, and you can see fair play."

They talked awhile; then Sunlight proposed to second the swag, while his mate supported the old man, and after some persuasion, Milky agreed, for the sake of the lark, to act as time-keeper and referee.

Rats entered into the spirit of the thing; he stripped to the waist, and while he was getting ready the travellers pretended to bet on the result.

Macquarie took his place behind the old man, and Sunlight up-ended the swag. Rats shaped and danced round; then he rushed, feinted, ducked, retreated, darted in once more, and suddenly went down like a shot on the broad of his back. No actor could have done it better; he went down from that imaginary blow as if a cannon-ball had struck him in the forehead.

Milky called time, and the old man came up, looking shaky. However, he got in a tremendous blow which knocked the swag into the bushes.

Several rounds followed with varying success.

The men pretended to get more and more excited, and betted freely; and Rats did his best. At last they got tired of the fun, Sunlight let the swag lie after Milky called time, and the jackaroo awarded the fight to Rats. They pretended to hand over the stakes, and then went back for their swags, while the old man put on his shirt.

Then he calmed down, carried his swag to the side of the track, sat down on it and talked rationally about bush matters for a while; but presently he grew silent and began to feel his muscles and smile idiotically.

"Can you len' us a bit o' meat?" said he suddenly.

They spared him half a pound; but he said he didn't want it all, and cut off about an ounce, which he laid on the end of his swag. Then he took the lid off his billy and produced a fishing-line. He baited the hook, threw the line across the track, and waited for a bite. Soon he got deeply interested in the line, jerked it once or twice, and drew it in rapidly. The bait had been rubbed off in the grass. The old man regarded the hook disgustedly.

"Look at that!" he cried. "I had him, only I was in such a hurry. I should ha' played him a little more."

Next time he was more careful. He drew the line in warily, grabbed an imaginary fish and laid it down on the grass. Sunlight and Co. were greatly interested by this time.

"Wot yer think o' that?" asked Rats. "It weighs thirty pound if it weighs an ounce! Wot yer think o' that for a cod? The hook's half-way down his blessed gullet!"

He caught several cod and a bream while they were there, and invited them to camp and have tea with him. But they wished to reach a certain shed next day, so—after the ancient had borrowed about a pound of meat for bait—they went on, and left him fishing contentedly.

But first Sunlight went down into his pocket and came up with half a crown, which he gave to the old man, along with some tucker. "You'd best push on to the water before dark, old chap," he said, kindly.

When they turned their heads again, Rats was still fishing but when they looked back for the last time before entering the timber, he was having another row with his swag; and Sunlight reckoned that the trouble arose out of some lies which the swag had been telling about the bigger fish it caught.

MITCHELL: A CHARACTER SKETCH

It was a very mean station, and Mitchell thought he had better go himself and beard the overseer for tucker. His mates were for waiting till the overseer went out on the run, and then trying their luck with the cook; but the self-assertive and diplomatic Mitchell decided to go.

"Good day," said Mitchell.

"Good day," said the manager.

"It's hot," said Mitchell.

"Yes, it's hot."

"I don't suppose," said Mitchell; "I don't suppose it's any use asking you for a job?"

"Naw."

"Well, I won't ask you," said Mitchell, "but I don't suppose you want any fencing done?"

"Naw."

"Nor boundary-riding'?"

"Naw."

"You ain't likely to want a man to knock round?"

"Naw."

"I thought not. Things are pretty bad just now."

"Na—yes—they are."

"Ah, well; there's a lot to be said on the squatter's side as well as the men's. I suppose I can get a bit of rations?"

"Ye-yes." (Shortly)—"Wot d'yer want?"

"Well, let's see; we want a bit of meat and flour—I think that's all. Got enough tea and sugar to carry us on."

"All right. Cook! have you got any meat?"

"No!"

To Mitchell: "Can you kill a sheep?"

"Rather!"

To the cook: "Give this man a cloth and knife and steel, and let him go up to the yard and kill a sheep." (To Mitchell) "You can take a fore-quarter and get a bit of flour."

Half an hour later Mitchell came back with the carcass wrapped in the cloth.

"Here yer are; here's your sheep," he said to the cook. "That's all right; hang it in there. Did you take a forequarter?"'

"No."

"Well, why didn't you? The boss told you to."

"I didn't want a fore-quarter. I don't like it. I took a hind-quarter."

So he had.

The cook scratched his head; he seemed to have nothing to say. He thought about trying to think, perhaps, but gave it best. It was too hot and he was out of practice.

"Here, fill these up, will you?" said Mitchell. "That's the tea-bag, and that's the sugar-bag, and that's the flour-bag." He had taken them from the front of his shirt.

"Don't be frightened to stretch 'em a little, old man. I've got two mates to feed."

The cook took the bags mechanically and filled them well before he knew what he was doing. Mitchell talked all the time.

"Thank you," said he—"got a bit of baking-powder?"

"Ye-yes, here you are."

"Thank you. Find it dull here, don't you?"

"Well, yes, pretty dull. There's a bit of cooked beef and some bread and cake there, if you want it!"

"Thanks," said Mitchell, sweeping the broken victuals into an old pillow-slip which he carried on his person for such an emergency. "I s'pose you find it dull round here."

"Yes, pretty dull."

"No one to talk to much?" "No, not many."

"Tongue gets rusty?"

"Ye—es, sometimes."

"Well, so long, and thank yer."

"So long," said the cook (he nearly added "thank yer").

"Well, good day; I'll see you again."

"Good day."

Mitchell shouldered his spoil and left.

The cook scratched his head; he had a chat with the overseer afterwards, and they agreed that the traveller was a bit gone.

But Mitchell's head wasn't gone—not much: he had been round a bit—that was all.

THE BUSH UNDERTAKER

"Five Bob!"

The old man shaded his eyes and peered through the dazzling glow of that broiling Christmas Day. He stood just within the door of a slab-and-bark hut situated upon the bank of a barren creek; sheep-yards lay to the right, and a low line of bare, brown ridges formed a suitable background to the scene.

"Five Bob!" shouted he again; and a dusty sheep-dog rose wearily from the shaded side of the but and looked inquiringly at his master, who pointed towards some sheep which were straggling from the flock.

"Fetch 'em back," he said confidently.

The dog went off, and his master returned to the interior of the hut.

"We'll yard 'em early," he said to himself; "the super won't know. We'll yard 'em early, and have the afternoon to ourselves."

"We'll get dinner," he added, glancing at some pots on the fire. "I cud do a bit of doughboy, an' that theer boggabri'll eat like tater-marrer along of the salt meat." He moved one of the black buckets from the blaze. "I likes to keep it jist on the sizzle," he said in explanation to himself; "hard bilin' makes it tough—I'll keep it jist a-simmerin'."

Here his soliloquy was interrupted by the return of the dog.

"All right, Five Bob," said the hatter, "dinner'll be ready dreckly. Jist keep yer eye on the sheep till I calls yer; keep 'em well rounded up, an' we'll yard 'em afterwards and have a holiday."

This speech was accompanied by a gesture evidently intelligible, for the dog retired as though he understood English, and the cooking proceeded.

"I'll take a pick an' shovel with me an' root up that old blackfellow," mused the shepherd, evidently following up a recent train of thought; "I reckon it'll do now. I'll put in the spuds."

The last sentence referred to the cooking, the first to a blackfellow's grave about which he was curious.

"The sheep's a-campin'," said the soliloquizer, glancing through the door. "So me an' Five Bob'll be able to get our dinner in peace. I wish I had just enough fat to make the pan siss; I'd treat myself to a leather-jacket; but it took three weeks' skimmin' to get enough for them theer doughboys."

In due time the dinner was dished up; and the old man seated himself on a block, with the lid of a gin-case across his knees for a table. Five Bob squatted opposite with the liveliest interest and appreciation depicted on his intelligent countenance.

Dinner proceeded very quietly, except when the carver paused to ask the dog how some tasty morsel went with him, and Five Bob's tail declared that it went very well indeed.

"Here y'are, try this," cried the old man, tossing him a large piece of doughboy. A click of Five Bob's jaws and the dough was gone.

"Clean into his liver!" said the old man with a faint smile. He washed up the tinware in the water the duff had been boiled in, and then, with the assistance of the dog, yarded the sheep.

This accomplished, he took a pick and shovel and an old sack, and started out over the ridge, followed, of course, by his four-legged mate. After tramping some three miles he reached a spur, running out from the main ridge. At the extreme end of this, under some gum-trees, was a little mound of earth, barely defined in the grass, and indented in the centre as all blackfellows' graves were.

He set to work to dig it up, and sure enough, in about half an hour he bottomed on payable dirt.

When he had raked up all the bones, he amused himself by putting them together on the grass and by speculating as to whether they had belonged to black or white, male or female. Failing, however, to arrive at any satisfactory conclusion, he dusted them with great care, put them in the bag, and started for home.

He took a short cut this time over the ridge and down a gully which was full of ring-barked trees and long white grass. He had nearly reached its mouth when a great greasy black goanna clambered up a sapling from under his feet and looked fightable.

"Dang the jumpt-up thing!" cried the old man. "It 'gin me a start!"

At the foot of the sapling he espied an object which he at first thought was the blackened carcass of a sheep, but on closer examination discovered to be the body of a man; it lay with its forehead resting on its hands, dried to a mummy by the intense heat of the western summer.

"Me luck's in for the day and no mistake!" said the shepherd, scratching the back of his head, while he took stock of the remains. He picked up a stick and tapped the body on the shoulder; the flesh sounded like leather. He turned it over on its side; it fell flat on its back like a board, and the shrivelled eyes seemed to peer up at him from under the blackened wrists.

He stepped back involuntarily, but, recovering himself, leant on his stick and took in all the ghastly details.

There was nothing in the blackened features to tell aught of name or race, but the dress proclaimed the remains to be those of a European. The old man caught sight of a black bottle in the grass, close beside the corpse. This set him thinking. Presently he knelt down and examined the soles of the dead man's blucher boots, and then, rising with an air of conviction, exclaimed: "Brummy! by gosh!—busted up at last!

"I tole yer so, Brummy," he said impressively, addressing the corpse. "I allers told yer as how it 'ud be—an' here y'are, you thundering jumpt-up cuss-o'-God fool. Yer cud earn more'n any man in the colony, but yer'd lush it all away. I allers sed as how it 'ud end, an' now yer kin see fur y'self.

"I spect yer was a-comin' t' me t' get fixt up an' set straight agin; then yer was a-goin' to swear off, same as yer 'allers did; an' here y'are, an' now I expect I'll have t' fix yer up for the last time an' make yer decent, for 'twon't do t' leave yer alyin' out here like a dead sheep."

He picked up the corked bottle and examined it. To his great surprise it was nearly full of rum.

"Well, this gits me," exclaimed the old man; "me luck's in, this Christmas, an' no mistake. He must 'a' got the jams early in his spree, or he wouldn't be a-making for me with near a bottleful left. Howsomenever, here goes."

Looking round, his eyes lit up with satisfaction as he saw some bits of bark which had been left by a party of strippers who had been getting bark there for the stations. He picked up two pieces, one about four and the other six feet long, and each about two feet wide, and brought them over to the body. He laid the longest strip by the side of the corpse, which he proceeded to lift on to it.

"Come on, Brummy," he said, in a softer tone than usual, "ye ain't as bad as yer might be, considerin' as it must be three good months since yer slipped yer wind. I spect it was the rum as preserved yer. It was the death of yer when yer was alive, an' now yer dead, it preserves yer like—like a mummy."

Then he placed the other strip on top, with the hollow side downwards—thus sandwiching the defunct between the two pieces—removed the saddle-strap, which he wore for a belt, and buckled it round one end, while he tried to think of something with which to tie up the other.

"I can't take any more strips off my shirt," he said, critically examining the skirts of the old blue overshirt he wore. "I might get a strip or two more off, but it's short enough already. Let's see; how long have I been a-wearin' of that shirt; oh, I remember, I bought it jist two days afore Five Bob was pupped. I can't afford a new shirt jist yet; howsomenever, seein' it's Brummy, I'll jist borrow a couple more strips and sew 'em on agen when I git home."

He up-ended Brummy, and placing his shoulder against the middle of the lower sheet of bark, lifted the corpse to a horizontal position; then, taking the bag of bones in his hand, he started for home.

"I ain't a-spendin' sech a dull Christmas arter all," he reflected, as he plodded on; but he had not walked above a hundred yards when he saw a black goanna sidling into the grass.

"That's another of them theer dang things!" he exclaimed. "That's two I've seed this mornin'."

Presently he remarked: "Yer don't smell none too sweet, Brummy. It must 'a' been jist about the middle of shearin' when yer pegged out. I wonder who got yer last cheque. Shoo! theer's another black goanner—theer must be a flock of 'em."

He rested Brummy on the ground while he had another pull at the bottle, and, before going on, packed the bag of bones on his shoulder under the body, and he soon stopped again.

"The thunderin' jumpt-up bones is all skew-whift," he said. "'Ole on, Brummy, an' I'll fix 'em"—and he leaned the dead man against a tree while he settled the bones on his shoulder, and took another pull at the bottle.

About a mile further on he heard a rustling in the grass to the right, and, looking round, saw another goanna gliding off sideways, with its long snaky neck turned towards him.

This puzzled the shepherd considerably, the strangest part of it being that Five Bob wouldn't touch the reptile, but slunk off with his tail down when ordered to "sick 'em."

"Theer's sothin' comic about them theer goanners," said the old man at last. "I've seed swarms of grasshoppers an' big mobs of kangaroos, but dang me if ever I seed a flock of black goanners afore!"

On reaching the hut the old man dumped the corpse against the wall, wrong end up, and stood scratching his head while he endeavoured to collect his muddled thoughts; but he had not placed Brummy at the correct angle, and, consequently, that individual fell forward and struck him a violent blow on the shoulder with the iron toes of his blucher boots.

The shock sobered him. He sprang a good yard, instinctively hitching up his moleskins in preparation for flight; but a backward glance revealed to him the true cause of this supposed attack from the rear. Then he lifted the body, stood it on its feet against the chimney, and ruminated as to where he should lodge his mate for the night, not noticing that the shorter sheet of bark had slipped down on the boots and left the face exposed.

"I spect I'll have ter put yer into the chimney-trough for the night, Brummy," said he, turning round to confront the corpse. "Yer can't expect me to take yer into the hut, though I did it when yer was in a worse state than—Lord!"

The shepherd was not prepared for the awful scrutiny that gleamed on him from those empty sockets; his nerves received a shock, and it was some time before he recovered himself sufficiently to speak.

"Now, look a-here, Brummy," said he, shaking his finger severely at the delinquent, "I don't want to pick a row with yer; I'd do as much for yer an' more than any other man, an' well yer knows it; but if yer starts playin' any of yer jumpt-up pranktical jokes on me, and a-scarin' of me after a-humpin' of yer 'ome, by the 'oly frost I'll kick yer to jim-rags, so I will."

This admonition delivered, he hoisted Brummy into the chimney-trough, and with a last glance towards the sheep-yards, he retired to his bunk to have, as he said, a snooze.

He had more than a snooze, however, for when he woke, it was dark, and the bushman's instinct told him it must be nearly nine o'clock.

He lit a slush-lamp and poured the remainder of the rum into a pannikin; but, just as he was about to lift the draught to his lips, he heard a peculiar rustling sound overhead, and put the pot down on the table with a slam that spilled some of the precious liquor.

Five Bob whimpered, and the old shepherd, though used to the weird and dismal, as one living alone in the bush must necessarily be, felt the icy breath of fear at his heart.

He reached hastily for his old shot-gun, and went out to investigate. He walked round the but several times and examined the roof on all sides, but saw nothing. Brummy appeared to be in the same position.

At last, persuading himself that the noise was caused by possums or the wind, the old man went inside, boiled his billy, and, after composing his nerves somewhat with a light supper and a meditative smoke, retired for the night. He was aroused several times before midnight by the same mysterious sound overhead, but, though he rose and examined the roof on each occasion by the light of the rising moon, he discovered nothing.

At last he determined to sit up and watch until daybreak, and for this purpose took up a position on a log a short distance from the hut, with his gun laid in readiness across his knee.

After watching for about an hour, he saw a black object coming over the ridge-pole. He grabbed his gun and fired. The thing disappeared. He ran round to the other side of the hut, and there was a great black goanna in violent convulsions on the ground.

Then the old man saw it all. "The thunderin' jumpt-up thing has been a-havin' o' me," he exclaimed. "The same cuss-o'-God wretch has a-follered me 'ome, an' has been a-havin' its Christmas dinner off of Brummy, an' a-hauntin' o' me into the bargain, the jumpt-up tinker!"

As there was no one by whom he could send a message to the station, and the old man dared not leave the sheep and go himself, he determined to bury the body the next afternoon, reflecting that the authorities could disinter it for inquest if they pleased.

So he brought the sheep home early and made arrangements for the burial by measuring the outer casing of Brummy and digging a hole according to those dimensions.

"That 'minds me," he said. "I never rightly knowed Brummy's religion, blest if ever I did. Howsomenever, there's one thing sartin—none o' them theer pianer-fingered parsons is a-goin' ter take the trouble ter travel out inter this God-forgotten part to hold sarvice over him, seein' as how his last cheque's blued. But, as I've got the fun'ral arrangements all in me own hands, I'll do jestice to it, and see that Brummy has a good comfortable buryin'—and more's unpossible."

"It's time yer turned in, Brum," he said, lifting the body down.

He carried it to the grave and dropped it into one corner like a post. He arranged the bark so as to cover the face, and, by means of a piece of clothes-line, lowered the body to a horizontal position. Then he threw in an armful of gum-leaves, and then, very reluctantly, took the shovel and dropped in a few shovelfuls of earth.

"An' this is the last of Brummy," he said, leaning on his spade and looking away over the tops of the ragged gums on the distant range.

This reflection seemed to engender a flood of memories, in which the old man became absorbed. He leaned heavily upon his spade and thought.

"Arter all," he murmured sadly, "arter all—it were Brummy."

"Brummy," he said at last. "It's all over now; nothin' matters now—nothin' didn't ever matter, nor—nor don't. You uster say as how it 'ud be all right termorrer" (pause); "termorrer's come, Brummy—come fur you—it ain't come fur me yet, but—it's a-comin'."

He threw in some more earth.

"Yer don't remember, Brummy, an' mebbe yer don't want to remember—I don't want to remember—but—well, but, yer see that's where yer got the pull on me."

He shovelled in some more earth and paused again.

The dog rose, with ears erect, and looked anxiously first at his master and then into the grave.

"Theer oughter be somethin' sed," muttered the old man; "'tain't right to put 'im under like a dog. Theer oughter be some sort o' sarmin." He sighed heavily in the listening silence that followed this remark and proceeded with his work. He filled the grave to the brim this time, and fashioned the mound carefully with his spade. Once or twice he muttered the words, "I am the rassaraction." As he laid the tools quietly aside, and stood at the head of the grave, he was evidently trying to remember the something that ought to be said. He removed his hat, placed it carefully on the grass, held his hands out from his sides and a little to the front, drew a long deep breath, and said with a solemnity that greatly disturbed Five Bob: "Hashes ter hashes, dus ter dus, Brummy—an'—an' in hopes of a great an' gerlorious rassaraction!"

He sat down on a log near by, rested his elbows on his knees and passed his hand wearily over his forehead—but only as one who was tired and felt the heat; and presently he rose, took up the tools, and walked back to the hut.

And the sun sank again on the grand Australian bush—the nurse and tutor of eccentric minds, the home of the weird.

OUR PIPES

The moon rose away out on the edge of a smoky plain, seen through a sort of tunnel or arch in the fringe of mulga behind which we were camped—Jack Mitchell and I. The timber proper was just behind us, very thick and very dark. The moon looked like a big new copper boiler set on edge on the horizon of the plain, with the top turned towards us and a lot of old rags and straw burning inside.

We had tramped twenty-five miles on a dry stretch on a hot day—swagmen know what that means. We reached the water about two hours "after dark "—swagmen know what that means. We didn't sit down at once and rest—we hadn't rested for the last ten miles. We knew that if we sat down we wouldn't want to get up again in a hurry—that, if we did, our leg-sinews, especially those of our calves, would "draw" like red-hot wire's. You see, we hadn't been long on the track this time—it was only our third day out. Swagmen will understand.

We got the billy boiled first, and some leaves laid down for our beds and the swags rolled out. We thanked the Lord that we had some cooked meat and a few johnny-cakes left, for we didn't feel equal to cooking. We put the billy of tea and our tucker-bags between the heads of our beds, and the pipes and tobacco in the crown of an old hat, where we could reach them without having to get up. Then we lay down on our stomachs and had a feed. We didn't eat much—we were too tired for that—but we drank a lot of tea. We gave our calves time to tone down a bit; then we lit up and began to answer each other. It got to be pretty comfortable, so long as we kept those unfortunate legs of ours straight and didn't move round much.

We cursed society because we weren't rich men, and then we felt better and conversation drifted lazily round various subjects and ended in that of smoking.

"How came to start smoking?" said Mitchell. "Let's see." He reflected. "I started smoking first when I was about fourteen or fifteen. I smoked some sort of weed—I forget the name of it—but it wasn't tobacco; and then I smoked cigarettes—not the ones we get now, for those cost a penny each. Then I reckoned that, if I could smoke those, I could smoke a pipe."

He reflected.

"We lived in Sydney then—Surry Hills. Those were different times; the place was nearly all sand. The old folks were alive then, and we were all at home, except Tom."

He reflected.

"Ah, well!... Well, one evening I was playing marbles out in front of our house when a chap we knew gave me his pipe to mind while he went into a church-meeting. The little church was opposite—a 'chapel' they called it."

He reflected.

"The pipe was alight. It was a clay pipe and niggerhead tobacco. Mother was at work out in the kitchen at the back, washing up the tea-things, and, when I went in, she said: 'You've been smoking!'

"Well, I couldn't deny it—I was too sick to do so, or care much, anyway.

"'Give me that pipe!' she said.

"I said I hadn't got it.

"'Give—me—that—pipe!' she said.

"I said I hadn't got it.

"'Where is it?' she said.

"'Jim Brown's got it,' I said, 'it's his.'

"'Then I'll give it to Jim Brown,' she said; and she did; though it wasn't Jim's fault, for he only gave it to me to mind. I didn't smoke the pipe so much because I wanted to smoke a pipe just then, as because I had such a great admiration for Jim."

Mitchell reflected, and took a look at the moon. It had risen clear and had got small and cold and pure-looking, and had floated away back out amongst the stars.

"I felt better towards morning, but it didn't cure me—being sick and nearly dead all night, I mean. I got a clay pipe and tobacco, and the old lady found it and put it in the stove. Then I got another pipe and tobacco, and she laid for it, and found it out at last; but she didn't put the tobacco in the stove this time—she'd got experience. I don't know what she did with it. I tried to find it, but couldn't. I fancy the old man got hold of it, for I saw him with a plug that looked very much like mine."

He reflected.

"But I wouldn't be done. I got a cherry pipe. I thought it wouldn't be so easy to break if she found it. I used to plant the bowl in one place and the stem in another because I reckoned that if she found one she mightn't find the other. It doesn't look much of an idea now, but it seemed like an inspiration then. Kids get rum ideas."

He reflected.

"Well, one day I was having a smoke out at the back, when I heard her coming, and I pulled out the stem in a hurry and put the bowl behind the water-butt and the stem under the house. Mother was coming round for a dipper of water. I got out of her way quick, for I hadn't time to look innocent; but the bowl of the pipe was hot and she got a whiff of it. She went sniffing round, first on one side of the cask and then on the other, until she got on the scent and followed it up and found the bowl. Then I had only the stem left. She looked for that, but she couldn't scent it. But I couldn't get much comfort out of that. Have you got the matches?

"Then I gave it best for a time and smoked cigars. They were the safest and most satisfactory under the circumstances, but they cost me two shillings a week, and I couldn't stand it, so I started a pipe again and then mother gave in at last. God bless her, and God forgive me, and us all—we deserve it. She's been at rest these seventeen long years."

Mitchell reflected.

"And what did your old man do when he found out that you were smoking?" I asked.

"The old man?"

He reflected.

"Well, he seemed to brighten up at first. You see, he was sort of pensioned off by mother and she kept him pretty well inside his income.... Well, he seemed to sort of brighten up—liven up—when he found out that I was smoking."

"Did he? So did my old man, and he livened me up, too. But what did your old man do—what did he say?"

"Well," said Mitchell, very slowly, "about the first thing he did was to ask me for a fill."

He reflected.

"Ah! many a solemn, thoughtful old smoke we had together on the quiet—the old man and me."

He reflected.

"Is your old man dead, Mitchell?" I asked softly. "Long ago—these twelve years," said Mitchell.

COMING ACROSS

We were delayed for an hour or so inside Sydney Heads, taking passengers from the Oroya, which had just arrived from England and anchored off Watson's Bay. An Adelaide boat went alongside the ocean liner, while we dropped anchor at a respectable distance. This puzzled some of us until one of the passengers stopped an ancient mariner and inquired. The sailor jerked his thumb upwards, and left. The passengers stared aloft till some of them got the lockjaw in the back of their necks, and then another sailor suggested that we had yards to our masts, while the Adelaide boat had not.

It seemed a pity that the new chums for New Zealand didn't have a chance to see Sydney after coming so far and getting so near. It struck them that way too. They saw Melbourne, which seemed another injustice to the old city. However, nothing matters much nowadays, and they might see Sydney in happier times.

They looked like new chums, especially the "furst clarsters," and there were two or three Scotsmen among them who looked like Scots, and talked like it too; also an Irishman. Great Britain and Ireland do not seem to be learning anything fresh about Australia. We had a yarn with one of these new arrivals, and got talking about the banks. It turned out that he was a radical. He spat over the side and said:

"It's a something shame the way things is carried on! Now, look here, a banker can rob hundreds of wimmin and children an' widders and orfuns, and nothin' is done to him; but if a poor man only embezzles a shilling he gets transported to the colonies for life." The italics are ours, but the words were his.

We explained to this new chum that transportation was done away with long ago, as far as Australia was concerned, that no more convicts were sent out here—only men who ought to be; and he seemed surprised. He did not call us a liar, but he looked as if he thought that we were prevaricating. We were glad that he didn't say so, for he was a bigger man. New chums are generally more robust than Australians.

When we got through the Heads someone pointed to the wrong part of the cliff and said:

"That's where the Dunbar was wrecked."

Shortly afterwards another man pointed to another wrong part of the cliffs and observed incidentally:

"That's where the Dunbar was wrecked."

Pretty soon a third man came along and pointed to a third wrong part of the cliff, and remarked casually:

"That's where the Dunbar was wrecked."

We moved aft and met the fourth mate, who jerked his thumb over his shoulder at the cliffs in general, and muttered condescendingly:

"That's where the Dunbar was wrecked."

It was not long before a woman turned round and asked "Was that the place where the Dunbar was wrecked, please?"

We said "Yes," and she said "Lor," and beckoned to a friend.

We went for'ard and met an old sailor, who glared at us, jerked his thumb at the coast and growled:

"That's where the Dunbar went down."

Then we went below; but we felt a slight relief when he said "went down" instead of "was wrecked."

It is doubtful whether a passenger boat ever cleared Sydney Heads since the wild night of that famous wreck without someone pointing to the wrong part of the cliffs, and remarking:

"That's where the Dunbar was wrecked."

The Dunbar fiend is inseparable from Australian coasting steamers.

We travelled second-class in the interests of journalism. You get more points for copy in the steerage. It was a sacrifice; but we hope to profit by it some day.

There were about fifty male passengers, including half a dozen New Zealand shearers, two of whom came on board drunk—their remarks for the first night mainly consisted of "gory." "Gory" is part of the Australian language now—a big part.

The others were chiefly tradesmen, labourers, clerks and bagmen, driven out of Australia by the hard times there, and glad, no doubt, to get away. There was a jeweller on board, of course, and his name was Moses or Cohen. If it wasn't it should have been—or Isaacs. His christian name was probably Benjamin. We called him Jacobs. He passed away most of his time on board in swopping watch lies with the other passengers and good-naturedly spoiling their Waterburys.

One commercial traveller shipped with a flower in his buttonhole. His girl gave it to him on the wharf, and told him to keep it till it faded, and then press it. She was a barmaid. She thought he was "going saloon," but he came forward as soon as the wharf was out of sight. He gave the flower to the stewardess, and told us about these things one moonlight night during the voyage.

There was another—a well-known Sydney man—whose friends thought he was going saloon, and turned up in good force to see him off. He spent his last shilling "shouting," and kept up his end of the pathetic little farce out of consideration for the feelings of certain proud female relatives, and not because he was "proud"—at least in that way. He stood on a conspicuous part of the saloon deck and waved his white handkerchief until Miller's Point came between. Then he came forward where he belonged. But he was proud—bitterly so. He had a flower too, but he did not give it to the stewardess. He had it pressed, we think (for we knew him), and perhaps he wears it now over the place where his heart used to be.

When Australia was fading from view we shed a tear, which was all we had to shed; at least, we tried to shed a tear, and could not. It is best to be exact when you are writing from experience.

Just as Australia was fading from view, someone looked through a glass, and said in a sad, tired kind of voice that he could just see the place where the Dunbar was wrecked.

Several passengers were leaning about and saying "Europe! E-u-rope!" in agonized tones. None of them were going to Europe, and the new chums said nothing about it. This reminds us that some people say "Asia! Asia! Ak-kak-Asia!" when somebody spills the pepper. There was a pepper-box without a stopper on the table in our cabin. The fact soon attracted attention.

A new chum came along and asked us whether the Maoris were very bad round Sydney. He'd heard that they were. We told him that we had never had any trouble with them to speak of, and gave him another show.

"Did you ever hear of the wreck of the Dunbar?" we asked. He said that he never "heerd tell" of it, but he had heerd of the wreck of the Victoria.

We gave him best.

The first evening passed off quietly, except for the vinously-excited shearers. They had sworn eternal friendship with a convivial dude from the saloon, and he made a fine specimen fool of himself for an hour or so. He never showed his nose for'ard again.

Now and then a passenger would solemnly seek the steward and have a beer. The steward drew it out of a small keg which lay on its side on a shelf with a wooden tap sticking out of the end of it—out of the end of the keg, we mean. The beer tasted like warm but weak vinegar, and cost sixpence per small glass. The bagman told the steward that he could not compliment him on the quality of his liquor, but the steward said nothing. He did not even seem interested—only bored. He had heard the same remark often before, no doubt. He was a fat, solemn steward—not formal, but very reticent—unresponsive. He looked like a man who had conducted a religious conservative paper once and failed, and had then gone into the wholesale produce line, and failed again, and finally got his present billet through the influence of his creditors and two clergymen. He might have been a sociable fellow, a man about town, even a gay young dog, and a radical writer before he was driven to accept the editorship of the aforesaid periodical. He probably came of a "good English family." He was now, very likely, either a rigid Presbyterian or an extreme freethinker. He thought a lot, anyway, and looked as if he knew a lot too—too much for words, in fact.

We took a turn on deck before turning in, and heard two men arguing about the way in which the Dunbar was wrecked.

The commercial travellers, the jeweller, and one or two new chums who were well provided with clothing undressed deliberately and retired ostentatiously in pyjamas, but there were others—men of better days—who turned in either very early or very late, when the cabin was quiet, and slipped hurriedly and furtively out of their clothes and between the blankets, as if they were ashamed of the poverty of their underwear. It is well that the Lord can see deep down into the hearts of men, for He has to judge them; it is well that the majority of mankind cannot, because, if they could, the world would be altogether too sorrowful to live in; and we do not think the angels can either, else they would not be happy—if they could and were they would not be angels any longer—they would be devils. Study it out on a slate.

We turned in feeling comfortably dismal, and almost wishing that we had gone down with the Dunbar.

The intoxicated shearers and the dude kept their concert up till a late hour that night—or, rather, a very early hour next morning; and at about midnight they were reinforced by the commercial traveller and Moses, the jeweller, who had been visiting acquaintances aft. This push was encouraged by voices from various bunks, and enthusiastically barracked for by a sandy-complexioned, red-headed comedian with twinkling grey eyes, who occupied the berth immediately above our own.

They stood with their backs to the bunks, and their feet braced against the deck, or lurched round, and took friendly pulls from whisky flasks, and chyacked each other, and laughed, and blowed, and lied like—like Australian bushmen; and occasionally they broke out into snatches of song—and as often broke down. Few Englishmen know more than the first verse, or two lines, of even their most popular song, and, where elevated enough to think they can sing, they repeat the first verse over and over again, with the wrong words, and with a sort of "Ta-ra-ra-rum-ti-tooral, ta-ra-ra-ra-ra-rum-ti, ta-ra-ra-rum-tum-ti-rum-rum-tum-ti-dee-e-e," by way of variation.

Presently—suddenly, it seemed to our drowsy senses—two of the shearers and the bagman commenced arguing with drunken gravity and precision about politics, even while a third bushman was approaching the climax of an out-back yarn of many adjectives, of which he himself was the hero. The scraps of conversation that we caught were somewhat as follow. We leave out most of the adjectives.

First Voice: "Now, look here. The women will vote for men, not principles. That's why I'm against women voting. Now, just mark my—"

Third Voice (trying to finish yarn): "Hold on. Just wait till I tell yer. Well, this bloomin' bloke, he says—"

Second Voice (evidently in reply to first): "Principles you mean, not men. You're getting a bit mixed, old man." (Smothered chuckle from comedian over our head.)

Third Voice (seeming to drift round in search of sympathy): "'You will!' sez I. 'Yes, I will,' he sez. 'Oh, you will, will yer?' I sez; and with that I—"

Second Voice (apparently wandering from both subjects) "Blanker has always stuck up for the workin' man, an' he'll get in, you'll see. Why, he's a bloomin' workin' man himself. Me and Blanker—"

Disgusted voice from a bunk: "Oh, that's damn rot! We've had enough of lumpers in parliament! Horny hands are all right enough, but we don't want any more blanky horny heads!"

Third Voice (threateningly): "Who's talkin' about 'orny heads? That pitch is meant for us, ain't it? Do you mean to say that I've got a 'orny head?"

Here two men commenced snarling at each other, and there was some talk of punching the causes of the dispute; but the bagman interfered, a fresh flask was passed round, and some more eternal friendship sworn to.

We dozed off again, and the next time we were aware of anything the commercial and Moses had disappeared, the rest were lying or sitting in their bunks, and the third shearer was telling a yarn about an alleged fight he had at a shed up-country; and perhaps he was telling it for the benefit of the dissatisfied individual who made the injudicious remark concerning horny heads.

"So I said to the boss-over-the-board, 'you're a nice sort of a thing,' I sez. 'Who are you talkin' to?' he says. 'You, bless yer,' I says. 'Now, look here,' he says, 'you get your cheque and clear! 'All right,' I says, 'you can take that!' and I hauled off and landed him a beauty under the butt of the listener. Then the boss came along with two blacklegs, but the boys made a ring, and I laid out the blanks in just five minutes. Then I sez to the boss, 'That's the sort of cove I am,' I sez, 'an' now, if you—"

But just here there came a deep, growling voice—seemingly from out of the depths of the forehold—anyway, there came a voice, and it said:

"For the Lord's sake give her a rest!"

The steward turned off the electricity, but there were two lanterns dimly burning in our part of the steerage. It was a narrow compartment running across the width of the boat, and had evidently been partitioned off from the top floor of the hold to meet the emigration from Australia to New Zealand. There were three tiers of bunks, two deep, on the far side, three rows of single bunks on the other, and two at each end of the cabin, the top ones just under the portholes.

The shearers had turned in "all standing;" two of them were lying feet to feet in a couple of outside lower berths. One lay on his stomach with his face turned outwards, his arm thrown over the side of the bunk, and his knuckles resting on the deck, the other rested on the broad of his back with his arm also hanging over the side and his knuckles resting on the floor. And so they slept the sleep of the drunk.

A fair, girl-faced young Swiss emigrant occupied one of the top berths, with his curly, flaxen head resting close alongside one of the lanterns that were dimly burning, and an Anglo-foreign dictionary in his hand. His mate, or brother, who resembled him in everything except that he had dark hair, lay asleep alongside; and in the next berth a long consumptive-looking new chum sat in his pyjamas, with his legs hanging over the edge, and his hands grasping the sideboard, to which, on his right hand, a sort of tin-can arrangement was hooked. He was staring intently at nothing, and seemed to be thinking very hard.

We dozed off again, and woke suddenly to find our eyes wide open, and the young Swiss still studying, and the jackaroo still sitting in the same position, but with a kind of waiting expression on his face—a sort of expectant light in his eyes. Suddenly he lurched for the can, and after awhile he lay back looking like a corpse.

We slept again, and finally awoke to daylight and the clatter of plates. All the bunks were vacated except two, which contained corpses, apparently.

Wet decks, and a round, stiff, morning breeze, blowing strongly across the deck, abeam, and gustily through the open portholes. There was a dull grey sky, and the sea at first sight seemed to be of a dark blue or green, but on closer inspection it took a dirty slate colour, with splashes as of indigo in the hollows. There was one of those near, yet far-away horizons.

About two-thirds of the men were on deck, but the women had not shown up yet—nor did they show up until towards the end of the trip.

Some of the men were smoking in a sheltered corner, some walking up and down, two or three trying to play quoits, one looking at the poultry, one standing abaft the purser's cabin with hands in the pockets of his long ragged overcoat, watching the engines, and two more—carpenters—were discussing a big cedar log, about five feet in diameter, which was lashed on deck alongside the hatch.

While we were waiting for the Oroya some of the ship's officers came and had a consultation over this log and called up part of the crew, who got some more ropes and a chain on to it. It struck us at the time that that log would make a sensation if it fetched loose in rough weather. But there wasn't any rough weather.

The fore-cabin was kept clean; the assistant steward was good-humoured and obliging; his chief was civil enough to freeze the Never-Never country; but the bill of fare was monotonous.

During the afternoon a first-salooner made himself obnoxious by swelling round for'ard. He was a big bull-necked "Britisher" (that word covers it) with a bloated face, prominent gooseberry eyes, fore 'n' aft cap, and long tan shoes. He seemed as if he'd come to see a "zoo," and was dissatisfied with it—had a fine contempt for it, in fact, because it did not come up to other zoological gardens that he had seen in London, and on the aw—continong and in the—aw-er—aw—the States, dontcherknow. The fellows reckoned that he ought to be "took down a peg" (dontcherknow) and the sandy-complexioned comedian said he'd do it. So he stepped softly up to the swell, tapped him lightly on the shoulder, and pointed aft—holding his arm out like a pump handle and his forefinger rigid.

The Britisher's face was a study; it was blank at first and then it went all colours, and wore, in succession, every possible expression except a pleasant one. He seemed bursting with indignation, but he did not speak—could not, perhaps; and, as soon as he could detach his feet from the spot to which they had been nailed in the first place by astonishment, he stalked aft. He did not come to see the zoo any more.

The fellows in the fore-cabin that evening were growling about the bad quality of the grub supplied.

Then the shearer's volcano showed signs of activity. He shifted round, spat impatiently, and said:

"You chaps don't know what yer talkin' about. You want something to grumble about. You should have been out with me last year on the Paroo in Noo South Wales. The meat we got there was so bad that it uster travel!"

"What?"

"Yes! travel! take the track! go on the wallaby! The cockies over there used to hang the meat up on the branches of the trees, and just shake it whenever they wanted to feed the fowls. And the water was so bad that half a pound of tea in the billy wouldn't make no impression on the colour—nor the taste. The further west we went the worse our meat got, till at last we had to carry a dog-chain to chain it up at night. Then it got worse and broke the chain, and then we had to train the blessed dogs to shepherd it and bring it back. But we fell in with another chap with a bad old dog—a downright knowing, thieving, old hard-case of a dog; and this dog led our dogs astray—demoralized them—corrupted their morals— and so one morning they came home with the blooming meat inside them, instead of outside—and we had to go hungry for breakfast."

"You'd better turn in, gentlemen. I'm going to turn off the light," said the steward.

The yarn reminded the Sydney man of a dog he had, and he started some dog lies.

"This dog of mine," he said, "knowed the way into the best public-houses. If I came to a strange town and wanted a good drink, I'd only have to say, 'Jack, I'm dry,' and he'd lead me all right. He always knew the side entrances and private doors after hours, and I—"

But the yarn did not go very well—it fell flat in fact. Then the commercial traveller was taken bad with an anecdote. "That's nothing," he said, "I had a black bag once that knew the way into public-houses."

"A what?"

"Yes. A black bag. A long black bag like that one I've got there in my bunk. I was staying at a boarding-house in Sydney, and one of us used to go out every night for a couple of bottles of beer, and we carried the bottles in the bag; and when we got opposite the pub the front end of the bag would begin to swing round towards the door. It was wonderful. It was just as if there was a lump of steel in the end of the bag and a magnet in the bar. We tried it with ever so many people, but it always acted the same. We couldn't use that bag for any other purpose, for if we carried it along the street it would make our wrists ache trying to go into pubs. It twisted my wrist one time, and it ain't got right since—I always feel the pain in dull weather. Well, one night we got yarning and didn't notice how the time was going, and forgot to go for the beer till it was nearly too late. We looked for the bag and couldn't find it—we generally kept it under a side-table, but it wasn't there, and before we were done looking, eleven o'clock went. We sat down round the fire, feeling pretty thirsty, and were just thinking about turning in when we heard a thump on the table behind us. We looked round, and there was that bag with two full bottles of English ale in it."

"Then I remembered that I'd left a bob in the bottom of the bag, and—"

The steward turned off the electric light.

There were some hundreds of cases of oranges stacked on deck, and made fast with matting and cordage to the bulwarks. That night was very dark, and next morning there was a row. The captain said he'd "give any man three months that he caught at those oranges."

"Wot, yer givin' us?" said a shearer. "We don't know anything about yer bloomin' oranges.... I seen one of the saloon passengers moochin' round for'ard last night. You'd better search the saloon for your blarsted oranges, an' don't come round tacklin' the wrong men."

It was not necessary to search our quarters, for the "offside" steward was sweeping orange peel out of the steerage for three days thereafter.

And that night, just as we were about to fall asleep, a round, good-humoured face loomed over the edge of the shelf above and a small, twinkling, grey eye winked at us. Then a hand came over, gave a jerk, and something fell on our nose. It was an orange. We sent a "thank you" up through the boards and commenced hurriedly and furtively to stow away the orange. But the comedian had an axe to grind—most people have—wanted to drop his peel alongside our berth; and it made us uneasy because we did not want circumstantial evidence lying round us if the captain chanced to come down to inquire. The next man to us had a barney with the man above him about the same thing. Then the peel was scattered round pretty fairly, or thrown into an empty bunk, and no man dared growl lest he should come to be regarded as a blackleg—a would-be informer.

The men opposite the door kept a look out; and two Australian jokers sat in the top end berth with their legs hanging over and swinging contentedly, and the porthole open ready for a swift and easy disposal of circumstantial evidence on the first alarm. They were eating a pineapple which they had sliced and extracted in sections from a crate up on deck. They looked so chummy, and so school-boyishly happy and contented, that they reminded us of the days long ago, when we were so high.

The chaps had talk about those oranges on deck next day. The commercial traveller said we had a right to the oranges, because the company didn't give us enough to eat. He said that we were already suffering from insufficient proper nourishment, and he'd tell the doctor so if the doctor came on board at Auckland. Anyway, it was no sin to rob a company.

"But then," said our comedian, "those oranges, perhaps, were sent over by a poor, struggling orange grower, with a wife and family to keep, and he'll have to bear the loss, and a few bob might make a lot of difference to him. It ain't right to rob a poor man."

This made us feel doubtful and mean, and one or two got uncomfortable and shifted round uneasily. But presently the traveller came to the rescue. He said that no doubt the oranges belonged to a middleman, and the middleman was the curse of the country. We felt better.

Towards the end of the trip the women began to turn up. There were five grass widows, and every female of them had a baby. The Australian marries young and poor; and, when he can live no longer in his native land, he sells the furniture, buys a steerage ticket to New Zealand or Western Australia, and leaves his wife with her relatives or friends until he earns enough money to send for her. Four of our women were girl-wives, and mostly pretty. One little handful of a thing had a fine baby boy, nearly as big as herself, and she looked so fragile and pale, and pretty and lonely, and had such an appealing light in her big shadowed brown eyes, and such a pathetic droop at the corners of her sweet little mouth, that you longed to take her in your manly arms—baby and all—and comfort her.

The last afternoon on high seas was spent in looking through glasses for the Pinnacles, off North Cape. And, as we neared the land, the commercial traveller remarked that he wouldn't mind if there was a wreck now—provided we all got saved. "We'd have all our names in the papers," he said. "Gallant conduct of the passengers and crew. Heroic rescue by Mr So-and-so-climbing the cliffs with a girl under his arm, and all that sort of thing."

The chaps smiled a doleful smile, and turned away again to look at the Promised Land. They had had no anxiety to speak of for the last two or three days; but now they were again face to face with the cursed question, "How to make a living." They were wondering whether or no they would get work in New Zealand, and feeling more doubtful about it than when they embarked.

Pity we couldn't go to sea and sail away for ever, and never see land any more—or, at least, not till better and brighter days—if they ever come.

THE STORY OF MALACHI

Malachi was very tall, very thin, and very round-shouldered, and the sandiness of his hair also cried aloud for an adjective. All the boys considered Malachi the greatest ass on the station, and there was no doubt that he was an awful fool. He had never been out of his native bush in all his life, excepting once, when he paid a short visit to Sydney, and when he returned it was evident that his nerves had received a shaking. We failed to draw one word out of Malachi regarding his views on the city—to describe it was not in his power, for it had evidently been something far beyond his comprehension. Even after his visit had become a matter of history, if you were to ask him what he thought of Sydney the dazed expression would come back into his face, and he would scratch his head and say in a slow and deliberate manner, "Well, there's no mistake, it's a caution." And as such the city remained, so far as Malachi's opinion of it was concerned.

Malachi was always shabbily dressed, in spite of his pound a week and board, and "When Malachi gets a new suit of clothes" was the expression invariably used by the boys to fix a date for some altogether improbable event. We were always having larks with Malachi, for we looked upon him as our legitimate butt. He seldom complained, and when he did his remonstrance hardly ever went beyond repeating the words, "Now, none of your pranktical jokes!" If this had not the desired effect, and we put up some too outrageous trick on him, he would content himself by muttering with sorrowful conviction, "Well, there's no mistake, it's a caution."

We were not content with common jokes, such as sewing up the legs of Malachi's trousers while he slept, fixing his bunk, or putting explosives in his pipe—we aspired to some of the higher branches of the practical joker's art. It was well known that Malachi had an undying hatred for words of four syllables and over, and the use of them was always sufficient to forfeit any good opinions he might have previously entertained concerning the user. "I hate them high-flown words," he would say—"I got a book at home that I could get them out of if I wanted them; but I don't." The book referred to was a very dilapidated dictionary. Malachi's hatred for high-flown words was only equalled by his aversion to the opposite sex; and, this being known, we used to write letters to him in a feminine hand, threatening divers breach of promise actions, and composed in the high-flown language above alluded to. We used to think this very funny, and by these means we made his life a burden to him. Malachi put the most implicit faith in everything we told him; he would take in the most improbable yarn provided we preserved a grave demeanour and used no high-flown expressions. He would indeed sometimes remark that our yarns were a caution, but that was all.

We played upon him the most gigantic joke of all during the visit of a certain bricklayer, who came to do some work at the homestead. "Bricky" was a bit of a phrenologist, and knew enough of physiognomy and human nature to give a pretty fair delineation of character. He also went in for spirit-rapping, greatly to the disgust of the two ancient housekeepers, who declared that they'd have "no dalins wid him and his divil's worruk."'

The bricklayer was from the first an object of awe to Malachi, who carefully avoided him; but one night we got the butt into a room where the artisan was entertaining the boys with a seance. After the table-rapping, during which Malachi sat with uncovered head and awe-struck expression, we proposed that he should have his bumps read, and before he could make his escape Malachi was seated in a chair in the middle of the room and the bricklayer was running his fingers over his head. I really believe that Malachi's hair bristled between the phrenologist's fingers. Whenever he made a hit his staunch admirer, "Donegal," would exclaim "Look at that now!" while the girls tittered and said, "Just fancy!" and from time to time Malachi would be heard to mutter to himself, in a tone of the most intense conviction, that, "without the least mistake it was a caution." Several times at his work the next day Malachi was observed to rest on his spade, while he tilted his hat forward with one hand and felt the back of his head as though he had not been previously aware of its existence.

We "ran" Malachi to believe that the bricklayer was mad on the subject of phrenology, and was suspected of having killed several persons in order to obtain their skulls for experimental purposes. We further said that he had been heard to say that Malachi's skull was a most extraordinary one, and so we advised him to be careful.

Malachi occupied a hut some distance from the station, and one night, the last night of the bricklayer's stay, as Malachi sat smoking over the fire the door opened quietly and the phrenologist entered. He carried a bag with a pumpkin in the bottom of it, and, sitting down on a stool, he let the bag down with a bump on the floor between his feet. Malachi was badly scared, but he managed to stammer out—

"'Ello!" "'Ello!" said the phrenologist.

There was an embarrassing silence, which was at last broken by "Bricky" saying "How are you gettin' on, Malachi?"

"Oh, jist right," replied Malachi.

Nothing was said for a while, until Malachi, after fidgeting a good deal on his stool, asked the bricklayer when he was leaving the station.

"Oh, I'm going away in the morning, early," said he. "I've jist been over to Jimmy Nowlett's camp, and as I was passing I thought I'd call and get your head."

"What?"

"I come for your skull.

"Yes," the phrenologist continued, while Malachi sat horror-stricken; "I've got Jimmy Nowlett's skull here," and he lifted the bag and lovingly felt the pumpkin—it must have weighed forty pounds. "I spoilt one of his best bumps with the tomahawk. I had to hit him twice, but it's no use crying over spilt milk." Here he drew a heavy shingling-hammer out of the bag and wiped off with his sleeve something that looked like blood. Malachi had been edging round for the door, and now he made a rush for it. But the skull-fancier was there before him.

"Gor-sake you don't want to murder me!" gasped Malachi.

"Not if I can get your skull any other way," said Bricky.

"Oh!" gasped Malachi—and then, with a vague idea that it was best to humour a lunatic, he continued, in a tone meant to be off-hand and careless—"Now, look here, if yer only waits till I die you can have my whole skelington and welcome."

"Now Malachi," said the phrenologist sternly, "d'ye think I'm a fool? I ain't going to stand any humbug. If yer acts sensible you'll be quiet, and it'll soon be over, but if yer—"

Malachi did not wait to hear the rest. He made a spring for the back of the hut and through it, taking down a large new sheet of stringy-bark in his flight. Then he could be heard loudly ejaculating "It's a caution!" as he went through the bush like a startled kangaroo, and he didn't stop till he reached the station.

Jimmy Nowlett and I had been peeping through a crack in the same sheet of bark that Malachi dislodged; it fell on us and bruised us somewhat, but it wasn't enough to knock the fun out of the thing.

When Jimmy Nowlett crawled out from under the bark he had to lie down on Malachi's bunk to laugh, and even for some time afterwards it was not unusual for Jimmy to wake up in the' night and laugh till we wished him dead.

I should like to finish here, but there remains something more to be said about Malachi.

One of the best cows at the homestead had a calf, about which she made a great deal of fuss. She was ordinarily a quiet, docile creature, and, though somewhat fussy after calving no one ever dreamed that she would injure anyone. It happened one day that the squatter's daughter and her intended husband, a Sydney exquisite, were strolling in a paddock where the cow was. Whether the cow objected to the masher or his lady love's red parasol, or whether she suspected designs upon her progeny, is not certain; anyhow, she went for them. The young man saw the cow coming first, and he gallantly struck a bee-line for the fence, leaving the girl to manage for herself. She wouldn't have managed very well if Malachi hadn't been passing just then. He saw the girl's danger and ran to intercept the cow with no weapon but his hands.

It didn't last long. There was a roar, a rush, and a cloud of dust, out of which the cow presently emerged, and went scampering back to the bush in which her calf was hidden.

We carried Malachi home and laid him on a bed. He had a terrible wound in the groin, and the blood soaked through the bandages like water. We did all that was possible for him, the boys killed the squatter's best horse and spoilt two others riding for a doctor, but it was of no use. In the last half-hour of his life we all gathered round Malachi's bed; he was only twenty-two. Once he said:

"I wonder how mother'll manage now?"

"Why, where's your mother?" someone asked gently; we had never dreamt that Malachi might have someone to love him and be proud of him.

"In Bathurst," he answered wearily—"she'll take on awful, I 'spect, she was awful fond of me—we've been pulling together this last ten years—mother and me—we wanted to make it all right for my little brother Jim—poor Jim!"

"What's wrong with Jim?" someone asked.

"Oh, he's blind," said Malachi "always was—we wanted to make it all right for him agin time he grows up—I—I managed to send home about—about forty pounds a year—we bought a bit of ground, and—and—I think—I'm going now. Tell 'em, Harry—tell 'em how it was—"

I had to go outside then. I couldn't stand it any more. There was a lump in my throat and I'd have given anything to wipe out my share in the practical jokes, but it was too late now.

Malachi was dead when I went in again, and that night the hat went round with the squatter's cheque in the bottom of it and we made it "all right" for Malachi's blind brother Jim.

TWO DOGS AND A FENCE

"Nothing makes a dog madder," said Mitchell, "than to have another dog come outside his fence and sniff and bark at him through the cracks when he can't get out. The other dog might be an entire stranger; he might be an old chum, and he mightn't bark—only sniff—but it makes no difference to the inside dog. The inside dog generally starts it, and the outside dog only loses his temper and gets wild because the inside dog has lost his and got mad and made such a stinking fuss about nothing at all; and then the outside dog barks back and makes matters a thousand times worse, and the inside dog foams at the mouth and dashes the foam about, and goes at it like a million steel traps.

"I can't tell why the inside dog gets so wild about it in the first place, except, perhaps, because he thinks the outside dog has taken him at a disadvantage and is 'poking it at him;' anyway, he gets madder the longer it lasts, and at last he gets savage enough to snap off his own tail and tear it to bits, because he can't get out and chew up that other dog; and, if he did get out, he'd kill the other dog, or try to, even if it was his own brother.

"Sometimes the outside dog only smiles and trots off; sometimes he barks back good-humouredly; sometimes he only just gives a couple of disinterested barks as if he isn't particular, but is expected, because of his dignity and doghood, to say something under the circumstances; and sometimes, if the outside dog is a little dog, he'll get away from that fence in a hurry on the first surprise, or, if he's a cheeky little dog, he'll first make sure that the inside dog can't get out, and then he'll have some fun.

"It's amusing to see a big dog, of the Newfoundland kind, sniffing along outside a fence with a broad, good-natured grin on his face all the time the inside dog is whooping away at the rate of thirty whoops a second, and choking himself, and covering himself with foam, and dashing the spray through the cracks, and jolting and jerking every joint in his body up to the last joint in his tail.

"Sometimes the inside dog is a little dog, and the smaller he is the more row he makes—but then he knows he's safe. And, sometimes, as I said before, the outside dog is a short-tempered dog who hates a row, and never wants to have a disagreement with anybody—like a good many peaceful men, who hate rows, and are always nice and civil and pleasant, in a nasty, unpleasant, surly, sneering sort of civil way that makes you want to knock their heads off; men who never start a row, but keep it going, and make it a thousand times worse when it's once started, just because they didn't start it—and keep on saying so, and that the other party did. The short-tempered outside dog gets wild at the other dog for losing his temper, and says:

"'What are you making such a fuss about? What's the matter with you, anyway? Hey?'

"And the inside dog says:

"'Who do you think you're talking to? You—! I'll—' etc., etc., etc.

"Then the outside dog says:

"'Why, you're worse than a flaming old slut!'

"Then they go at it, and you can hear them miles off, like a Chinese war—like a hundred great guns firing eighty blank cartridges a minute, till the outside dog is just as wild to get inside and eat the inside dog as the inside dog is to get out and disembowel him. Yet if those same two dogs were to meet casually outside they might get chummy at once, and be the best of friends, and swear everlasting mateship, and take each other home."

She lived in Jones's Alley. She cleaned offices, washed, and nursed from daylight until any time after dark, and filled in her spare time cleaning her own place (which she always found dirty—in a "beastly filthy state," she called it—on account of the children being left in possession all day), cooking, and nursing her own sick—for her family, though small, was so in the two senses of the word, and sickly; one or another of the children was always sick, but not through her fault. She did her own, or rather the family washing, at home too, when she couldn't do it by kind permission, or surreptitiously in connection with that of her employers. She was a haggard woman. Her second husband was supposed to be dead, and she, lived in dread of his daily resurrection. Her eldest son was at large, but, not being yet sufficiently hardened in misery, she dreaded his getting into trouble even more than his frequent and interested appearances at home. She could buy off the son for a shilling or two and a clean shirt and collar, but she couldn't purchase the absence of the father at any price—he claimed what he called his "conzugal rights" as well as his board, lodging, washing and beer. She slaved for her children, and nag-nag-nagged them everlastingly, whether they were in the right or in the wrong, but they were hardened to it and took small notice. She had the spirit of a bullock. Her whole nature was soured. She had those "worse troubles" which she couldn't tell to anybody, but had to suffer in silence.

She also, in what she called her "spare time," put new cuffs and collar-bands on gentlemen's shirts. The gentlemen didn't live in Jones's Alley—they boarded with a patroness of the haggard woman; they didn't know their shirts were done there—had they known it, and known Jones's Alley, one or two of them, who were medical students, might probably have objected. The landlady charged them just twice as much for repairing their shirts as she paid the haggard woman, who, therefore, being unable to buy the cuffs and collar-bands ready-made for sewing on, had no lack of employment with which to fill in her spare time.

Therefore, she was a "respectable woman," and was known in Jones's Alley as "Misses" Aspinall, and called so generally, and even by Mother Brock, who kept "that place" opposite. There is implied a world of difference between the "Mother" and the "Misses," as applied to matrons in Jones's Alley; and this distinction was about the only thing—always excepting the everlasting "children"—that the haggard woman had left to care about, to take a selfish, narrow-minded sort of pleasure in—if, indeed, she could yet take pleasure, grim or otherwise, in anything except, perhaps, a good cup of tea and time to drink it in.

Times were hard with Mrs Aspinall. Two coppers and two half-pence in her purse were threepence to her now, and the absence of one of the half-pence made a difference to her, especially in Paddy's market—that eloquent advertisement of a young city's sin and poverty and rotten wealth—on Saturday night. She counted the coppers as anxiously and nervously as a thirsty dead-beat does. And her house was "falling down on her" and her troubles, and she couldn't get the landlord to do a "han'stern" to it.

At last, after persistent agitation on her part (but not before a portion of the plastered ceiling had fallen and severely injured one of her children) the landlord caused two men to be sent to "effect necessary repairs" to the three square, dingy, plastered holes—called "three rooms and a kitchen"—for the privilege of living in which, and calling it "my place," she paid ten shillings a week.

Previously the agent, as soon as he had received the rent and signed the receipt, would cut short her reiterated complaints—which he privately called her "clack"—by saying that he'd see to it, he'd speak to the landlord; and, later on, that he had spoken to him, or could do nothing more in the matter—that it wasn't his business. Neither it was, to do the agent justice. It was his business to collect the rent, and thereby earn the means of paying his own. He had to keep a family on his own account, by assisting the Fat Man to keep his at the expense of people—especially widows with large families, or women, in the case of Jones's Alley—who couldn't afford it without being half-starved, or running greater and unspeakable risks which "society" is not supposed to know anything about.

So the agent was right, according to his lights. The landlord had recently turned out a family who had occupied one of his houses for fifteen years, because they were six weeks in arrears. He let them take their furniture, and explained: "I wouldn't have been so lenient with them only they were such old tenants of mine." So the landlord was always in the right according to his lights.

But the agent naturally wished to earn his living as peacefully and as comfortably as possible, so, when the accident occurred, he put the matter so persistently and strongly before the landlord that he said at last: "Well, tell her to go to White, the contractor, and he'll send a man to do what's to be done; and don't bother me any more."

White had a look at the place, and sent a plasterer, a carpenter, and a plumber. The plasterer knocked a bigger hole in the ceiling and filled it with mud; the carpenter nailed a board over the hole in the floor; the plumber stopped the leak in the kitchen, and made three new ones in worse places; and their boss sent the bill to Mrs Aspinall.

She went to the contractor's yard, and explained that the landlord was responsible for the debt, not she. The contractor explained that he had seen the landlord, who referred him to her. She called at the landlord's private house, and was referred through a servant to the agent. The agent was sympathetic, but could do nothing in the matter—it wasn't his business; he also asked her to put herself in his place, which she couldn't, not being any more reasonable than such women are in such cases. She let things drift, being powerless to prevent them from doing so; and the contractor sent another bill, then a debt collector and then another bill, then the collector again, and threatened to take proceedings, and finally took them. To make matters worse, she was two weeks in arrears with the rent, and the wood-and-coalman's man (she had dealt with them for ten years) was pushing her, as also were her grocers, with whom she had dealt for fifteen years and never owed a penny before.

She waylaid the landlord, and he told her shortly that he couldn't build houses and give them away, and keep them in repair afterwards.

She sought for sympathy and found it, but mostly in the wrong places. It was comforting, but unprofitable. Mrs Next-door sympathized warmly, and offered to go up as a witness—she had another landlord. The agent sympathized wearily, but not in the presence of witnesses—he wanted her to put herself in his place. Mother Brock, indeed, offered practical assistance, which offer was received in breathlessly indignant silence. It was Mother Brock who first came to the assistance of Mrs Aspinall's child when the plaster accident took place (the mother being absent at the time), and when Mrs Aspinall heard of it, her indignation cured her of her fright, and she declared to Mrs Next-door that she would give "that woman"—meaning Mother Brock—"in char-rge the instant she ever dared to put her foot inside her (Mrs A.'s) respectable door-step again. She was a respectable, honest, hard-working woman, and—" etc.

Whereat Mother Brock laughed good-naturedly. She was a broad-minded bad woman, and was right according to her lights. Poor Mrs A. was a respectable, haggard woman, and was right according to her lights, and to Mrs Next-door's, perfectly so—they being friends—and vice versa. None of them knew, or would have taken into consideration, the fact that the landlord had lost all his money in a burst financial institution, and half his houses in the general depression, and depended for food for his family on the somewhat doubtful rents of the remainder. So they were all right according to their different lights.

Mrs Aspinall even sought sympathy of "John," the Chinaman (with whom she had dealt for four months only), and got it. He also, in all simplicity, took a hint that wasn't intended. He said: "Al li'. Pay bimeby. Nexy time Flyday. Me tlust." Then he departed with his immortalized smile. It would almost appear that he was wrong—according to our idea of Chinese lights.

Mrs Aspinall went to the court—it was a small local court. Mrs Next-door was awfully sorry, but she couldn't possibly get out that morning. The contractor had the landlord up as a witness. The landlord and the P.M. nodded pleasantly to each other, and wished each other good morning.... Verdict for plaintiff with costs... Next case!... "You mustn't take up the time of the court, my good woman.".. "Now, constable!"..."Arder in the court!"... "Now, my good woman," said the policeman in an undertone, "you must go out; there's another case on-come now." And he steered her—but not unkindly—through the door.

"My good woman" stood in the crowd outside, and looked wildly round for a sympathetic face that advertised sympathetic ears. But others had their own troubles, and avoided her. She wanted someone to relieve her bursting heart to; she couldn't wait till she got home.

Even "John's" attentive ear and mildly idiotic expression would have been welcome, but he was gone. He had been in court that morning, and had won a small debt case, and had departed cheerfully, under the impression that he lost it.

"Y'aw Mrs Aspinall, ain't you?"

She started, and looked round. He was one of those sharp, blue or grey-eyed, sandy or freckled complexioned boys-of-the-world whom we meet everywhere and at all times, who are always going on towards twenty, yet never seem to get clear out of their teens, who know more than most of us have forgotten, who understand human nature instinctively—perhaps unconsciously—and are instinctively sympathetic and diplomatic; whose satire is quick, keen, and dangerous, and whose tact is often superior to that of many educated men-of-the-world. Trained from childhood in the great school of poverty, they are full of the pathos and humour of it.

"Don't you remember me?"

"No; can't say I do. I fancy I've seen your face before somewhere."

"I was at your place when little Arvie died. I used to work with him at Grinder Brothers', you know."

"Oh, of course I remember you! What was I thinking about? I've had such a lot of worry lately that I don't know whether I'm on my head or my heels. Besides, you've grown since then, and changed a lot. You're Billy—Billy—"

"Billy Anderson's my name."

"Of course! To be sure! I remember you quite well."

"How've you been gettin' on, Mrs Aspinall?"

"Ah! Don't mention it—nothing but worry and trouble—nothing but worry and trouble. This grinding poverty! I'll never have anything else but worry and trouble and misery so long as I live."

"Do you live in Jones's Alley yet?"

"Yes."

"Not bin there ever since, have you?"

"No; I shifted away once, but I went back again. I was away nearly two years."

"I thought so, because I called to see you there once. Well, I'm goin' that way now. You goin' home, Mrs Aspinall?"

"Yes."

"Well, I'll go along with you, if you don't mind."

"Thanks. I'd be only too glad of company."

"Goin' to walk, Mrs Aspinall?" asked Bill, as the tram stopped in their way.

"Yes. I can't afford trams now—times are too hard."

"Sorry I don't happen to have no tickets on me!"

"Oh, don't mention it. I'm well used to walking. I'd rather walk than ride."

They waited till the tram passed.

"Some people"—said Bill, reflectively, but with a tinge of indignation in his tone, as they crossed the street—"some people can afford to ride in trams.

"What's your trouble, Mrs Aspinall—if it's a fair thing to ask?" said Bill, as they turned the corner.

This was all she wanted, and more; and when, about a mile later, she paused for breath, he drew a long one, gave a short whistle, and said:

"Well, it's red-hot!"

Thus encouraged, she told her story again, and some parts of it for the third and fourth and even fifth time—and it grew longer, as our stories have a painful tendency to do when we re-write them with a view to condensation.

But Bill heroically repeated that it was "red-hot."

"And I dealt off the grocer for fifteen years, and the wood-and-coal man for ten, and I lived in that house nine years last Easter Monday and never owed a penny before," she repeated for the tenth time.

"Well, that's a mistake," reflected Bill. "I never dealt off nobody more'n twice in my life.... I heerd you was married again, Mrs Aspinall—if it's a right thing to ask?"

"Wherever did you hear that? I did get married again—to my sorrow."

"Then you ain't Mrs Aspinall—if it's a fair thing to ask?"

"Oh, yes! I'm known as Mrs Aspinall. They all call me Mrs Aspinall."

"I understand. He cleared, didn't he? Run away?"

"Well, yes—no—he—"

"I understand. He's s'posed to be dead?"

"Yes."

"Well, that's red-hot! So's my old man, and I hope he don't resurrect again."

"You see, I married my second for the sake of my children."

"That's a great mistake," reflected Bill. "My mother married my step-father for the sake of me, and she's never been done telling me about it."

"Indeed! Did your mother get married again?"

"Yes. And he left me with a batch of step-sisters and step-brothers to look after, as well as mother; as if things wasn't bad enough before. We didn't want no help to be pinched, and poor, and half-starved. I don't see where my sake comes in at all."

"And how's your mother now?"

"Oh, she's all right, thank you. She's got a hard time of it, but she's pretty well used to it."

"And are you still working at Grinder Brothers'?"

"No. I got tired of slavin' there for next to nothing. I got sick of my step-father waitin' outside for me on pay-day, with a dirty, drunken, spieler pal of his waitin' round the corner for him. There wasn't nothin' in it. It got to be too rough altogether.... Blast Grinders!"

"And what are you doing now?"

"Sellin' papers. I'm always tryin' to get a start in somethin' else, but I ain't got no luck. I always come back to, sellin' papers."

Then, after a thought, he added reflectively: "Blast papers!"

His present ambition was to drive a cart.

"I drove a cart twice, and once I rode a butcher's horse. A bloke worked me out of one billet, and I worked myself out of the other. I didn't know when I was well off. Then the banks went bust, and my last boss went insolvent, and one of his partners went into Darlinghurst for suicide, and the other went into Gladesville for being mad; and one day the bailiff seized the cart and horse with me in it and a load of timber. So I went home and helped mother and the kids to live on one meal a day for six months, and keep the bum-bailiff out. Another cove had my news-stand."

Then, after a thought "Blast reconstriction!"

"But you surely can't make a living selling newspapers?"

"No, there's nothin' in it. There's too many at it. The blessed women spoil it. There's one got a good stand down in George Street, and she's got a dozen kids sellin'—they can't be all hers-and then she's got the hide to come up to my stand and sell in front of me.... What are you thinkin' about doin', Mrs Aspinall?"

"I don't know," she wailed. "I really don't know what to do."

And there still being some distance to go, she plunged into her tale of misery once more, not forgetting the length of time she had dealt with her creditors.

Bill pushed his hat forward and walked along on the edge of the kerb.

"Can't you shift? Ain't you got no people or friends that you can go to for a while?"

"Oh, yes; there's my sister-in-law; she's asked me times without number to come and stay with her till things got better, and she's got a hard enough struggle herself, Lord knows. She asked me again only yesterday."

"Well, that ain't too bad," reflected Bill. "Why don't you go?"

"Well, you see, if I did they wouldn't let me take my furniture, and she's got next to none."

"Won't the landlord let you take your furniture?"

"No, not him! He's one of the hardest landlords in Sydney—the worst I ever had."

"That's red-hot!... I'd take it in spite of him. He can't do nothin'."

"But I daren't; and even if I did I haven't got a penny to pay for a van."

They neared the alley. Bill counted the flagstones, stepping from one to another over the joints. "Eighteen-nineteen-twenty-twenty-one!" he counted mentally, and came to the corner kerbing. Then he turned suddenly and faced her.

"I'll tell you what to do," he said decidedly. "Can you get your things ready by to-night? I know a cove that's got a cart."

"But I daren't. I'm afraid of the landlord."

"The more fool you," said Bill. "Well, I'm not afraid of him. He can't do nothin'. I'm not afraid of a landlady, and that's worse. I know the law. He can't do nothin'. You just do as I tell you."

"I'd want to think over it first, and see my sister-in-law."

"Where does your sister-'n-law live?"

"Not far."

"Well, see her, and think over it—you've got plenty of time to do it in—and get your things ready by dark. Don't be frightened. I've shifted mother and an aunt and two married sisters out of worse fixes than yours. I'll be round after dark, and bring a push to lend a hand. They're decent coves."

"But I can't expect your friend to shift me for nothing. I told you I haven't got a—"

"Mrs Aspinall, I ain't that sort of a bloke, neither is my chum, and neither is the other fellows—'relse they wouldn't be friends of mine. Will you promise, Mrs Aspinall?"

"I'm afraid—I—I'd like to keep my few things now. I've kept them so long. It's hard to lose my few bits of things—I wouldn't care so much if I could keep the ironin' table."

"So you could, by law—it's necessary to your living, but it would cost more'n the table. Now, don't be soft, Mrs Aspinall. You'll have the bailiff in any day, and be turned out in the end without a rag. The law knows no 'necessary.' You want your furniture more'n the landlord does. He can't do nothin'. You can trust it all to me.... I knowed Arvie.... Will you do it?"

"Yes, I will."

At about eight o'clock that evening there came a mysterious knock at Mrs Aspinall's door. She opened, and there stood Bill. His attitude was business-like, and his manner very impressive. Three other boys stood along by the window, with their backs to the wall, deeply interested in the emptying of burnt cigarette-ends into a piece of newspaper laid in the crown of one of their hats, and a fourth stood a little way along the kerb casually rolling a cigarette, and keeping a quiet eye out for suspicious appearances. They were of different makes and sizes, but there seemed an undefined similarity between them.

"This is my push, Mrs Aspinall," said Bill; "at least," he added apologetically, "it's part of 'em. Here, you chaps, this is Mrs Aspinall, what I told you about."

They elbowed the wall back, rubbed their heads with their hats, shuffled round, and seemed to take a vacant sort of interest in abstract objects, such as the pavement, the gas-lamp, and neighbouring doors and windows.

"Got the things ready?" asked Bill.

"Oh, yes."

"Got 'em downstairs?"

"There's no upstairs. The rooms above belong to the next house."

"And a nice house it is," said Bill, "for rooms to belong to. I wonder," he reflected, cocking his eye at the windows above; "I wonder how the police manage to keep an eye on the next house without keepin' an eye on yours—but they know."

He turned towards the street end of the alley and gave a low whistle. Out under the lamp from behind the corner came a long, thin, shambling, hump-backed youth, with his hat down over his head like an extinguisher, dragging a small bony horse, which, in its turn, dragged a rickety cart of the tray variety, such as is used in the dead marine trade. Behind the cart was tied a mangy retriever. This affair was drawn up opposite the door.

"The cove with a cart" was introduced as 'Chinny'. He had no chin whatever, not even a receding chin. It seemed as though his chin had been cut clean off horizontally. When he took off his hat he showed to the mild surprise of strangers a pair of shrewd grey eyes and a broad high forehead. Chinny was in the empty bottle line.

"Now, then, hold up that horse of yours for a minute, Chinny," said Bill briskly, "'relse he'll fall down and break the shaft again." (It had already been broken in several places and spliced with strips of deal, clothes-line, and wire.) "Now, you chaps, fling yourselves about and get the furniture out."

This was a great relief to the push. They ran against each other and the door-post in their eagerness to be at work. The furniture—what Mrs A. called her "few bits of things"—was carried out with elaborate care. The ironing table was the main item. It was placed top down in the cart, and the rest of the things went between the legs without bulging sufficiently to cause Chinny any anxiety.

Just then the picket gave a low, earnest whistle, and they were aware of a policeman standing statue-like under the lamp on the opposite corner, and apparently unaware of their existence. He was looking, sphinx-like, past them towards the city.

"It can't be helped; we must put on front an' go on with it now," said Bill.

"He's all right, I think," said Chinny. "He knows me."

"He can't do nothin'," said Bill; "don't mind him, Mrs Aspinall. Now, then (to the push), tie up. Don't be frightened of the dorg-what are you frightened of? Why! he'd only apologize if you trod on his tail."

The dog went under the cart, and kept his tail carefully behind him.

The policeman—he was an elderly man—stood still, looking towards the city, and over it, perhaps, and over the sea, to long years agone in Ireland when he and the boys ducked bailiffs, and resisted evictions with "shticks," and "riz" sometimes, and gathered together at the rising of the moon, and did many things contrary to the peace of Gracious Majesty, its laws and constitutions, crown and dignity; as a reward for which he had helped to preserve the said peace for the best years of his life, without promotion; for he had a great aversion to running in "the boys"—which included nearly all mankind—and preferred to keep, and was most successful in keeping, the peace with no other assistance than that of his own rich fatherly brogue.

Bill took charge of two of the children; Mrs Aspinall carried the youngest.

"Go ahead, Chinny," said Bill.

Chinny shambled forward, sideways, dragging the horse, with one long, bony, short-sleeved arm stretched out behind holding the rope reins; the horse stumbled out of the gutter, and the cart seemed to pause a moment, as if undecided whether to follow or not, and then, with many rickety complaints, moved slowly and painfully up on to the level out of the gutter. The dog rose with a long, weary, mangy sigh, but with a lazy sort of calculation, before his rope (which was short) grew taut—which was good judgment on his part, for his neck was sore; and his feet being tender, he felt his way carefully and painfully over the metal, as if he feared that at any step he might spring some treacherous, air-trigger trap-door which would drop and hang him.

"Nit, you chaps," said Bill, "and wait for me." The push rubbed its head with its hat, said "Good night, Mrs Ashpennel," and was absent, spook-like.

When the funeral reached the street, the lonely "trap" was, somehow, two blocks away in the opposite direction, moving very slowly, and very upright, and very straight, like an automaton.

BOGG OF GEEBUNG

At the local police court, where the subject of this sketch turned up periodically amongst the drunks, he had "James" prefixed to his name for the sake of convenience and as a matter of form previous to his being fined forty shillings (which he never paid) and sentenced to "a month hard" (which he contrived to make as soft as possible). The local larrikins called him "Grog," a very appropriate name, all things considered; but to the Geebung Times he was known until the day of his death as "a well-known character named Bogg." The antipathy of the local paper might have been accounted for by the fact that Bogg strayed into the office one day in a muddled condition during the absence of the staff at lunch and corrected a revise proof of the next week's leader, placing bracketed "query" and "see proof" marks opposite the editor's most flowery periods and quotations, and leaving on the margin some general advice to the printers to "space better." He also corrected a Latin quotation or two, and added a few ideas of his own in good French.

But no one, with the exception of the editor of the Times, ever dreamed that there was anything out of the common in the shaggy, unkempt head upon which poor Bogg used to "do his little time," until a young English doctor came to practise at Geebung. One night the doctor and the manager of the local bank and one or two others wandered into the bar of the Diggers' Arms, where Bogg sat in a dark corner mumbling to himself as usual and spilling half his beer on the table and floor. Presently some drunken utterances reached the doctor's ear, and he turned round in a surprised manner and looked at Bogg. The drunkard continued to mutter for some time, and then broke out into something like the fag-end of a song. The doctor walked over to the table at which Bogg was sitting, and, seating himself on the far corner, regarded the drunkard attentively for some minutes; but the latter's voice ceased, his head fell slowly on his folded arms, and all became silent except the drip, drip of the overturned beer falling from the table to the form and from the form to the floor.

The doctor rose and walked back to his friends with a graver face.

"You seem interested in Bogg," said the bank manager.

"Yes," said the doctor.

"What was he mumbling about?"

"Oh, that was a passage from Homer."

"What?"

The doctor repeated his answer.

"Then do you mean to say he understands Greek?"

"Yes," said the doctor, sadly; "he is, or must have been, a classical scholar."

The manager took time to digest this, and then asked:

"What was the song?"

"Oh, that was an old song we used to sing at the Dublin University," said the doctor.

During his sober days Bogg used to fossick about among the old mullock heaps, or split palings in the bush, and just managed to keep out of debt. Strange to say, in spite of his drunken habits, his credit was as good as that of any man in the town. He was very unsociable, seldom speaking, whether drunk or sober; but a weary, hard-up sundowner was always pretty certain to get a meal and a shake-down at Bogg's lonely but among the mullock heaps. It happened one dark night that a little push of local larrikins, having nothing better to amuse them, wended their way through the old mullock heaps in the direction of the lonely little bark hut, with the object of playing off an elaborately planned ghost joke on Bogg. Prior to commencing operations, the leader of the jokers put his eye to a crack in the bark to reconnoitre. He didn't see much, but what he did see seemed to interest him, for he kept his eye there till his mates grew impatient. Bogg sat in front of his rough little table with his elbows on the same, and his hands supporting his forehead. Before him on the table lay a few articles such as lady novelists and poets use in their work, and such as bitter cynics often wear secretly next their bitter, cynical hearts.

There was the usual faded letter, a portrait of a girl, something that looked like a pressed flower, and, of course, a lock of hair. Presently Bogg folded his arms over these things, and his face sank lower and lower, till nothing was visible to the unsuspected watcher except the drunkard's rough, shaggy hair; rougher and wilder looking in the uncertain light of the slush-lamp.

The larrikin turned away, and beckoned his comrades to follow him.

"Wot is it?" asked one, when they had gone some distance. The leader said, "We're a-goin' ter let 'im alone; that's wot it is."

There was some demur at this, and an explanation was demanded; but the boss bully unbuttoned his coat, and spat on his hands, and said:

"We're a-goin' ter let Bogg alone; that's wot it is."

So they went away and let Bogg alone.

A few days later the following paragraph appeared in the Geebung Times: "A well-known character named Bogg was found drowned in the river on Sunday last, his hat and coat being found on the bank. At a late hour on Saturday night a member of our staff saw a man walking slowly along the river bank, but it was too dark to identify the person."

We suppose it was Bogg whom the Times reported, but of course we cannot be sure. The chances are that it was Bogg. It was pretty evident that he had committed suicide, and being "a well-known character," no doubt he had reasons for his rash act. Perhaps he was walking by himself in the dark along the river bank, and thinking of those reasons when the Times man saw him. Strange to say, the world knows least about the lives and sorrows of "well-known characters" of this kind, no matter what their names might be, and—well, there is no reason why we should bore a reader, or waste any more space over a well-known character named Bogg.

SHE WOULDN'T SPEAK

Well, we reached the pub about dinner-time, dropped our swags outside, had a drink, and then went into the dinin'-room. There was a lot of jackaroo swells, that had been on a visit to the squatter, or something, and they were sittin' down at dinner; and they seemed to think by their looks that we ought to have stayed outside and waited till they were done—we was only two rough shearers, you know. There was a very good-looking servant girl waitin' on 'em, and she was all smiles—laughin', and jokin', and chyackin', and barrickin' with 'em like anything.

I thought a damp expression seemed to pass across her face when me and my mate sat down, but she served us and said nothing—we was only two dusty swaggies, you see. Dave said "Good day" to her when we came in, but she didn't answer; and I could see from the first that she'd made up her mind not to speak to us.

The swells finished, and got up and went out, leaving me and Dave and the servant girl alone in the room; but she didn't open her mouth—not once. Dave winked at her once or twice as she handed his cup, but it wasn't no go. Dave was a good-lookin' chap, too; but we couldn't get her to say a word—not one.

We finished the first blanky course, and, while she was gettin' our puddin' from the side-table, Dave says to me in a loud whisper, so's she could hear: "Ain't she a stunner, Joe! I never thought there was sich fine girls on the Darlin'!"

But no; she wouldn't speak.

Then Dave says: "They pitch a blanky lot about them New Englan' gals; but I'll back the Darlin' girls to lick 'em holler as far's looks is concerned," says Dave.

But no; she wouldn't speak. She wouldn't even smile. Dave didn't say nothing for awhile, and then he said: "Did you hear about that red-headed barmaid at Stiffner's goin' to be married to the bank manager at Bourke next month, Joe?" says Dave.

But no, not a single word out of her; she didn't even look up, or look as if she wanted to speak.

Dave scratched his ear and went on with his puddin' for awhile. Then he said: "Joe, did you hear that yarn about young Scotty and old whatchisname's missus?"

"Yes," I says; "but I think it was the daughter, not the wife, and young Scotty," I says.

But it wasn't no go; that girl wouldn't speak.

Dave shut up for a good while, but presently I says to Dave "I see that them hoops is comin' in again, Dave. The paper says that this here Lady Duff had one on when she landed."

"Yes, I heard about it," says Dave. "I'd like to see my wife in one, but I s'pose a woman must wear what all the rest does."

And do you think that girl would speak? Not a blanky word.

We finished our second puddin' and fourth cup of tea, and I was just gettin' up when Dave catches holt on my arm, like that, and pulls me down into my chair again.

"'Old on," whispers Dave; "I'm goin' to make that blanky gal speak."

"You won't," I says.

"Bet you a five-pound note," says Dave.

"All right," I says.

So I sits down again, and Dave whistles to the girl, and he passes along his cup and mine. She filled 'em at once, without a word, and we got outside our fifth cup of tea each. Then Dave jingled his spoon, and passed both cups along again. She put some hot water in the pot this time, and, after we'd drunk another couple of cups, Dave muttered somethin' about drownin' the miller.

"We want tea, not warm water," he growled, lookin' sulky and passin' along both cups again.

But she never opened her mouth; she wouldn't speak. She didn't even, look cross. She made a fresh pot of tea, and filled our cups again. She didn't even slam the cups down, or swamp the tea over into the saucers—which would have been quite natural, considerin'.

"I'm about done," I said to Dave in a low whisper. "We'll have to give it up, I'm afraid, Dave," I says.

"I'll make her speak, or bust myself," says Dave.

And I'm blest if he didn't go on till I was so blanky full of tea that it brimmed over and run out the corners of my mouth; and Dave was near as bad. At last I couldn't drink another teaspoonful without holding back my head, and then I couldn't keep it down, but had to let it run back into the blanky cup again. The girl began to clear away at the other end of the table, and now and then she'd lay her hand on the teapot and squint round to see if we wanted any more tea. But she never spoke. She might have thought a lot—but she never opened her lips.

I tell you, without a word of a lie, that we must have drunk about a dozen cups each. We made her fill the teapot twice, and kept her waitin' nearly an hour, but we couldn't make her say a word. She never said a single word to us from the time we came in till the time we went out, nor before nor after. She'd made up her mind from the first not to speak to us.

We had to get up and leave our cups half full at last. We went out and sat down on our swags in the shade against the wall, and smoked and gave that tea time to settle, and then we got on to the track again.

THE GEOLOGICAL SPIELER

There's nothing so interesting as Geology, even to common and ignorant people, especially when you have a bank or the side of a cutting, studded with fossil fish and things and oysters that were stale when Adam was fresh to illustrate by. (Remark made by Steelman, professional wanderer, to his pal and pupil, Smith.)

The first man that Steelman and Smith came up to on the last embankment, where they struck the new railway line, was a heavy, gloomy, labouring man with bowyangs on and straps round his wrists. Steelman bade him the time of day and had a few words with him over the weather. The man of mullock gave it as his opinion that the fine weather wouldn't last, and seemed to take a gloomy kind of pleasure in that reflection; he said there was more rain down yonder, pointing to the southeast, than the moon could swallow up—the moon was in its first quarter, during which time it is popularly believed in some parts of Maoriland that the south-easter is most likely to be out on the wallaby and the weather bad.

Steelman regarded that quarter of the sky with an expression of gentle remonstrance mingled as it were with a sort of fatherly indulgence, agreed mildly with the labouring man, and seemed lost for a moment in a reverie from which he roused himself to inquire cautiously after the boss. There was no boss, it was a co-operative party. That chap standing over there by the dray in the end of the cutting was their spokesman—their representative: they called him boss, but that was only his nickname in camp. Steelman expressed his thanks and moved on towards the cutting, followed respectfully by Smith.

Steelman wore a snuff-coloured sac suit, a wide-awake hat, a pair of professional-looking spectacles, and a scientific expression; there was a clerical atmosphere about him, strengthened, however, by an air as of unconscious dignity and superiority, born of intellect and knowledge. He carried a black bag, which was an indispensable article in his profession in more senses than one. Smith was decently dressed in sober tweed and looked like a man of no account, who was mechanically devoted to his employer's interests, pleasures, or whims.

The boss was a decent-looking young fellow, with a good face—rather solemn—and a quiet manner.

"Good day, sir," said Steelman.

"Good day, sir," said the boss.

"Nice weather this."

"Yes, it is, but I'm afraid it won't last."

"I am afraid it will not by the look of the sky down there," ventured Steelman.

"No, I go mostly by the look of our weather prophet," said the boss with a quiet smile, indicating the gloomy man.

"I suppose bad weather would put you back in your work?"

"Yes, it will; we didn't want any bad weather just now."

Steelman got the weather question satisfactorily settled; then he said:

"You seem to be getting on with the railway."

"Oh yes, we are about over the worst of it."

"The worst of it?" echoed Steelman, with mild surprise: "I should have thought you were just coming into it," and he pointed to the ridge ahead.

"Oh, our section doesn't go any further than that pole you see sticking up yonder. We had the worst of it back there across the swamps—working up to our waists in water most of the time, in midwinter too—and at eighteenpence a yard."

"That was bad."

"Yes, rather rough. Did you come from the terminus?"

"Yes, I sent my baggage on in the brake."

"Commercial traveller, I suppose?" asked the boss, glancing at Smith, who stood a little to the rear of Steelman, seeming interested in the work.

"Oh no," said Steelman, smiling—"I am—well—I'm a geologist; this is my man here," indicating Smith. "(You may put down the bag, James, and have a smoke.) My name is Stoneleigh—you might have heard of it."

The boss said, "Oh," and then presently he added "indeed," in an undecided tone.

There was a pause—embarrassed on the part of the boss—he was silent not knowing what to say. Meanwhile Steelman studied his man and concluded that he would do.

"Having a look at the country, I suppose?" asked the boss presently.

"Yes," said Steelman; then after a moment's reflection: "I am travelling for my own amusement and improvement, and also in the interest of science, which amounts to the same thing. I am a member of the Royal Geological Society—vice-president in fact of a leading Australian branch;" and then, as if conscious that he had appeared guilty of egotism, he shifted the subject a bit. "Yes. Very interesting country this—very interesting indeed. I should like to make a stay here for a day or so. Your work opens right into my hands. I cannot remember seeing a geological formation which interested me so much. Look at the face of that cutting, for instance. Why! you can almost read the history of the geological world from yesterday—this morning as it were—beginning with the super-surface on top and going right down through the different layers and stratas—through the vanished ages—right down and back to the pre-historical—to the very primeval or fundamental geological formations!" And Steelman studied the face of the cutting as if he could read it like a book, with every layer or stratum a chapter, and every streak a note of explanation. The boss seemed to be getting interested, and Steelman gained confidence and proceeded to identify and classify the different "stratas and layers," and fix their ages, and describe the conditions and politics of man in their different times, for the boss's benefit.

"Now," continued Steelman, turning slowly from the cutting, removing his glasses, and letting his thoughtful eyes wander casually over the general scenery—"now the first impression that this country would leave on an ordinary intelligent mind—though maybe unconsciously, would be as of a new country—new in a geological sense; with patches of an older geological and vegetable formation cropping out here and there; as for instance that clump of dead trees on that clear alluvial slope there, that outcrop of limestone, or that timber yonder," and he indicated a dead forest which seemed alive and green because of the parasites. "But the country is old—old; perhaps the oldest geological formation in the world is to be seen here, the oldest vegetable formation in Australasia. I am not using the words old and new in an ordinary sense, you understand, but in a geological sense."

The boss said, "I understand," and that geology must be a very interesting study.

Steelman ran his eye meditatively over the cutting again, and turning to Smith said:

"Go up there, James, and fetch me a specimen of that slaty outcrop you see there—just above the coeval strata."

It was a stiff climb and slippery, but Smith had to do it, and he did it.

"This," said Steelman, breaking the rotten piece between his fingers, "belongs probably to an older geological period than its position would indicate—a primitive sandstone level perhaps. Its position on that layer is no doubt due to volcanic upheavals—such disturbances, or rather the results of such disturbances, have been and are the cause of the greatest trouble to geologists—endless errors and controversy. You see we must study the country, not as it appears now, but as it would appear had the natural geological growth been left to mature undisturbed; we must restore and reconstruct such disorganized portions of the mineral kingdom, if you understand me."

The boss said he understood.

Steelman found an opportunity to wink sharply and severely at Smith, who had been careless enough to allow his features to relapse into a vacant grin.

"It is generally known even amongst the ignorant that rock grows—grows from the outside—but the rock here, a specimen of which I hold in my hand, is now in the process of decomposition; to be plain it is rotting—in an advanced stage of decomposition—so much so that you are not able to identify it with any geological period or formation, even as you may not be able to identify any other extremely decomposed body."

The boss blinked and knitted his brow, but had the presence of mind to say: "Just so."

"Had the rock on that cutting been healthy—been alive, as it were—you would have had your work cut out; but it is dead and has been dead for ages perhaps. You find less trouble in working it than you would ordinary clay or sand, or even gravel, which formations together are really rock in embryo—before birth as it were."

The boss's brow cleared.

"The country round here is simply rotting down—simply rotting down."

He removed his spectacles, wiped them, and wiped his face; then his attention seemed to be attracted by some stones at his feet. He picked one up and examined it.

"I shouldn't wonder," he mused, absently, "I shouldn't wonder if there is alluvial gold in some of these creeks and gullies, perhaps tin or even silver, quite probably antimony."

The boss seemed interested.

"Can you tell me if there is any place in this neighbourhood where I could get accommodation for myself and my servant for a day or two?" asked Steelman presently. "I should very much like to break my journey here."

"Well, no," said the boss. "I can't say I do—I don't know of any place nearer than Pahiatua, and that's seven miles from here."'

"I know that," said Steelman reflectively, "but I fully expected to have found a house of accommodation of some sort on the way, else I would have gone on in the van.'

"Well," said the boss. "If you like to camp with us for to night, at least, and don't mind roughing it, you'll be welcome, I'm sure."

"If I was sure that I would not be putting you to any trouble, or interfering in any way with your domestic economy—"

"No trouble at all," interrupted the boss. "The boys will be only too glad, and there's an empty whare where you can sleep. Better stay. It's going to be a rough night."

After tea Steelman entertained the boss and a few of the more thoughtful members of the party with short chatty lectures on geology and other subjects.

In the meantime Smith, in another part of the camp, gave selections on a tin whistle, sang a song or two, contributed, in his turn, to the sailor yarns, and ensured his popularity for several nights at least. After several draughts of something that was poured out of a demijohn into a pint-pot, his tongue became loosened, and he expressed an opinion that geology was all bosh, and said if he had half his employer's money he'd be dashed if he would go rooting round in the mud like a blessed old ant-eater; he also irreverently referred to his learned boss as "Old Rocks" over there. He had a pretty easy billet of it though, he said, taking it all round, when the weather was fine; he got a couple of notes a week and all expenses paid, and the money was sure; he was only required to look after the luggage and arrange for accommodation, grub out a chunk of rock now and then, and (what perhaps was the most irksome of his duties) he had to appear interested in old rocks and clay.

Towards midnight Steelman and Smith retired to the unoccupied whare which had been shown them, Smith carrying a bundle of bags, blankets, and rugs, which had been placed at their disposal by their good-natured hosts. Smith lit a candle and proceeded to make the beds. Steelman sat down, removed his specs and scientific expression, placed the glasses carefully on a ledge close at hand, took a book from his bag, and commenced to read. The volume was a cheap copy of Jules Verne's Journey to the Centre of the Earth. A little later there was a knock at the door. Steelman hastily resumed the spectacles, together with the scientific expression, took a note-book from his pocket, opened it on the table, and said, "Come in." One of the chaps appeared with a billy of hot coffee, two pint-pots, and some cake. He said he thought you chaps might like a drop of coffee before you turned in, and the boys had forgot to ask you to wait for it down in the camp. He also wanted to know whether Mr Stoneleigh and his man would be all right and quite comfortable for the night, and whether they had blankets enough. There was some wood at the back of the whare and they could light a fire if they liked.

Mr Stoneleigh expressed his thanks and his appreciation of the kindness shown him and his servant. He was extremely sorry to give them any trouble.

The navvy, a serious man, who respected genius or intellect in any shape or form, said that it was no trouble at all, the camp was very dull and the boys were always glad to have someone come round.

Then, after a brief comparison of opinions concerning the probable duration of the weather which had arrived, they bade each other good night, and the darkness swallowed the serious man.

Steelman turned into the top bunk on one side and Smith took the lower on the other. Steelman had the candle by his bunk, as usual; he lit his pipe for a final puff before going to sleep, and held the light up for a moment so as to give Smith the full benefit of a solemn, uncompromising wink. The wink was silently applauded and dutifully returned by Smith. Then Steelman blew out the light, lay back, and puffed at his pipe for a while. Presently he chuckled, and the chuckle was echoed by Smith; by and by Steelman chuckled once more, and then Smith chuckled again. There was silence in the darkness, and after a bit Smith chuckled twice. Then Steelman said:

"For God's sake give her a rest, Smith, and give a man a show to get some sleep."

Then the silence in the darkness remained unbroken.

The invitation was extended next day, and Steelman sent Smith on to see that his baggage was safe. Smith stayed out of sight for two or three hours, and then returned and reported all well.

They stayed on for several days. After breakfast and when the men were going to work Steelman and Smith would go out along the line with the black bag and poke round amongst the "layers and stratas" in sight of the works for a while, as an evidence of good faith; then they'd drift off casually into the bush, camp in a retired and sheltered spot, and light a fire when the weather was cold, and Steelman would lie on the grass and read and smoke and lay plans for the future and improve Smith's mind until they reckoned it was about dinner-time. And in the evening they would come home with the black bag full of stones and bits of rock, and Steelman would lecture on those minerals after tea.

On about the fourth morning Steelman had a yarn with one of the men going to work. He was a lanky young fellow with a sandy complexion, and seemingly harmless grin. In Australia he might have been regarded as a "cove" rather than a "chap," but there was nothing of the "bloke" about him. Presently the cove said:

"What do you think of the boss, Mr Stoneleigh? He seems to have taken a great fancy for you, and he's fair gone on geology."

"I think he is a very decent fellow indeed, a very intelligent young man. He seems very well read and well informed."

"You wouldn't think he was a University man," said the cove.

"No, indeed! Is he?"

"Yes. I thought you knew!"

Steelman knitted his brows. He seemed slightly disturbed for the moment. He walked on a few paces in silence and thought hard.

"What might have been his special line?" he asked the cove.

"Why, something the same as yours. I thought you knew. He was reckoned the best—what do you call it?—the best minrologist in the country. He had a first-class billet in the Mines Department, but he lost it—you know—the booze."

"I think we will be making a move, Smith," said Steelman, later on, when they were private. "There's a little too much intellect in this camp to suit me. But we haven't done so bad, anyway. We've had three days' good board and lodging with entertainments and refreshments thrown in." Then he said to himself: "We'll stay for another day anyway. If those beggars are having a lark with us, we're getting the worth of it anyway, and I'm not thin-skinned. They're the mugs and not us, anyhow it goes, and I can take them down before I leave."

But on the way home he had a talk with another man whom we might set down as a "chap."

"I wouldn't have thought the boss was a college man," said Steelman to the chap.

"A what?"

"A University man—University education."

"Why! Who's been telling you that?"

"One of your mates."

"Oh, he's been getting at you. Why, it's all the boss can do to write his own name. Now that lanky sandy cove with the birth-mark grin—it's him that's had the college education."

"I think we'll make a start to-morrow," said Steelman to Smith in the privacy of their where. "There's too much humour and levity in this camp to suit a serious scientific gentleman like myself."

MACQUARIE'S MATE

The chaps in the bar of Stiffner's shanty were talking about Macquarie, an absent shearer—who seemed, from their conversation, to be better known than liked by them.

"I ain't seen Macquarie for ever so long," remarked Box-o'-Tricks, after a pause. "Wonder where he could 'a' got to?"

"Jail, p'r'aps—or hell," growled Barcoo. "He ain't much loss, any road."

"My oath, yer right, Barcoo!" interposed "Sally" Thompson. "But, now I come to think of it, Old Awful Example there was a mate of his one time. Bless'd if the old soaker ain't comin' to life again!"

A shaky, rag-and-dirt-covered framework of a big man rose uncertainly from a corner of the room, and, staggering forward, brushed the staring thatch back from his forehead with one hand, reached blindly for the edge of the bar with the other, and drooped heavily.

"Well, Awful Example," demanded the shanty-keeper. "What's up with you now?"

The drunkard lifted his head and glared wildly round with bloodshot eyes.

"Don't you—don't you talk about him! Drop it, I say! DROP it!"

"What the devil's the matter with you now, anyway?" growled the barman. "Got 'em again? Hey?"

"Don't you—don't you talk about Macquarie! He's a mate of mine! Here! Gimme a drink!"

"Well, what if he is a mate of yours?" sneered Barcoo. "It don't reflec' much credit on you—nor him neither."

The logic contained in the last three words was unanswerable, and Awful Example was still fairly reasonable, even when rum oozed out of him at every pore. He gripped the edge of the bar with both hands, let his ruined head fall forward until it was on a level with his temporarily rigid arms, and stared blindly at the dirty floor; then he straightened himself up, still keeping his hold on the bar.

"Some of you chaps," he said huskily; "one of you chaps, in this bar to-day, called Macquarie a scoundrel, and a loafer, and a blackguard, and—and a sneak and a liar."

"Well, what if we did?" said Barcoo, defiantly. "He's all that, and a cheat into the bargain. And now, what are you going to do about it?"

The old man swung sideways to the bar, rested his elbow on it, and his head on his hand.

"Macquarie wasn't a sneak and he wasn't a liar," he said, in a quiet, tired tone; "and Macquarie wasn't a cheat!"

"Well, old man, you needn't get your rag out about it," said Sally Thompson, soothingly. "P'r'aps we was a bit too hard on him; and it isn't altogether right, chaps, considerin' he's not here. But, then, you know, Awful, he might have acted straight to you that was his mate. The meanest blank—if he is a man at all— will do that."

"Oh, to blazes with the old sot!" shouted Barcoo. "I gave my opinion about Macquarie, and, what's more, I'll stand to it."

"I've got—I've got a point for the defence," the old man went on, without heeding the interruptions. "I've got a point or two for the defence."

"Well, let's have it," said Stiffner.

"In the first place—in the first place, Macquarie never talked about no man behind his back."

There was an uneasy movement, and a painful silence. Barcoo reached for his drink and drank slowly; he needed time to think—Box-o'-Tricks studied his boots—Sally Thompson looked out at the weather—the shanty-keeper wiped the top of the bar very hard—and the rest shifted round and "s'posed they'd try a game er cards."

Barcoo set his glass down very softly, pocketed his hands deeply and defiantly, and said:

"Well, what of that? Macquarie was as strong as a bull, and the greatest bully on the river into the bargain. He could call a man a liar to his face—and smash his face afterwards. And he did it often, too, and with smaller men than himself."

There was a breath of relief in the bar.

"Do you want to make out that I'm talking about a man behind his back?" continued Barcoo, threateningly, to Awful Example. "You'd best take care, old man."

"Macquarie wasn't a coward," remonstrated the drunkard, softly, but in an injured tone.

"What's up with you, anyway?" yelled the publican. "What yer growling at? D'ye want a row? Get out if yer can't be agreeable!"

The boozer swung his back to the bar, hooked himself on by his elbows, and looked vacantly out of the door.

"I've got—another point for the defence," he muttered. "It's always best—it's always best to keep the last point to—the last."

"Oh, Lord! Well, out with it! Out with it!"

"Macquarie's dead! That—that's what it is!"

Everyone moved uneasily: Sally Thompson turned the other side to the bar, crossed one leg behind the other, and looked down over his hip at the sole and heel of his elastic-side—the barman rinsed the glasses vigorously—Longbones shuffled and dealt on the top of a cask, and some of the others gathered round him and got interested—Barcoo thought he heard his horse breaking away, and went out to see to it, followed by Box-o'-Tricks and a couple more, who thought that it might be one of their horses.

Someone—a tall, gaunt, determined-looking bushman, with square features and haggard grey eyes—had ridden in unnoticed through the scrub to the back of the shanty and dismounted by the window.

When Barcoo and the others re-entered the bar it soon became evident that Sally Thompson had been thinking, for presently he came to the general rescue as follows:

"There's a blessed lot of tommy-rot about dead people in this world—a lot of damned old-woman nonsense. There's more sympathy wasted over dead and rotten skunks than there is justice done to straight, honest-livin' chaps. I don't b'lieve in this gory sentiment about the dead at the expense of the living. I b'lieve in justice for the livin'—and the dead too, for that matter—but justice for the livin'. Macquarie was a bad egg, and it don't alter the case if he was dead a thousand times."

There was another breath of relief in the bar, and presently somebody said: "Yer tight, Sally!"

"Good for you, Sally, old man!" cried Box-o'-Tricks, taking it up. "An', besides, I don't b'lieve Macquarie is dead at all. He's always dyin', or being reported dead, and then turnin' up again. Where did you hear about it, Awful?"

The Example ruefully rubbed a corner of his roof with the palm of his hand.

"There's—there's a lot in what you say, Sally Thompson," he admitted slowly, totally ignoring Box-o'-Tricks. "But—but—'

"Oh, we've had enough of the old fool," yelled Barcoo. "Macquarie was a spieler, and any man that ud be his mate ain't much better."

"Here, take a drink and dry up, yer ole hass!" said the man behind the bar, pushing a bottle and glass towards the drunkard. "D'ye want a row?"

The old man took the bottle and glass in his shaking bands and painfully poured out a drink.

"There's a lot in what Sally Thompson says," he went on, obstinately, "but—but," he added in a strained tone, "there's another point that I near forgot, and none of you seemed to think of it—not even Sally Thompson nor—nor Box-o'-Tricks there."

Stiffner turned his back, and Barcoo spat viciously and impatiently.

"Yes," drivelled the drunkard, "I've got another point for—for the defence—of my mate, Macquarie—"

"Oh, out with it! Spit it out, for God's sake, or you'll bust!" roared Stiffner. "What the blazes is it?"

"HIS MATE'S ALIVE!" yelled the old man. "Macquarie's mate's alive! That's what it is!"

He reeled back from the bar, dashed his glass and hat to the boards, gave his pants, a hitch by the waistband that almost lifted him off his feet, and tore at his shirt-sleeves.

"Make a ring, boys," he shouted. "His mate's alive! Put up your hands, Barcoo! By God, his mate's alive!"

Someone had turned his horse loose at the rear and had been standing by the back door for the last five minutes. Now he slipped quietly in.

"Keep the old fool off, or he'll get hurt," snarled Barcoo.

Stiffner jumped the counter. There were loud, hurried words of remonstrance, then some stump-splitting oaths and a scuffle, consequent upon an attempt to chuck the old man out. Then a crash. Stiffner and Box-o'-Tricks were down, two others were holding Barcoo back, and someone had pinned Awful Example by the shoulders from behind.

"Let me go!" he yelled, too blind with passion to notice the movements of surprise among the men before him. "Let me go! I'll smash—any man—that—that says a word again' a mate of mine behind his back. Barcoo, I'll have your blood! Let me go! I'll, I'll, I'll— Who's holdin' me? You—you—"

"It's Macquarie, old mate!" said a quiet voice.

Barcoo thought he heard his horse again, and went out in a hurry. Perhaps he thought that the horse would get impatient and break loose if he left it any longer, for he jumped into the saddle and rode off.

BALDY THOMPSON

Rough, squarish face, curly auburn wig, bushy grey eyebrows and moustache, and grizzly stubble—eyes that reminded one of Dampier the actor. He was a squatter of the old order—new chum, swagman, drover, shearer, super, pioneer, cocky, squatter, and finally bank victim. He had been through it all, and knew all about it.

He had been in parliament, and wanted too again; but the men mistrusted him as Thompson, M.P., though they swore by him as old Baldy Thompson the squatter. His hobby was politics, and his politics were badly boxed. When he wasn't cursing the banks and government he cursed the country. He cursed the Labour leaders at intervals, and seemed to think that he could run the unions better than they could. Also, he seemed to think that he could run parliament better than any premier. He was generally voted a hard case, which term is mostly used in a kindly sense out back.

He was always grumbling about the country. If a shearer or rouseabout was good at argument, and a bit of a politician, he hadn't to slave much at Thompson's shed, for Baldy would argue with him all day and pay for it.

"I can't put on any more men," he'd say to travellers. "I can't put on a lot of men to make big cheques when there's no money in the bank to pay 'em—and I've got all I can do to get tucker for the family. I shore nothing but burrs and grass-seed last season, and it didn't pay carriage. I'm just sending away a flock of sheep now, and I won't make threepence a head on 'em. I had twenty thousand in the bank season before last, and now I can't count on one. I'll have to roll up my swag and go on the track myself next."

"All right, Baldy," they'd say, "git out your blooming swag and come along with us, old man; we'll stick to you and see you through."

"I swear I'd show you round first," he'd reply. "Go up to the store and get what rations you want. You can camp in the huts to-night, and I'll see you in the morning."

But most likely he'd find his way over after tea, and sit on his heels in the cool outside the hut, and argue with the swagmen about unionism and politics. And he'd argue all night if he met his match.

The track by Baldy Thompson's was reckoned as a good tucker track, especially when a dissolution of parliament was threatened. Then the guileless traveller would casually let Baldy know that he'd got his name on the electoral list, and show some interest in Baldy's political opinions, and oppose them at first, and finally agree with them and see a lot in them—be led round to Baldy's way of thinking, in fact; and ultimately depart, rejoicing, with a full nose-bag, and a quiet grin for his mate.

There are many camp-fire yarns about old Baldy Thompson.

One New Year the shearers—shearing stragglers—roused him in the dead of night and told him that the shed was on fire. He came out in his shirt and without his wig. He sacked them all there and then, but of course they went to work as usual next morning. There is something sad and pathetic about that old practical joke—as indeed there is with all bush jokes. There seems a quiet sort of sadness always running through outback humour—whether alleged or otherwise.

There's the usual yarn about a jackaroo mistaking Thompson for a brother rouser, and asking him whether old Baldy was about anywhere, and Baldy said:

"Why, are you looking for a job?"

"Yes, do you think I stand any show? What sort of a boss is Baldy?"

"You'd tramp from here to Adelaide," said Baldy, "and north to the Gulf country, and wouldn't find a worse. He's the meanest squatter in Australia. The damned old crawler! I grafted like a nigger for him for over fifty years"—Baldy was over sixty—"and now the old skunk won't even pay me the last two cheques he owes me—says the bank has got everything he had—that's an old cry of his, the damned old sneak; seems to expect me to go short to keep his wife and family and relations in comfort, and by God I've done it for the last thirty or forty years, and I might go on the track to-morrow worse off than the meanest old whaler that ever humped bluey. Don't you have anything to do with Scabby Thompson, or you'll be sorry for it. Better tramp to hell than take a job from him."

"Well, I think I'll move on. Would I stand any show for some tucker?"

"Him! He wouldn't give a dog a crust, and like as not he'd get you run in for trespass if he caught you camping on the run. But come along to the store and I'll give you enough tucker to carry you on."

He patronized literature and arts, too, though in an awkward, furtive way. We remember how we once turned up at the station hard up and short of tucker, and how we entertained Baldy with some of his own ideas as ours—having been posted beforehand by our mate—and how he told us to get some rations and camp in the hut and see him in the morning.

And we saw him in the morning, had another yarn with him, agreed and sympathized with him some more, were convinced on one or two questions which we had failed to see at first, cursed things in chorus with him, and casually mentioned that we expected soon to get some work on a political paper.

And at last he went inside and brought out a sovereign. "Wrap this in a piece of paper and put it in your pocket, and don't lose it," he said.

But we learnt afterwards that the best way to get along with Baldy, and secure his good will, was to disagree with him on every possible point.

FOR AULD LANG SYNE

These were ten of us there on the wharf when our first mate left for Maoriland, he having been forced to leave Sydney because he could not get anything like regular work, nor anything like wages for the work he could get. He was a carpenter and joiner, a good tradesman and a rough diamond. He had got married and had made a hard fight for it during the last two years or so, but the result only petrified his conviction that "a lovely man could get no blessed show in this condemned country," as he expressed it; so he gave it best at last—"chucked it up," as he said—left his wife with her people and four pounds ten, until such time as he could send for her—and left himself with his box of tools, a pair of hands that could use them, a steerage ticket, and thirty shillings.

We turned up to see him off. There were ten of us all told and about twice as many shillings all counted. He was the first of the old push to go—we use the word push in its general sense, and we called ourselves the mountain push because we had worked in the tourist towns a good deal—he was the first of the mountain push to go; and we felt somehow, and with a vague kind of sadness or uneasiness, that this was the beginning of the end of old times and old things. We were plasterers, bricklayers, painters, a carpenter, a labourer, and a plumber, and were all suffering more or less—mostly more—and pretty equally, because of the dearth of regular graft, and the consequent frequency of the occasions on which we didn't hold it—the "it" being the price of one or more long beers. We had worked together on jobs in the city and up-country, especially in the country, and had had good times together when things were locomotive, as Jack put it; and we always managed to worry along cheerfully when things were "stationary." On more than one big job up the country our fortnightly spree was a local institution while it lasted, a thing that was looked forward to by all parties, whether immediately concerned or otherwise (and all were concerned more or less), a thing to be looked back to and talked over until next pay-day came. It was a matter for anxiety and regret to the local business people and publicans, and loafers and spielers, when our jobs were finished and we left.

There were between us the bonds of graft, of old times, of poverty, of vagabondage and sin, and in spite of all the right-thinking person may think, say or write, there was between us that sympathy which in our times and conditions is the strongest and perhaps the truest of all human qualities, the sympathy of drink. We were drinking mates together. We were wrong-thinking persons too, and that was another bond of sympathy between us.

There were cakes of tobacco, and books, and papers, and several flasks of "rye-buck"—our push being distantly related to a publican who wasn't half a bad sort—to cheer and comfort our departing mate on his uncertain way; and these tokens of mateship and the sake of auld lang syne were placed casually in his bunk or slipped unostentatiously into his hand or pockets, and received by him in short eloquent silence (sort of an aside silence), and partly as a matter of course. Every now and then there would be a surreptitious consultation between two of us and a hurried review of finances, and then one would slip quietly ashore and presently return supremely unconscious of a book, magazine, or parcel of fruit bulging out of his pocket.

You may battle round with mates for many years, and share and share alike, good times or hard, and find the said mates true and straight through it all; but it is their little thoughtful attentions when you are going away, that go right down to the bottom of your heart, and lift it up and make you feel inclined—as you stand alone by the rail when the sun goes down on the sea—to write or recite poetry and otherwise make a fool of yourself.

We helped our mate on board with his box, and inspected his bunk, and held a consultation over the merits or otherwise of its position, and got in his way and that of the under-steward and the rest of the crew right down to the captain, and superintended our old chum's general arrangements, and upset most of them, and interviewed various members of the crew as to when the boat would start for sure, and regarded their statements with suspicion, and calculated on our own account how long it would take to get the rest of the cargo aboard, and dragged our mate ashore for a final drink, and found that we had "plenty of time to slip ashore for a parting wet" so often that his immediate relations grew anxious and officious, and the universe began to look good, and kind, and happy, and bully, and jolly, and grand, and glorious to us, and we forgave the world everything wherein it had not acted straight towards us, and were filled full of love for our kind of both genders—for the human race at large—and with an almost irresistible longing to go aboard, and stay at all hazards, and sail along with our mate. We had just time "to slip ashore and have another" when the gangway was withdrawn and the steamer began to cast off. Then a rush down the wharf, a hurried and confused shaking of hands, and our mate was snatched aboard. The boat had been delayed, and we had waited for three hours, and had seen our chum nearly every day for years, and now we found we hadn't begun to say half what we wanted to say to him. We gripped his hand in turn over the rail, as the green tide came between, till there was a danger of one mate being pulled aboard—which he wouldn't have minded much—or the other mate pulled ashore, or one or both yanked overboard. We cheered the captain and cheered the crew and the passengers—there was a big crowd of them going and a bigger crowd of enthusiastic friends on the wharf—and our mate on the forward hatch; we cheered the land they were going to and the land they had left behind, and sang "Auld Lang Syne" and "He's a Jolly Good Fellow" (and so yelled all of us) and "Home Rule for Ireland Evermore"—which was, I don't know why, an old song of ours. And we shouted parting injunctions and exchanged old war cries, the meanings of which were only known to us, and we were guilty of such riotous conduct that, it being now Sunday morning, one or two of the quieter members suggested we had better drop down to about half-a-gale, as there was a severe-looking old sergeant of police with an eye on us; but once, in the middle of a heart-stirring chorus of "Auld Lang Sync," Jack, my especial chum, paused for breath and said to me:

"It's all right, Joe, the trap's joining in."

And so he was—and leading.

But I well remember the hush that fell on that, and several other occasions, when the steamer had passed the point.

And so our first mate sailed away out under the rising moon and under the morning stars. He is settled down in Maoriland now, in a house of his own, and has a family and a farm; but somehow, in the bottom of our hearts, we don't like to think of things like this, for they don't fit in at all with "Auld Lang Syne."'

There were six or seven of us on the wharf to see our next mate go. His ultimate destination was known to himself and us only. We had pickets at the shore end of the wharf, and we kept him quiet and out of sight; the send-off was not noisy, but the hand-grips were very tight and the sympathy deep. He was running away from debt, and wrong, and dishonour, a drunken wife, and other sorrows, and we knew it all.

Two went next—to try their luck in Western Australia; they were plasterers. Ten of us turned up again, the push having been reinforced by one or two new members and an old one who had been absent on the first occasion. It was a glorious send-off, and only two found beds that night—the government supplied the beds.

And one by one and two by two they have gone from the wharf since then. Jack went to-day; he was perhaps the most irreclaimable of us all—a hard case where all cases were hard; and I loved him best—anyway I know that, wherever Jack goes, there will be someone who will barrack for me to the best of his ability (which is by no means to be despised as far as barracking is concerned), and resent, with enthusiasm and force if he deems it necessary, the barest insinuation which might be made to the effect that I could write a bad line if I tried, or be guilty of an action which would not be straight according to the rules of mateship.

Ah well! I am beginning to think it is time I emigrated too; I'll pull myself together and battle round and raise the price of a steerage ticket, and maybe a pound or two over. There may not be anybody to see me off, but some of the boys are sure to be on the wharf or platform "over there," when I arrive. Lord! I almost hear them hailing now! and won't I yell back! and perhaps there won't be a wake over old times in some cosy bar parlour, or camp, in Western Australia or Maoriland some night in a year to come.

Henry Lawson – A Short Biography

Henry Archibald Hertzberg Lawson was born on the 17th June 1867 in a town on the Grenfell goldfields of New South Wales, Australia.

His parents, father Niel, a Norwegian born miner and mother Louisa, a noted poet, publisher and feminist were married on 7th July 1866 when he was 32 and she 18. On Henry's birth, the family surname was Anglicised to Lawson. The couple were to have an unhappy marriage despite producing three children.

Lawson attended school at Eurunderee from October 1876 but an ear infection he contracted left him partially deaf. By fourteen he had lost his hearing completely.

Lawson later attended a Catholic school at Mudgee, New South Wales where he developed an interest in poetry and, on his mother's influence, immersed himself in books given that learning in the classroom, with his deafness, was a major hurdle.

In 1883, after working on construction jobs with his father in the Blue Mountains, Lawson joined his mother in Sydney where she was living with his siblings. Here, Lawson worked during the day and studied at night for his matriculation in the hopes of enrolling at university. However, he failed his exams.

His first published poem was 'A Song of the Republic' in The Bulletin on 1st October 1887. This was quickly followed by other published poems with one recognising him as "a youth whose poetic genius here speaks eloquently for itself."

In 1890 he began a relationship with Mary Gilmore but it broke down due to his frequent absences from Sydney.

Lawson received an offer to write for the Brisbane Boomerang in 1891, but financial troubles at the magazine made this a short stint of only a few months. Despite writing for other magazines in Brisbane it was a dead end.

He returned to Sydney and continued to write for the Bulletin which, in 1892, engaged him for an inland trip where he could write articles about the harsh realities of life in drought-stricken New South Wales. He also took some time to work as a roustabout (an unskilled or semi-skilled worker) in the woolshed at Toorale Station. This resulted in his contributions to the Bulletin Debate and became the experience he used for a number of his stories in subsequent years. For Lawson this was an eye-opening period. His grim view of the outback was far removed from the romantic idyll of bravery and beauty inked in the poetry of his contemporary Banjo Paterson.

In 1896, Lawson married Bertha Bredt, Jr., daughter of Bertha Bredt, the prominent socialist. The marriage ended very unhappily in June 1903. They had two children.

Despite this Lawson was finding his way in the literary world. His writing was achieving recognition. His most successful prose collection 'While the Billy Boils', was published in 1896. In it he virtually reinvented Australian realism.

His writing style of short, sharp sentences with honed and sparse descriptions created a personal writing style that defined Australians: dryly laconic, passionately egalitarian and deeply humane. Most of Lawson's work centres on the Australian bush, it's fabled outback, such as in the desolate 'Past Carin', and is considered by many to vividly portray the real Australian life at that time.

Like the majority of Australians, Lawson lived in a city, but had had plenty of experience in outback life, these two outlooks helped shape a very individual talent. Unfortunately, his life was also flawed with other issues.

In Sydney in 1898 he was a prominent member of the Dawn and Dusk Club, a bohemian club of writer friends who met for drinks and conversation.

Sadly, for Lawson despite his growing recognition and fame he became withdrawn and unable to take part in the usual routines of life. His struggles with alcohol and mental health issues continued to drain him. His once prolific literary output began to decline. At times he was destitute mainly due, despite good sales and an enthusiastic audience, to ruinous publishing deals he had entered into.

In 1903 he bought a room at Mrs Isabel Byers' Coffee Palace in North Sydney. This near 20-year friendship between Mrs Byers and Lawson was a bedrock for him. Despite his position as the most celebrated Australian writer of the time, Lawson was deeply depressed and perpetually poor. His ex-wife repeatedly reported him for non-payment of child maintenance, which resulted in numerous jail terms or periods in psychiatric institutions. He was incarcerated at Darlinghurst Gaol for drunkenness, wife desertion, child desertion, and non-payment of child support seven times between 1905 and 1909 and spent a total of 159 days in prison. He wrote about these experiences in the haunting poem 'One Hundred and Three'—his prison number—which was published in 1908.

Mrs Byers was a good poet herself and, although of modest education, had been writing vivid poetry since her teens in a somewhat similar style to Lawson's. Long separated from her husband and elderly, Mrs Byers was, at the time she met Lawson, a woman of independent means looking forward to a comfortable retirement. She regarded Lawson as Australia's greatest living poet, and hoped to sustain him well enough to keep him writing. She acted as his agent in negotiations with publishers, helped to arrange contact with his children, contacted friends and supporters to help him financially, as well as assisting and nursing him through his mental health issues and problems with alcohol. She wrote countless letters on his behalf and pursued any avenue that could provide Lawson with financial support or a publishing deal.

Regardless of all else Lawson was a vocal nationalist and republican and took pride that many of his works were helping to establish the Australian vernacular in fiction.

Henry Archibald Hertzberg Lawson died, of a cerebral hemorrhage, in Mrs Byer's home in Abbotsford, Sydney on 2nd September 1922.

Lawson became the first Australian writer to be granted a state funeral. It was attended by the Prime Minister Billy Hughes and the (later) Premier of New South Wales, Jack Lang (the husband of Lawson's sister-in-law Hilda Bredt), as well as thousands of citizens.

Henry Lawson – A Concise Bibliography

Short Stories in Prose and Verse (1894)
While the Billy Boils (1896)
In the Days When the World was Wide and Other Verses (1896)
Verses, Popular and Humorous (1900)
On the Track (1900)
Over the Sliprails (1900)
On the Track, and, Over the Sliprails (1900)
Popular Verses (1900)
Humorous Verses (1900)
The Country I Come From (1901)
Joe Wilson and His Mates (1901)
Children of the Bush (1902)
When I Was King and Other Verses (1905)
The Elder Son (1905)
When I Was King (1905)
The Romance of the Swag (1907)
Send Round the Hat (1907)
The Skyline Riders and Other Verses (1910)
The Rising of the Court and Other Sketches in Prose and Verse (1910)
For Australia and Other Poems (1913)
Triangles of Life and Other Stories (1913)
My Army, O, My Army! and Other Songs (1915)
Song of the Dardanelles and Other Verses (1916)
Selected Poems of Henry Lawson (1918)